Marti

# The Comedown

Damned if they do, dead if they don't...

Grosvenor House
Publishing Limited

The right of Martin Doohan to be identified as the author of this
work has been asserted in accordance with Section 78
of the Copyright, Designs and Patents Act 1988

The book cover picture is copyright to Martin Doohan

This book is published by
Grosvenor House Publishing Ltd
Link House
140 The Broadway, Tolworth, Surrey, KT6 7HT.
www.grosvenorhousepublishing.co.uk

A CIP record for this book
is available from the British Library

ISBN 978-1-78623-102-4

# Acknowledgements / Big thanks...

Firstly, to Tom and June and my family for allowing my imagination to flourish and not getting me tested... To Louise Sears [Nee Duggan], Esther Roberts, Julian Raikes, Briony Adams [Nee Salton], Little Jo, Lee Bilham, Barney Vost, Elizabeth Haynes, Vicky Blunsden, Linda McQueen and Dawn Sackett for all their encouragement and help in finally putting this out there... Finally, to Stacy Tuffen, for just being Stacy Tuffen. I hope it makes you smile at least once...

For

Absent friends. I miss you all.

*When you choose your friends, don't be short changed by choosing personality over character.*

**William Somerset Maugham**

# 1 The Set Up

## 1.1 Taxi Driver

He didn't open his eyes as he reached across the bed and turned off the radio alarm.

*Vanilla fucking Ice?*

He shook his head, tugged up the duvet and dozed off. Exactly nine minutes later, another well aimed slap turned the radio off again. He rolled over, opened his eyes and looked across at the wardrobe. The suit hanging from its door was dark grey wool, not as expensive as he would have liked, but tidy enough – a job interview suit. And it wasn't as if he could afford a nice suit, he'd just been lucky enough to borrow one last night, right before last orders, and it had still cost him a tenner in a return cab fare.

He got out of bed and went to the bathroom to flick the switch for the immersion. He hated not having a shower. Baths took too much time and then all you did was wallow in your own dirt. While he was waiting for the water to heat he put on some Kate Bush, *The Whole Story*, and went downstairs for the iron and board humming the intro to 'Running up That Hill'.

Today, Tom Adams had to go to court. It wasn't his first choice for a Monday morning, but there wasn't much he could do about it. He thought about the last month or so as he ironed the right arm of the shirt. Everything had been alright. He didn't love what he had turned into but it kept him in booze and pub grub all week, and treats at the weekend. More

1

importantly it paid for his day release to college. Housing benefit and income support let him attend college so long as he said he would take a job if he was offered one, and that wasn't going to happen with his interview technique.

Tom thought of himself as a facilitator. He and a couple of friends provided a service that benefited all involved, but his heart hadn't been in it recently and being 'visited' by nine Old Bill and two dogs had told him his time was up. The crazy thing was though, he had moved twice recently, leaving him to assume that there must be someone feeding information to the police. Wanker.

Everyone was partied out and moving on, or if not, attempting to. There was still the hard core that would be there for the foreseeable, but it wasn't his thing anymore.

With the ironing done he put on the suit and went downstairs. He ate a small bowlful of Rice Krispies with tepid enthusiasm and called a cab.

*The suit looks good,* he thought as he caught his reflection in the side window of the car.

*Look at the baggy suit on this little tosser. The arsehole's off to court,* the taxi driver thought as he watched Tom. 'Morning, mate, where to?'

'Morning. Up to the train station please.' Tom grimaced as the taxi pulled away. He was already sweating inside the suit.

Tom looked again at the cab driver and realised he recognised him. He considered telling him that Lassie had taken his seventeen-year-old daughter's arse cherry the week before, but he did need to get to court.

'Cheers mate,' said Tom as he paid the driver, and tipped him.

'Yeah, thanks and have a great day!'

He walked into the station and bought a ticket to Colchester, grabbed a paper and slid onto the train as the beep, beep, beep sounded. Harwich was truly a dump. One shitty club, lots of shitty pubs, a shitty town centre and three shitty train stations. He looked at the paper, Monday 3 June 1991, the football was over and the back pages were full of gossip. He enjoyed the gossip almost as much as he enjoyed

2

the season. Who was going where, for how much? Who wanted to leave? Which famous footballer had been caught taking drugs this time? It amused him when other people's lives were in even more of a mess than his own.

At the court, he found the usher and gave his name. It was cold and depressing in the big building, but the usher had one leg shorter than the other and his robe kept lifting as he walked which amused Tom for about twenty seconds. He shuffled around in his suit until he caught sight of his solicitor coming towards him.

Tom respected Toby Charles. He was a bloke who had taken his chances.

'Hello Mr Adams. I trust you had a good journey?' he said as he offered Tom his hand.

Hi, please call me Tom.' He always remembered to be polite. After all, as his Nana used to say, manners cost nothing.

'Fine, Tom. So, we know why we're here, yes?' His eyebrows raised as he spoke and Tom instantly thought of Lassie. He'd love this bloke. *Nice tie,* Tom thought, and laughed inside at the way he'd said 'we', as if they were all in this together.

'I have the probation report from your case officer and I have to say it's very favourable.'

'Err, yeah, great. He's a nice bloke.' *Brogues, very cool.*

'Well, if all goes well today we should have no problem securing a non-custodial sentence, probably a community service order, a fine and/or probation.'

*Probably just in the right place at the right time. Bet he hadn't had to put up with the sort of bullshit I had when I left school. The YTS on £ 27 a week just so the Tory government could say that school leavers were 'in work' when really they were getting their arses felt cleaning out freezers for 50p a fucking hour. She was why he was there, in court today, it wasn't anything to do with what he'd done, it was her, and her fascist ideas. The bitch had only survived so long because the red-top readers loved her for going to war over a bit of ground*

3

*the size of Canvey Island, that was worth about the same too – fuck all.*

'Excellent Mr Charles, thank you very much for all your help,' he said, looking at his watch.

'Well, I see from the register you've contacted the usher. We've just got to wait to be called now. Did you bring a sandwich and a paper?'

*Bollocks,* Tom thought remembering the paper going in the bin at the bus stop. 'No, I forgot, I'll pop to the newsagents quickly now.'

Toby Charles waved his Guardian at him as he said 'Ok, be quick. There is one person you really don't want to upset today.'

## 1.2 Brown or Red?

Patrick Wherry's eyes didn't open as his brain began its slow rewiring job. The radio that had just sprung into life in the background began bringing him round with 'Groovy Train'. He slid his tongue along neglected teeth, a dirty fingernail along the inside of a molar and peered at the off-white paste under his nail. A slight gag followed and finished with a mouthful of thick phlegm. He needed a glass of water. He opened his eyes, hoping for the best, but found only a can of Vimto with a cigarette end hanging out the top of it. He stirred in anguish, he felt damp; he slouched back and considered his options. His hands slipped between his legs to investigate the potential damage. If he'd pissed himself it would be a long walk home with his legs chafing and his new denims humming of stale urine. Either way he had to move.

They were damp but it wasn't him, it was the chair. Closer inspection of the room and the wet wallpaper falling away from the walls, exposing a healthy covering of mould explained the situation which was better than he had hoped as he had form for a bladder that did its own thing. Delicately he picked the dried crustie's away from his sore eyes and looked around. He'd been asleep in an old cloth chair with worn wooden arms. The room smelt of old books and was a poor excuse for a home; the drawn orange curtains were a clear throwback to the 1970s sitcoms his family loved and the sun seeping through made the room glow. He felt like he was inside someone's guts waiting to be flushed away. He liked the idea... until he imagined being deposited into the Mersey with the rest of the needles, shopping trolleys and assorted other shite that found its way there.

Heaving himself up and forward he battered a trail to the door; he had to struggle against a pile of dirty clothes to get it open. *Jesus, student houses*, he thought as he made it into the hallway. How the bollocks was he meant to find the shithouse in this rabbit hutch?

He found the magic door that he needed thanks to a nice 'Men at work' road sign. He picked up the copy of Viz from the floor and sat down to contemplate the day with Roger Mellie. He hated this part of the weekend. It was Monday, it was, according to his watch, 08:13, and another depressing, weekend of hopelessness had passed. He needed, and wanted all this rubbish to end. It was boring, or it had become boring. It used to be fun, selling gear to the students in John Moore's halls, getting generally twisted, making a few quid and no stress. Things had escalated though and he and Razor were now being asked to do too much, and were getting too little. The last scrape was the line in the sand. He needed out.

He flushed and walked back to the room he'd started in, which smelt possibly even more disgusting than smell he'd left behind in the toilet. At first sight it looked like there was a mess of people in there, but really there seemed to be only five, including him. It looked so crowded because the room resembled the doorway of a charity shop after late night deliveries with shite everywhere, trousers, skirts, hats the lot. It looked like the Lime street tramps had had a feckin field day in there. He looked towards the old chair he had been sitting in. It was now occupied by an even bigger mess than when he had clawed his own eyes open. He stepped over a Woolworths placky bag and aimed a kick at the tramp who had nicked his seat.

'Fuck off', Razor said. 'Now!'

'Come on soft lad, it's time to trip the light fantastic and get the fuck out of here. We have to show our faces before ten if we want to eat anything in the next few hours.'

Razor stood up and ruffled his jacket. After consideration, Paddy decided not to take the piss. It was far too easy, far too early and Razor looked like he felt. They waded through the detritus that was the floor of the bed-sit towards the door.

'Cheers fellas,' said a voice from the floor, followed by a muffled, 'Yeah, thanks.'

*Leave us the fuck alone and let us get out of here with our dignity intact,* Paddy thought.

Don't say goodbye, or thanks for sorting us out. It embarrassed him; these were lads and lasses he was in awe of in a strange way. They were exciting. He liked them and would continue to do so, that is if they stopped chucking the Gary Abletts down their gates every weekend. He'd like people to ring him or Razor to ask if they wanted to go the football or for a game of snooker or a midweek drink. Not just every Thursday or Friday asking them to deliver gear for the weekend, with the ultimate piss-take being the late Saturday night call for a restock. He couldn't understand the brass on them ringing them at the end of a night, although he and Razor would always get over there to keep the party going.

'Yeah, cheers girls,' he heard Razor say as he pulled open the door into the mighty region of Anfield. They stepped past bin bags and a pram in the five yards of front garden before they reached the gate. An average day, Monday was. It was the kind of day to take stock of the weekend, and plan for a sunny future, unless that is you had to sign on. Paddy Wherry squinted up at a lovely blue sky and in a second went into what can only be described as a full body sweat. He grabbed Razor's arm and sat on the wall.

'Game weekend that, Paddy?'

'Yeah, ok I suppose.'

'Did you get anything out of those birds?'

'The one from Wycombe was up for it but she got a little too battered and started calling me Terry.'

'Who the fuck?'

'An ex-fella.' Paddy butted in to silence Razor. He looked at his scruffy Reeboks for a split second, and then they both fell about laughing.

Raymond Wilkins stood and considered the bag of humanity that had been his bezzie mate since they were kids for a few almost fatal seconds, and then started singing 'Groovy Train' to him.

'Please fuck off Razor, I'm having a moment here.'

Arm in arm the two boys staggered off in search of a sausage sandwich.

## 1.3 Cuckoo

'Read em for me then Razor.'

'Read what?'

Paddy had been sitting and watching his mate stare into a cup of shite brown tea for about a lifetime, or so it felt. They were in a café waiting on a couple of sausage sangers with brown sauce. It was always Brown. A friend of theirs, Donald, refused to even entertain brown sauce after 11 a.m. – it was a breakfast sauce. That had stayed with him.

He'd known Ray Wilkins for most of his life. They had lived on the same road since they were five and had gone to the same schools. Raymond was nicknamed Razor because of his razor sharp wit: basically he was a soft lad with no brains. He was also known as Butch, as a mark of respect to Ray 'Butch' Wilkins the England footballer, but Ray hated this even more as he was a skinny piece of piss and six foot tall.

'Read me feckin leaves soft lad.'

'Jesus.' Razor muttered. 'Ok then here we go...' He'd done this loads of times before, and began swishing his tea around the bottom of the mug.

It says here that you're going to be the next centre forward for Everton, then you're gonna be crowned the next Messiah and tell everyone that Jesus's church is bleedin the world and to do away with organised religion and just treat people nicely…'

'Fuck off yer fucking knob head. Firstly, me ma would kill me for doing away with the church, (crosses himself) and secondly, I'm shite at footie so no one will take us.'

'This is what is says my son.' Razor got up bowing like a Catholic cardinal.

'Dickhead, you've been wanking at your Nan's again, reading her *Peoples' Friend* and looking at the grannies!'

'Fuck off la, you're plain wrong.' Razor said, flicking a lonely cold, table stranded bean at Paddy.

Paddy ignored the bean attack and thought about their next move. He'd thought about it a lot lately, ever since he'd seen them all together in the kitchen at his Ma and Da's house, congratulating each other.

There had been a few raids lately in the district. None of his Dad's mob had been busted but things were edgy to say the least. His brother in-law and top boy, George Meachen, known by most as 'The Scouse', who he fucking hated, had sent him and Razor down the local to get them out of the way. They had come back later with some chips to watch the boxing. They both thought they had seen a few quid before and some weekends they were doing a grand each on the tablets, but it was a fucking shock when the pair of them opened the back door to his Ma and Da's; firstly, he had nearly had his fucking snout blown off by George and secondly, they had never seen a bin bag full to the top with cash before. They were both yanked through the door and stood in the corner and then told to fuck off upstairs with their food. It seemed that George had needed to count the money before a big deal in Manchester and had come to their house to do it.

Paddy and Razor hadn't really talked about that evening but it had been flying around in Paddy's head ever since. That money is what he, Razor and others around the city were making for that smug cunt. He disliked George for being with his sister, but hated him more because it seemed that he took no risks, just counted money and drove around in a flash motor, usually driven by one of his psycho mates. This got on his nerves. Where was his new motor or flash clothes?

'What's twisting your keks into a knot there, Paddy?' Razor asked with brown sauce slapped around his mouth.

'Nothing, mate,' he said laughing, "though you look like you've had your mush in someone's backside, la!'

'Do one, dickhead,' Razor replied as he dragged a skinny arm across his mouth and licked off the sauce.

Paddy smiled and drifted off again with his plan in the forefront of his mind. After that night things had moved quickly. He and Razor were now dealing a lot of gear to more people, doing less legwork themselves and making more money. It seemed that since they had seen the size of the business they were being lured with the promise of cash and responsibility. Things were talked about more in his kitchen. Things happened more in his kitchen too. It still didn't seem fair though the run to Warrington had been a disaster for all of them. It was since then that he'd been planning his exit strategy.

Paddy looked up at the old digital clock on the wall, it was 11:00 hours, Monday, 3rd June 1991.

'Penny for em, dickhead.'

Paddy Wherry sat, thinking, almost in a state of higher consciousness, fingering the mustard bottle in front of him.

'Answer me this, Razor,' Paddy said, staring intently into Razors eyes, 'how far would you go, or what would you do to have a new start, a new life somewhere else. A clean slate?'

Paddy watched as Razor considered this question with all the ease of a constipated horse. It seemed to totally confuse him and his eyes started to bulge; he looked as if he might cry.

'Err, erm. I'll get back to you,' he answered and fell back into the cheap white garden furniture that had been left to the rubbish men or for students to put in their kitchens and had ended up in the Star of the Sea café.

Paddy leant over the table and spoke softly and intently to Razor, making sure he understood every word. 'Remember Warrington, Razor?'

Razor nodded. How could he forget, it had only been a month or so ago.

*They had been sent to Warrington for a drop off and had ended up in a horrific crack flat on one of the estates. The buyers were all addicts and when they were in the flat they had become pretty sure they were not getting out of there with their drugs or payment for the drugs. He remembered looking at Paddy across the kitchen and nodding towards the bread bin, which had an old Luger hanging out of it. The conversation with the buyers had been tense, with them insisting they all tried the gear before any money changed hands.*

'That fucking Luger, eh? I thought we were going to get shot and robbed!'

Paddy's fist on the table startled Razor.

'What the fuck?'

This is my point, Razor – we are nothing but worker ants for those cunts. Those people are my blood. But my Da, George and all of them, they really don't give a fuck about anything but money. If it had gone wrong in there we were on our own. They sent us alone, with no warning, with no back up and no hardware, into the Lion's den, my friend. It was a new deal, new connection. So they send the young mugs, the dispensable mugs. Not a fully trained soldier. The ones that can fuck up a deal and not be missed. Then they know who they are dealing with and can act accordingly. We owe them nothing, Razor, not a fucking bean and the deeper we get the more chance we have of being shot, stabbed or banged up... which one do you prefer? Paddy stopped and wiped some white spittle from the sides of his mouth before settling and watching Razor, patiently waiting for his response. Razor just stared into the distance over Paddy's shoulder.

Paddy knew he was considering something stupid. He cast his mind back to Jack Nicholson in *One Flew Over the Cuckoo's Nest*; at least he'd have fucking tried... Was it a gamble? Yes. Was it potential death? Yes. Was he still considering it? Yes. He sat looking directly at Razor. His mate was still sat in some sort of catatonic state, either that or he was about to shit himself.

He returned to his own thoughts while he waited for Razor's brain to get into gear. He had come home from having a knock up at the park last week and had gone into the kitchen to make a drink – there was none there so he had gone into the pantry in search of a bottle of Ki-Ora when he noticed someone had been mucking about with the floorboards. He had understood straight away what it was and confirmed it minutes later when, having prized a board away, he saw the black bin bag. He had immediately pulled away, his arsehole as tight as his Nan's purse and had sat on the floor. Forgetting the squash he had gathered his thoughts before calmly walking out of the house, down to the boozer, stopping at the call box to ring Razor on the way. They had played a couple of games of pool when Razor had turned up. They had discussed it and forgot it. Seeing as it would probably mean the end of their meaningless little scally lives. But Paddy had not been able to think about anything else since.

Razor seemed to be back in the room. He stood up, wild-eyed and lent over to speak to Paddy quietly.

'I'll tell you what I wouldn't fucking do, you crazy little twat. I wouldn't even fucking dream of robbing your fucking brother-in-law, and in doing so, half of this city's fucking underworld. He'd finish you, you stupid cunt!' He then sat down and stared up at the ceiling, unable to work out if he felt sick because of the conversation or because of the colour of the fucking ceiling.

Paddy realised that Razor was well up for it.


## 1.4 Court

'Thomas Adams to court two please', the usher repeated as he limped through the crowd of people waiting to be punished. Tom tightened his tie and walked briskly, head down into the court. He was led towards the dock and asked to stand. Toby Charles approached the front of the court, shook hands with the prosecution and after everyone was put in the picture they were ready to start. Tom relaxed when he saw that everyone was smiling. It was really an open and shut case. Tom had instructed the court through Mr Charles that he would be pleading guilty to all charges. So this was just a get to know you and read a probation report, listen to any mitigating circumstances and then pass sentence.

'All rise.'

*Here we go* Tom thought, hoping to be on the train with the hour.

Then the door to the court opened with a low creak and he heard a giggle, a darting look from Charles and the gathered court population told Tom something was not going to plan. He turned towards the door and then towards the public gallery. Tom felt his heart jump as his thoughts nearly turned verbal. *Fucking hell. This is all I need.*

Into the gallery had just wandered some of the lads he knew from what he called 'going out and about'. Going out to Tom was his way of pigeonholing the people that didn't work much and went out all the time and were mostly off their heads mostly all of the time.

The magistrate looked horrified, Toby Charles looked annoyed and he felt very embarrassed. They were all looking very giggly and a bit spooked Tom immediately diagnosed this as Monday mushroom madness. This was confirmed when Danny leant over the rail, and apologised for giggling, explaining that they had been drinking mushroom tea for breakfast. Mushroom tea, that is, of the magic variety.

Tom smiled weakly, thinking *fuck off quickly, please...*

The magistrate had called for the court security guard and was in the process of explaining the problem to him. The lads, by this time, were in fits of laughter and Ally, a mad Scot, was shouting 'Free the Harwich one!'

The security guard politely asked the lads to leave, which they thought was hilarious. The pain continued as Justin then tried to offer everyone cold cans of orange Tango, complaining that it was hot in the courtroom and everyone deserved some refreshments. More security soon turned up and began, much to everyone's relief including Tom's, to shepherd the lunatics outside and off the premises. After a break of ten minutes the court was ready to start again. Although the magistrate and prosecution now looked more than ready to lock him up in time for lunch. He had after all, as his brief had pointed out, managed to piss off the one person he shouldn't have today.

The magistrate read out the charges.

'Are you Thomas Adams?'

'I am.'

'Do you reside at...'

Tom was quite confident that he would not be going to jail, even with all the goings on. She couldn't blame him for those silly fuckers, could she? He had been told this by his solicitor and by his probation officer, Richard Barford. A nice Irish fella with a big grey beard. He'd been in trouble before but nothing serious. It only bothered him that they were beginning to tot up and after this last one 'having a laugh' at the weekends didn't seem worth the agro. The bust at the house had revealed nothing, much to the amusement of himself and Lassie, who both felt so mightily happy afterwards that they had put on an old Braintree Barn tape of Mr C and Julian and had happily munched their way through a bag of pills. The local constabulary had torn the place apart, and even considered digging up the garden until they had found an ornamental machete and mask that Tom had bought at a car boot sale for a laugh. They were overjoyed at their 'find' and had arrested him for possession of an offensive weapon. A charge he was happy to consider would be his last. He looked at his watch and then up at the magistrate. He would have loved to have gone not-guilty and argued that the weapon was an ornament, but these fuckers in magistrate's courts were more corrupt than the old bill themselves. Do gooding wannabe freemasons who entered each other, as well as quiz shows, on a regular basis. *Come on then. Get on with it...*

He was embarrassed enough by today's proceedings already and just wanted to get back and clean the house.

'Mr Adams, you pleaded guilty to all charges and in consideration of your probation report I am willing to offer you a non-custodial sentence.'

*Nice.* He nodded his head in thanks.

'You will be required to carry out seventy-five...'

*Gutted, thought I wouldn't get any more than fifty.*

...hours of community service for your crime. However, for bringing this court into disrepute this will be increased by ten hours to eighty-five hours of community service. May this be a lesson to you not to invite your friends to court? Your crimes are serious and should not be trivialised by your own arrogance. Your order is to be carried out in your locality of Harwich. You may stand down.'

Tom looked down at his feet as he itched in his borrowed wool suit. *Fucking cow. What a liberty. I'm gonna kill those tossers.*

He stepped down and thanked Mr Charles.

'No problem, Tom. Hopefully this will be the last time you need my counsel. Good luck for the future.'

'Hope so,' he replied. They shook hands and Tom slunk off to meet the probation officer who was lurking in the shadows stage right.

The order would be every Sunday from 08.30–14.30. It would involve painting fences, cleaning gates and chopping down overgrown bushes. The major inconvenience was the fact that he'd have to watch himself on Saturday evening. Friday would now become his blow-out day.

Tom walked out of Colchester Magistrates' Court semi-relieved. He had a lot on his mind, including college on Wednesday. He loosened his tie, slung the suit jacket over his shoulders and wandered down the high street to the Castle, thinking a cool pint would sort his head out. He glanced at his watch and then up at the big clock to check the time, in doing so he nearly walked into a group of pissed squaddies and swerved into the chippy and was greeted by jeering and hot potato missiles. He promptly decided the squaddies would have been a better shout. Inside the chippy looked like a kid's

Play-Doh and paint party. He really couldn't believe the mess it was in. The woman behind the counter was shouting at a bloke who was covered in red sauce and was in the middle of downing the brown. He was happy to see that it was not only his day that this bunch of loons was intent on making a misery.

The woman behind the counter smiled at him and barked, 'Do you know this bunch of nutters?'

'Yeah unfortunately', Tom replied.

The four of them were now rolling around the floor laughing as Ally was puking red and brown sauce into a paper bag. There was a queue of people forming outside, some wanted to see the show, others just wanted to get their lunch.

In high-pitched desperation the woman called, 'Get them out of here and I'll give you free fish and chips.'

'OK! Salt and vinegar please, and a sachet of tartare sauce. And, give us some serviettes please to clean him up.' Tom nodded at the red and brown freak.

'Come on lads', Tom said pushing and pulling them, keeping out of the way of the sauce machine. 'Let's go to the pub.'

'Hey Tom!' Ally said. 'How's it going? Weren't you in court today?'

'Yeah, nice one,' he replied. 'I got eighty-five hours' community service.' He left it at that.

In the pub it was orange juices all round for the boys. He considered the fact that this may well bring them down from their buzz, he'd read somewhere that vitamin C has that effect on natural acid. He felt surprised that they even let them in, though they did hide Ally round the corner. This is no fun he thought. He wanted to get home.

It was late Monday afternoon and the story of the morning's proceedings twinned with more vitamin C had the desired effect. The lads were coming round as the mushiness wore off and all four had progressed to lager. They were all sorry they had cost him ten hours of his life and were promising to make it up to him. They were talking about getting some cars together for the weekend for a party in Oxford when Justin walked outside with a tray of drinks along with a bunch of older ladies, who looked like they had been drinking most of the day too. Louise, Louise, Sally and Karen were all very drunk, all very late twenties and all very pre-hen party.

They all sat down and began to talk shit to the assembled group. Tom surveyed the scene, thinking he was glad he wasn't on any gear as the assembled rotters in front of him would definitely send him over the edge. Squaddie's wives, mothers and divorcees all before thirty. Tom sat listening to the conversations, considering his options through another four or five rounds of drinks. It was half four. He thought he'd just head to the toilet and would then make tracks for home before he ended up out all night, again. The problem was, he was a bit pissed.

Tom promised himself that this lager would be his last. The girls were now friendly to the point that one of them, Louise was snogging Danny, the other Bean. Sally, Karen, Justin and Ally were happily watching.

'You bunch of sex cases.' Tom said as he sat down.

'Fucking right,' they all seemed to answer at once.

'I love watching,' said Karen, 'it really makes me wet.'

At this point Tom began to realise that he was coming up on an E. He sat down and took a gulp of lager; it tasted slightly bitter and fucking horrible as he finished it. As he put the glass down, Bang! He was up and flying, all at early o' clock on Monday, the day he had promised himself it would all end!

'You gang of absolute fuckers,' he gurned as he leant on the table, nibbling his bottom lip and rubbing the back of his head. He also felt the faint need to have a shit rising in his bowel.

'Told you we'd make it up to you mate,' said Bean.

'Back round to ours then,' one of the witches said.

Tom Adams closed his eyes and rocked back into his chair in ecstasy bliss. He knew he'd probably be spending the rest of the week off his face. He knew he should fight it, but what could he do? He stood up and put a hand on Bean's shoulder,

'You're a wanker,' he said, trying to eat his own tongue as his eyes rolled into the back of his head and the need to go to the toilet reached the peak of his need to do very soon list, 'but I loves ya.'

A group hug ensued and when he next consciously opened his eyes he was in a flat on the Grinstead Estate. A dirty little flat with toys strewn all over the front room. He looked at his watch – half six, he'd lost two hours, the usual really.

He considered how many hours of his life he had lost in these kinds of stupors, he'd paid for it even. He needed to get out of the flat and home as soon as possible. He looked up from his position next to the stereo and saw eight bodies jumping around shouting the words to 'Don't Make me Wait too Long'. He loved that song but not on a Monday, fuck he needed an e-vac fast. The song finished and Ally boomed out Doug Lazy's 'Let it Roll' for an encore. At this point he felt himself giving up again as he felt a wave of euphoria steaming through his body. He took a massive swig on a bottle of ready mixed JD and coke that was magically already in his hand and drifted off into ecstasy world, dreaming of being at home, sitting on the sofa, drinking a little wine and watching 'Cracker'.

He began to come around when he was half in, half out of a dream. He could hear noises, like some kind of vacuum cleaner. Was someone cleaning up? He tried to clear his mind and looked at his watch again, seven, he needed to call a cab. The sound was still there, this time clearer and almost like a broken vacuum cleaner, one with a teddy bear stuck in it. There was no sound of music now just this weird Hoover sound. When he opened his eyes Tom Adams knew that something was going very wrong in his life. Across from him on the floor, with her back to the sofa, was the woman he thought might be Karen. Her eyes were rolling round in her head and she was making a strange sound, almost like a vacuum cleaner. Lying on the floor in front of her was Ally, who seemed equally wasted and was making weird sounds too. The room was dotted with bottles of JD, wine and beer. There were also two bottles of champagne, one of which was next to Tom. The other bottle of Moet was in Ally's hand and it was sliding in and out of Karen's fanny, making the vacuum sounds. There was bubbling from the top of the bottle and this seemed to excite both Ally and Karen.

Tom staggered towards the kitchen, trying to work out how he felt about the scene He looked at the clock on the wall and then at his watch. He considered looking for the others, but glanced back into the front room and quickly decided to laugh off that idea. He moved toward the yellowing net curtain across the window, parted it with an empty Bic pen and wrote down the name of the road before going into the hallway and ringing a cab. A kind sounding girl promised him a cab as soon as humanly possible. He left, clicking the door shut and staggered to the end of the road. After five minutes of peering into the summer evening a cab turned up and Tom got in. 'Harwich please mate.' He glanced at the dashboard which winked back at him, 7.30. The whole day was a fucking write off.

'Fare upfront please, mate,' the cabby countered, 'there's some right twisted fuckers around here.'

'You're not fucking wrong, my friend,' Tom said handing him a score, 'You're not fucking wrong.'

## 1.5 Charles Bronson

Paddy nodded at Razor across the table as Razor stood up and took the plates and cups from their brunch back to the lovely Linda, a terrible looking thing whose neck was a sea of boils and make up. He watched him return to the table and raised his eyebrows when he didn't sit back down. Razor shook himself down and then spoke clearly, without much accent, as though he had been practising what he was going to say. 'You, la, are off you fucking tits. You are mad. Are you on a Charles Branson type death wish thing? Tell me you are fucking joking so I can fall about and you can call me a twat for believing you.' All this came out without Razor once taking a breath.

Paddy, impressed, looked at him and replied, equally slowly and methodically, though his motivation was more to allow understanding than thought process. 'There is a village in Cheshire missing an idiot and you are it Butch. You complete fucking imbecile. This is the chance of a lifetime, cash, lasses, cash and more lasses. I've got a plan... Are you listening to me Razor?' He slowed his speech down as much as he could. 'I have a fucking plan...' He paused before adding. "Oh, and it's Charles fucking Bronson you fucking lemon.'

'Fuck off, Pat-fucking-rick, you are a complete fucking knob head.'

'Come on soft lad, let's talk outside.' Paddy began shepherding Razor out of the door into the street with an arm around his best mate's shoulder.

'First, please tell me you're kidding,' said Razor hopefully.

'I can't do that fella, let's just talk outside.'

'I'm going home you fucking lunatic. You're on the fuckin scag. You're going to get us killed.'

Paddy watched as Razor left the café. He could have got the hump with the scag comment and Razor knew that. He and Razor both hated scag and scag heads. He shrugged his shoulders and followed slowly behind Razor. Neither said much. He thought he knew Razor. For all the laughs he wasn't that stupid and was deeply loyal. He was guessing he would go for it. He watched him. His shoulders were going up and down. He was kicking stones, and then looking to see where they ended up. He was, in Razor's own way, mulling over the idea. It wouldn't take long, of that Paddy was sure.

He'd known and hung around with Razor all his life. Except that is when he went off to join the Navy – something he was fiercely proud of and always talked about given the opportunity. Paddy, likewise, saw it as his duty not to tell anyone that he didn't pass his basic training because the lanky twat couldn't tread water for fifteen minutes. He was a sound lad though, as long as he was regularly fed with Burger King and strong cider. They had walked quite a way now and he had expected an answer before they got to the first Moby, the usual drunks were gathered outside with their wag and coupons. It must be around 11:30 he thought, quite a nice day, maybe he'd try his luck in the bookies later.

His thoughts were interrupted by Razor standing in front of him, casting a shadow over and beyond him and blocking out the heat of the morning rays. 'I have a few questions, la.'

The warmth returned to Paddy's body as he realised that Razor was halfway to saying yes. 'Go right ahead, I might not have all the answers though. That's why I need you with me.'

'Where the fuck will we go? Do you realise its forever? What will we do with all that money? How will we get to where we are going? How will we...'

Paddy stopped dead and held his arms up. 'Hold tight there, Razor, I don't know all this stuff. What I do know is this, if we take that money we're not the only ones in trouble. Yeah they'll want to kill us, but people will want to kill them too. It will create a fucking turf war. They will probably kill each other. They'll wipe a generation out trying to win the city. It's all scag, we hate scag. This could be a chance to make history, no?'

'Yeah, history in fucking silence, and fucking exile.'

'True.' Paddy smiled, 'But what an exile, Razor, think of all the places on earth we could go to, live in. Away from this place. Put another way, if we don't do this we will be working for George until we go to prison for him. We'll get no thanks, just a warning when we're nicked that grasses are easier to kill inside prison than out. Think on that soft lad.'

'Fuck it though, Paddy, not seeing me ma and pa? I don't think I could do it.'

They don't give a toss anyway, Razor. They're both rinses down the fucking Legion. There either in the boozer or in bed, too drunk to fuck.'

'Hey, Dickhead, you're out of order, that's my family, I'm not slagging yours but I could."

'Razor, I don't give a toss. Ma is dead, my Da's involved in peddling scag with my wanker of a brother in law. I really don't give one fuck at all, lad.'

Razor had started to realise what they were considering. They muted their conversation as a group of lads came towards them. There were some low-key nodded scally acknowledgments and shortly they were alone again.

Razor looked into Paddy's face, looking for some tip as to where he was leaning, he could see he'd go for it. His mind was made up. He had known him too long. He would be thinking through all the shots right now. Right down to the snooker on the black and the double to finish, remembering to chalk his cue after every shot and rubbing the end before giving it away. Liverpool was a great city. There were many in England. However some people in those cities got a bad deal, leaving them without much choice but to take their chances when they came. He'd miss his mum and dad but he kinda knew Paddy was right. This time the response was the one Patrick Wherry was looking for.

Let's do it, la. Let's do a runner.'

'Fucking boss!' Paddy grabbed Razor and gave him a hug. 'Come on pal, we've got loads to talk about.'

Paddy led them to a quiet boozer where he insisted they drank shandy, which not only shocked Razor but the barmaid too, who replied to the order, 'This is Liverpool boys, watch yerselves.'

Razor was furious, 'Knobhead, now you're pushing it, I'm fucking telling you.'

Paddy changed the order to a Strongbow for Razor and they retreated to a booth.

The plan was easy. Paddy explained in detail how they would do it. They would go for the two Scousers with forty grand in a holdall, on a weekend break in London look. They both laughed but it wasn't far from the truth. They didn't need clothes, they could buy new ones. All they needed to do was wash, wear clean clothes and Reeboks, and most importantly remember to bring their passports.

Razor's immediate thought was *For fuck's sake what are we doing?* But he decided to leave it well alone. After all, he'd just agreed to everything.

They agreed they would go their separate ways and sort their shit out, do what they had to do and meet at the Druid's Head near Lime Street. From there they would go to London and make a plan to get abroad as soon as possible.

Paddy wandered home deep in thought. He had gotten his own way and now had an assistant of sorts. He hoped Razor would be ok; after all he only had to keep his cool, get his passport and fill up a holdall for fuck's sake.

## 1.6 Gym

Paddy turned into his road and counted his footsteps, 172 to the point of turning the key in the door. The house was quiet. It would have only been his dad anyway since Ma had died of cancer two years back. At the thought of her he crossed himself and promised to attend confession and mass as soon as he could. His sister, dressed smartly in her school uniform, stared down at him from the wall in the hallway. She was much older now, was married to George and was a nutty bitch, he didn't speak to her. He still remembered being held down and his sister's friends practising their blowjob technique on him, fucking slags. It would have been ok if they were fit but they were all dogs. All of them. He realised then that he would miss none of them except Ma, and there wasn't anything he could do about that.

*Maybe I could give some cash to the Macmillan Fund. Jesus, Mary and Joseph, what a confession this would make!* He walked through the house into the kitchen grinning, and then spun around as the door clicked.

'Hello, Da.'

'What the fuck are you doing skulking about with a huge fucking grin on at this time of day, son?'

'I'm not skulking about anywhere. I've just got in and I'm off to bed for a kip.'

'Well don't kip too fucking long, George has you and Razor in mind for a little job later on.'

'Ok, Da.' Paddy retreated upstairs, eager to get away from his dad in case he smelt the betrayal coming. *Fuck you and that George twat. I'm gonna fuck you both over.* He smiled to himself as he sat down on the throne for part two of the morning's bum opera.

He heard his dad grab his coat and unlock the door chains and mortice lock. Things were looking up he thought.

'Paddy!' He shouted up the stairs. 'Another thing, if you see that Sean lad, you tell him I wanna word with the wee fucker.'

Paddy pulled the door open a few inches, 'What for Da?'

'Not that it's any of your fucking business, but I'm gonna shoot that fucking little turkey.' He then walked out and slammed the door shut.

Paddy heard him as he walked up the path, then strangely he heard him stop, turn around and walk back. He listened as his dad returned to the house, climbed the stairs and leered around the bathroom door looking straight into Paddy's eyes. Paddy felt his arse cheeks bubble as his dad began to speak.

'And I naa what you're up too with that soft-lad mate of yours too, you fucking little jockey, so if you fancy still having your knees where they should be leave the fuck well alone, you daft little cunt.'

Paddy blinked. Blinked again and stared at his dad in total disbelief. His dad was still speaking to him and he needed to concentrate on what he was saying, how did he fucking know?

'I said, make sure you check in on that pissy uncle of yours tonight before you do anything, he's a fucking liability.' He felt like he'd had some kind of flashback, like he'd seen in films. He felt faint and for the first time has misgivings about what he and Razor were going to do.

'OK.' Paddy gasped in some very important oxygen and felt his eyes slip back into their sockets as he watched his Da walk away back down the stairs and out before he leant back against the cistern and mopped his brow of the beads of sweat that had gathered there.

Paddy thought about what his dad had just said, and what he had thought he had said at first, before he had got his composure and listened properly. He made a mental note to pop into see his uncle Joey before he left. He finished and wandered downstairs, munched on a cold bit of toast and considered his next move. While eating the toast he realised he was shaking like a leaf. He threw the toast in the bin. He didn't want to think about his next move just yet.

Razor was very scared; he had always wanted to go abroad but this wasn't how he'd imagined it – forever abroad, never home. Just constantly on holiday, it sounded good the first time he said it to himself but on reflection he wasn't so sure. He fished around for his key and couldn't find it, an extra deep rummage finally struck gold and he retrieved the key from his trousers, he looked up and saw two girls who had obviously been laughing at him groping himself outside his own front door. He smiled behind a weak laugh and a semi-blush as he pushed open the door and closed it behind him. He still lived with his Ma and Da who, unlike most in the area, were both at work. He went to the kitchen and grabbed a piece of scrap paper, scribbling down toothpaste/passport/clean clothes/cash/train times and then opened the fridge and made himself a cheese and pickle sandwich. Half an hour later he was at the front door, he checked the list and everything on it was in his bag. He was pulling the door shut when he realised a he had made a small but very important mistake – he had left Crispy Sue under the bed and needed to get rid of her before his mum cleaned the room. Back upstairs the offending sock which was stiff with masturbatory residue was removed from her hiding place and ceremoniously placed in the bin in the kitchen as he knew this was the one that would be emptied most regularly. As the door fell into place and he made his way toward the city centre he wondered if he'd be shot, caught, tortured or killed before the end of June 1991.

Paddy was ahead of himself and the 3.30 train seemed ages off, so he decided he had time to change his clothes again – the sweat, paranoia and emotional turmoil that had been spent in moving the forty grand from under the floorboards into his Head holdall had left him drained and looking as if he'd been mugged in a water-park. He put the bag in the hallway and slipped his passport and smellies into the side compartment. One of the zippers had bust and he considered this piece of good fortune as he wrapped some plasters around the top, after all, the last thing he needed was someone else picking up the wrong bag and becoming the recipient of his balls of steel moment in sunny Liverpool. It was 2.00 and time for the visit to Uncle Joey's could become a problem. The only reason his Da wanted him to go round was to make sure his Auntie Breda hadn't killed Joey in another of their pisshead fights.

He didn't bother looking back as he walked out of the house he had lived in for twenty-one years carrying forty grand, not one penny of which was his own. The door slammed and he did a right at the end of the gate and headed towards Joey and Breda's counting his steps as he went. Their house wasn't far, it would be a 10-minute stop over and then away to Lime Street and away for good.

He reached the top of the road and walked toward the crossing that would take him over and past the Leek and Whistle. The lights changed, red, red-amber, green. The sound of the pelican crossing pierced his ears and he stepped out into the road. At this point he could see the pub car park and in it a black BMW, barely a few months old. His guts lurched and he had to concentrate to stop himself from instantly throwing up on the pavement. He readjusted his bag and put his head down as he quickened his step. Then there it was, a loud bang. Was it in his head? No, there it was again. A bang on the window, and another. This time only harder. He ignored it and tried to walk on. The next bang felt like the window had broken, he looked up and waved, there was a massive crack in one of the decorated windows in the pub. Behind the broken window was his brother-in-law holding a pool cue and gesturing that he wanted Paddy to come inside.

Paddy's thoughts were racing, should he run? Cry? Fuck, he was probably going to die. He began to recite a 'Hail Mary' as he approached the front door of the Leek, they never fucking drank in this boozer, it was a shit hole. It had gone up in flames three times this year, all of them insurance jobs and the like. Why the fuck were they in there? Time seemed to slow down and he seemed to be able to pick out the smallest details on the doors and posters, screws missing and tired wooden furniture outside, begging like him, for salvation from the pain of existence. He put his hand on the dirty brass door plate and pushed the door open. Inside, by the pool table and surrounded by the Stones brothers stood George Meachen and Gary Sparks. All nasty cunts in their own right.

'Hey, look who it fucking is; it's my fucking brother-in law!'

'Alright lad.' They all seemed to say in unison, like fucking parrots in a cage.

Paddy nodded to the man he had just relieved of £40,000.

'Will ya have a drink with us, Patrick?'

'No, I can't really. I got shit to do.'

George's face pulled into a cold stare as he surveyed the pool table for his next shot. He looked up at the group with him and then over towards Paddy. He spoke in a cold menacing way that made it clear he should stay and respect the offer of a drink.

'We've all got shit to do. Have a drink with me.'

Paddy Wherry could feel sweat running down his legs, chilling as it met the top of his socks. He thought he'd try one more time to get out of this potential death sequence in his tortured life.

'I'd love to George, but I'm off to the gym,' motioning with his bag in the air.

In a blur George was round the table and had grabbed Paddy's holdall. George, bag in hand looked at him, 'Fuck the gym you little cunt, have a fucking drink when it's offered.'

Paddy watched in slow motion as the bag of money was launched through the air and landed by the bar. He flinched as he saw the open end with the broken zip. His passport was just visible. His voice choked back into life, 'I'll have a bottle please.'

George turned to the barman, 'A bottle of Export, please.'

The beer duly arrived and Paddy gulped at it, trying to finish it as soon as it hit the bar, eyes constantly watching the bag, sat alone on the floor almost screaming, 'George, open me, your brother-in-law is a thieving little cunt.'

At any moment, Patrick Wherry knew it could be all over. George would also work out he wasn't in this alone.

An arm flew round his neck and he his head was pulled into a huge armpit with a sweet but off-putting odour. They had probably been up on it all night.

'You alright, you wee little fucker?'

'Yeah I'm fine cheers. Thanks for the beer.'

Bottles were raised and the Stones brothers argued about who was actually playing his brother in law at pool. In the space of five minutes all four of them had been in and out of the toilet. Clearly of all them were fully charged on the marching powder.

Paddy began to look for an exit.

George had won the last game but the mood had gone weird.

'So, what are you boys doing down this way today?'

Gary Sparks looked incapable of speaking; the Charlie must be superb.

'Just a little visit to see a friend.' George made a gesture for another round of drinks.

'No thanks, mate, really.'

'Fuck off la, I want to show you something.'

This was serious. Paddy still had to visit Breda and Joey and then meet Razor at Lime Street, and that would only happen if he could get out of here with his life. He looked at the clock on the wall and gulped down more booze, he looked at George.

'What do you wanna show me, la?'

At this point the barman had just arrived with a new set of drinks for them which he placed down carefully on the bar. As he did George swung around and smashed the barman round the face with the pool cue. Paddy heard the crack of bone as the nose split, along with the top of his eye. He fell back into the bar area and was followed by George who lined up the cue and smashed it into the barman's legs, causing him to scream out in pain. He then stood over him with glass, crisps and beer towels everywhere and started stamping on his body and face.

The bar emptied in seconds and another female member of staff ran in and tried to hit a panic alarm in the bar area, she was met by one of the Stones brothers who grabbed her, pulled her arms down onto the bar and smashed both her hands with a hammer. Paddy did not know what the fuck to do. This had all happened in seconds and been done in absolute silence. The woman was howling, with massive open wounds to both hands, the barman had passed out. He saw George lean over and pull the barman's head up, bloodied and broken. At last he spoke, quietly and under his breath, 'Don't ever, ever fuck about with me la.'

Paddy looked towards the Stones brother who was holding the woman's head against the bar. She was screaming and her hands were bleeding heavily, with bits of loose skin hanging off them. He pulled her up to his face height and said, 'You fucking talk to anyone bitch and I'll cut your cunt out with a jigsaw, got it?'

He then smashed his head into her face, sending her reeling back into the optics; her broken body fell on the floor with whiskey and vodka dripping all over her. He reached into his pocket and pulled out a zippo. 'Shall I fucking burn her?'

'Leave her, she knows.' George Meachen then turned to Paddy grinning, with hands and forehead covered in blood. He grabbed a beer cloth and rubbed his face and hands,

'See la, you're in the firm. Let's make some fucking money, eh!'

Paddy grabbed the bag and made toward the door.

'I'm getting the fuck out of here George.'

'Us too, wanna lift to the gym?' George spoke as if he was just out on a shopping trip looking for socks.

Paddy, his head screaming, turned down the offer and left the pub, swinging a hard left as soon as he could. As he turned he looked back and saw George and the others calmly leave the pub, get in the BMW and drive off. He sat on the wall and cried. Jesus fucking Christ he thought. He looked down at the bag and thought of Razor. He'd killed them both. He had fucking killed them both.

He got himself together as he heard the wail of the sirens flying down the road. He turned and walked, rubbing his streaming eyes with his arm. As he walked he decided that none of this would ever reach Razor's ears. It would be unfair and if they were going to die for this they were going to have a right good fucking laugh before they were caught. It was done now. No going back, unless it was for their own funeral.

## 1.7 Wag

After a steady ten minute walk he bowled into Joey's street feeling slightly better, it was a normal Liverpudlian street, of old back-to-back cotton industry workers' houses where the front doors opened onto the streets and everybody knew everyone. He remembered it well from days spent in the back room while people from the bank or other lenders knocked on the door and waited for a response. No one opened their door to anyone that knocked at that time in the morning, even now in Liverpool, and the stupid thing was everybody's doors were always unlocked, it was a trust thing, and no one had anything to steal anyway. He got to the front door of Joey and Breda's house and saw the door was ajar; it kind of gave him a sense of home, that nothing had changed. He smiled to himself as he pushed the door open and called a greeting to those inside, the greeting stopped abruptly and was replaced by 'What the fuck is going on here' followed as fast as he could spit it out.

'Hello, Paddy son,' Joey said, completely ignoring the fact that he was kneeling down in the front room with a plastic knife and fork in his pants with some fish n' chips in newspaper surrounded by bottles of Merrydown Silver.

Paddy looked at Joey like a Huntsman would look at his favourite gundog before he shot him. 'Come on, you crazy old sod' he said, and pushed a few bottles of cider out the way so as to able to help him up. It was at that moment that he smelt a terrific smell of shit, he reeled away and knocked over a half drunk bottle of cider, fell into a chair and sat looking in disbelief at his uncle Joey. He hadn't noticed that the newspaper did not in fact contain a fish 'n' chip tea but about half a pound of human waste. At this moment Breda came steaming in and grabbed Paddy's bag.

'Wouldya watch what the feck you're doing there Joey, you've gone and got Paddy's bag all wet,' she scolded his uncle.

Paddy jumped up and grabbed the bag. 'It's fine Breda, honestly, it'll be all right.'

'Will it fuck yer silly sod,' she said, grabbing the bag. 'We'll put the wet stuff on the horse and yer'll have yer tea here yer little fecker.'

Paddy clung on to the bag, feeling new beads of sweat start to run down his back,

'No Breda, honestly, you need to concentrate on Joey for Christ's sake, he's having his own shite for tea!'

This seemed to calm Breda down and Paddy too. She fell about laughing and Joey just sat there bemused, slowly cutting his own excrement into little pieces as Breda explained that the night before had been a particular heavy night; her Housing Benefit had come in and a friend down the road had a little win on the Bingo. She carried on to say that after a long afternoon she and Joey had come home and had a blistering row that ended with her knocking him out and in the process dislodging his gold tooth, which he had then swallowed. His uncle was now in the process of retrieving the tooth.

Today was becoming slightly too weird for Paddy and he asked for and received a cup of tea with lots of sugar. The parcel of shit was hastily put away, though not thrown away as the tooth had not yet been recovered. He sat and explained he was away to play five-a-side later with Razor and had to get off as he was only meant to pop in and make sure they were alright. He made his way to the door, told them he loved them and would see them soon and left. Out on the street he felt cooler if not safer and a glance at his watch told him it was just after 3 o'clock. A fifteen-minute walk would put him in the centre of town with time to grab some food and a drink.

He met Raymond on busy Lord Nelson Street with a wink and smile as he shook the bag. Purchases of tickets, beers, sweets, a newspaper and a Burger King for Razor accomplished, they boarded the train and took their seats in first class looking forward to the ticket collector coming round and asking them to move. They cracked a can and Paddy Wherry used his feet to push the bag under the seat but remembered to still leave a leg in the holdall handle, old habits dying hard. The cold 1664 tasted great and Paddy leant back in his seat and began to plan their next move in his head. He looked across at Razor who had instantly fallen asleep. He smiled and wondered to himself what the hell he had gotten them into. Looking out of the window he yawned, and finished his can. He cracked another and placed it on the small table under the window before resting his head in the plush comfort of the first class accommodation. Paddy woke just as they pulled into Crewe and instantly shuffled his leg, checking the holdall was still attached to him. Paddy grabbed his can from earlier, it was warmer but ultimately still drinkable. Razor was still asleep across from him and he gazed out of the window, not wanting to wake him. By the time the train pulled away both were sound asleep and on the way to London.

Paddy was dreaming that he was on an island somewhere in South East Asia, which could only be reached by little boats and they only came twice a day, there was beer but not many people. He wandered up and down the beach in his dream and then back to his little hut just a short distance away. Then he was poking fish in the sea with a big stick, trying to catch some food, prod, prod, prod...

'Wake up son,' prodded the ticket collector, 'tickets please and I hope you two have both got first class ones for the WHOLE of your journey!'

Paddy smiled and gestured towards sleeping beauty,

'We've both got tickets, hang on a sec,' Paddy kicked Razor and nodded towards the guard, they both went into their pockets while one of Paddy's legs instinctively pulled his bag toward him.

The guard scanned the tickets and looked them both up and down. 'So boys, off to the bright lights of Amsterdam for the week?'

Paddy looked at the guard with a stare that stretched between puzzled and are you working for the dole? 'How do you know that?' he enquired with a suspicious look.

'Easy one that lads,' the guard mused, 'you've got tickets to Harwich, and the last time I looked no great football side plays in Harwich, in fact the only reason someone usually goes to Harwich is to get to Holland and Amsterdam.' The guard looked at them with a 'look at me, I'm fucking Columbo' grin on his face, gave them their tickets and sauntered off into the next carriage.

They looked at each other and shrugged. Neither of them had looked at the paper and both seemed too caught up in their own thoughts to bother. Paddy stared out of the window, his mind back in Asia, and Razor sat mulling over the possible ways that his body could be disposed of that would leave him unrecognisable to his family. He shuddered and tried not to think about gangster films. They shot past Rugby station and Paddy looked into the bright summer afternoon as it started to subside into the hills. All was going well so far. Milton Keynes was next: a true shit hole he'd heard, with a living boil on the side called Leighton Buzzard, which was a very cool name. Watford came and went like Elton John at a Texan dinner party and they were in London. London always had something to offer. The trip round the circle line to Liverpool street featured a man in a suit who was crying, shouting at what must have been his girlfriend, that she had bought the wrong sausages, that these really wouldn't do and she was going to have to go back to Farringdon and get some more. He was in bits. Paddy was intrigued by this conversation, as was Razor. They got off at Liverpool Street, looked at the man, looked at each other and shrugged the 'wanker' shrug. Paddy considered giving him a couple of fifty pound notes and telling him to get his own fucking sausages but thought better of it. They negotiated the building site that was the station, huge signs informing them that it would be finished in December that year. Razor pointed out the pub in the corner, but the Harwich train was leaving in 10 minutes and Paddy wanted them both to be on it.

## 1.8 Poison

The taxi driver was clearly a U2 fan, which wasn't a problem at all, but Tom did think he had the wrong album on.

'You got the *Joshua Tree*,' Tom asked hopefully, as 'New Year's Day' crashed around the cab, almost killing him.

'I have indeed,' said the cabbie. 'A sublime album.'

'Could you put it on?'

'Are you ok son?' the cabbie ventured.

'No I'm fucking not, mate,' Tom wailed, 'I've had a fucking beast of a day. Can you just put on 'One Tree Hill'?'

'Sorry, mate, I'd love to but the tapes fucked, and anyway I'm no one's fucking Tony Blackburn, shitty day or not!'

Tom subsided into silence. 'New Year's Day' was replaced by some Madonna and 15 minutes later they were outside Tom's place. He told the driver to keep the change and walked up the path to what he hoped would be a house with the hot water on. He found Lassie in the kitchen, who greeted him with: 'I didn't think you were coming home today.'

'Good one dog boy, why don't you take yourself for a shit over the park?'

Tom opened the fridge and cracked two beers, sat down and began to tell his mate about the day's proceedings.

Lassie doubled up with laughter and spluttered: 'I really can't believe it, lad. Jesus, you bring it on yourself don't you?'

Please, I don't need a lecture,' Tom answered, as stared at the wall. It made him feel a lot better. The wall just stood there, like a big magnolia concrete pillow. It seemed to make sense, just sitting there looking at the wall.

'Wake up, freak,' Lassie said. 'You were zoning out there, fella.'

Lassie stood over the dishevelled looking Tom and thought about throwing a blanket over him, instead he wandered off into the kitchen and made himself a nice cheese and salad cream sandwich. He pondered toasting it, but realised it would make a hell of a mess in the new Breville. He picked up a half smoked spliff, lit it and took a chunk out of the meal he had made himself. He heard Tom go upstairs.

Tom spent ten minutes standing under the shower, switching from cold to hot, and making sure he was still alive or at least had nerve endings. Then he lay back on his bed listening to Talking Heads while he finished his beer and decided that a few drinks on the seafront with Lassie were what he needed to finish off his day.

Lassie appeared to be dead. Tom felt his neck and the confirmed the worse – he was still alive. The pointer to his catatonic state was the huge reefer in the ashtray. Lassie looked the same as he had when they had left school: massively stoned. Tom had known James Lassiter since they were at school and had shared a house with him for nearly two years, even though Lassie was a massive stoner. Tom hated smoking and usually made him do it in the garden. Shithead he thought, turning off the TV. He picked up the phone in the hallway and called a cab. Ten minutes later he was in the Cliff Hotel. He took a stool at the bar. To his left was the jukebox and the right a 'hot peanut' machine he had never seen before, a new gimmick just waiting to be launched he guessed, but which would probably end up being properly launched out of the door by some maniac at the weekend.

He smiled at the young filly behind the bar, had he slept with her? He didn't remember, but had a vague recollection of intimacy. Pretty and a lovely bottom too he thought as she opened the fridge for a bottle of Holsten Pils. He nodded at a couple of the pool or maybe darts team as they left for an away match. The pub was verging on empty and his first bottle was gone in seconds. The next followed, though the complete lack of attention the barmaid was paying him led him to conclude that he must indeed have slept with her. He would make an effort to grab her again after he put some tunes on. Flicking the buttons on the jukebox he thought again about the bottle of champagne thrusting into Sandra, or was it Lucy? He didn't remember. Filthy bastards he thought, and ten extra hours of community service for the privilege. He would just do the time, and keep his head down. He carried on choosing tunes, five for a quid it said. The first one came on, 'We Built This City' by Starship. He looked up as the barmaid began to giggle and blushed.

'That one's a mistake, sorry. Can you eject it please?'

She walked towards him smiling, 'Pardon?'

'Err, that's a mistake, can you get rid for me?'

'Of course, Tom,' she said, bending over to find the correct button and giving him the beginnings of a semi.

'Cheers, you've saved my blushes there. Can I buy you a drink?'

'Not allowed to drink on duty,' she purred. 'It'll have to be after work.'

Worked every fucking time he thought. Now he just had to get her to say her fucking name!

'No problem, I'll just have a few drinks here and wait for you, my sweet.' He leant back on his bar stool and sipped his Pils, while the jukebox whirred and the Happy Mondays came on. He sang along in his head and felt a little bit more relaxed.

## 1.9 Travel

Razor had never really left Liverpool and he was enjoying the journey. There was a woman sitting directly opposite him, kinda city type he'd thought. Black suit, shoes and bag, with harsh almost black eyes. As the train approached Colchester she stood to get off and smiled at him, in pity he thought, as she walked to the exit. He was admiring her arse as she went when she looked over her shoulder and winked back at him. Razor sat there, bulging out of his trousers. He glanced up at the wall to see which way the toilet was, left... He wanted to tear the head off his old man while that wink was still in his memory.

The train moved and Paddy awoke with a start, 'Where the fuck are we?'

'Fuck me, la, a city bird just gave me the come on! A cracking skirt type, honest,' he blurted out with one hand on his throbbing cock. 'I gotta get to the bog, la, let me outta me seat.'

Paddy stood up laughing to let Razor out and looked down, 'Where's the fecking bag, Razor?' he said in panic.

Razor looked at his best mate. He looked like a smack head from home, with sweat beads forming all across his forehead. 'It's here,' he said, pulling the Head bag from under the seat. 'It's here.' His knob now resembled a winter acorn in his pants.

They sat in silence, starring at the bag as the train rolled along, each wondering who was going to bottle it first. When they reached Harwich Town they grabbed their holdalls and headed outside, where they found a bus station with no buses and a solitary taxi. The taxi driver, *Racing Post* in hand, was half asleep but quickly roused by their broad Scouse. You couldn't trust Scousers.

'Hello mate,' Paddy ventured. 'Can you take us to a decent hotel?'

The driver looked around, put his paper down and replied, 'Sure, lads, there's only one half decent one round these parts, the Cliff Hotel.'

The driver watched as the two young lads, early twenties he thought, put their gear in on the back seat and got in. Neither of them went for the front seat, which suggested they were up for doing a runner. *Fucking Scousers, always on the fucking rob. Cunts. Wankers. They were sure to try to leg it.* He looked into the rear-view mirror. They weren't scruffy, but they weren't well dressed either. *Thieving fucking shit bag Scouse cunts.*

'There you go lads,' he said, as he stopped the cab. 'Best one in town, and it's got a bar.' *Thieving wankers.*

Paddy pressed twenty into the driver's hand. 'Cheers,' he and Razor chimed. 'You're a gent.'

The driver watched the two lads walk into the hotel before pulling away. *Nice lads those two.*

Paddy and Razor found no one in the lobby of the hotel except a large African Grey parrot sitting in a cage. It stared at them, unfurling the red plume of feathers on its head. Razor approached the beast with a finger to stroke it. WHAM! The beak of the monster struck a huge blow on the cage making a loud clanging sound. Through his laughter Paddy noticed a girl of about twenty, dressed in black trousers and a white top watching them.

'Can I help you?', she said.

Twenty minutes later the two of them were sat in a nice twin room overlooking a beach. There was a bathroom with a shower and a small mini bar. It would do fine. The TV flickered into life and again an uneasy silence settled over them.

Razor broke it. 'Right, we're here now lad. What the fuck do we do now? You do know we are far from safe, fella, they WILL come for us.'

Paddy pulled himself up and looked over towards Razor. 'They'll come for us. As soon as they know where we are. We have to get out of the country as soon as possible.' He stood up, thinking about the pub earlier, he wanted to talk about it but it might well break Razor if he knew. He walked to the sink and splashed some water over his face and then stuck his hand in the holdall, pulling out a handful of notes. 'Come on, let's go and have a drink.'

They went downstairs and followed the signs to the bar. Razor stopped on the way in to say, 'Eh, la, things are looking up! Listen to that: 'Wrote for Luck', fucking mega tune!'

The room was empty except for one lad sitting at the bar, a couple of blokes at the end playing darts and the barmaid. The girl smiled and asked them what they would like to drink. They were both mesmerised by the unfamiliar accent and stared at her, until she asked again and stirred them into action.

They took their Carlsberg's to a seat by the window and listened to the Happy Mondays. They both loved the Mondays but equally hated the fact they were Mancs.

## 1.10 Hello Mum

Tom Adams sat at the bar, engrossed by the tune, he'd seen them live with the Stone Roses at the Alexandra Palace; first E in fact. It had ripped him apart. He'd necked it and then stood around waiting, drinking and wondering what all the fuss was about. Twenty minutes later he'd been sat on the toilet breathing in, licking his lips like a lizard on speed. Rushes hitting him every thirty seconds until the buzz nearly made him faint. Waves of electricity surging through his body as he wandered back, smiling and hanging on to a bottle of warm lager for the next three hours while he stomped up and down to the best music he had ever heard in his life. He'd ended so sweaty he'd looked like he'd jumped in a swimming pool, wandering round vaguely searching for the car in the car park clutching a bottle of water. He couldn't even remember what car he had come in. He smiled and laughed to himself. What a fucking top night. Fancying another drink, he stuck his hand in his pocket for some cash and felt a plastic bag. He looked around and pulled it out, 14 Es. Fuck, he didn't even know he'd had them. What a twat!

It was at this moment he noticed the two lads come in. He quickly shoved the bag back in his jeans. Must be staying in the hotel he thought as he discreetly looked them up and down, he'd never seen them before. Scousers, he realised when they gave their order. A long way from home. They were probably on the way to Holland, Amsterdam most likely. Drugs and fucking. A great trip and one all lads should experience as many times as possible before they die, go to jail or get married.

He listened to them, as they sat behind him discussing the Happy Mondays. He was glad he'd put the tune on; he'd pleased someone on what had been a very shitty day so far. He ordered another Pils, left some money on the bar and went to the toilet. On the way back to the bar he rang home to invite Lassie down for a few beers. He could be here in fifteen minutes, and if he did it in ten he'd buy him an Indian. The phone rang and rang. He waited for ten rings or so before putting the receiver down. His bottle of Pils and his change was on the bar. He smiled at the barmaid with No Name and sat down. The lads in the window seat were now raving about the new tune, 'Fool's Gold'. Tom had put on the 10:09 minute version and the Scouse lads were lapping it up. He swigged his beer and thought about an Indian, if Lassie wasn't going to join him perhaps No Name girl would. He took another gulp of his lager, motioned for another and put his hand in his pocket for cash.

The beer arrived and No Name girl winked at him... 'Don't get too drunk.' She walked back down the bar swinging her petite little arse and all thoughts of using the phone were gone.

He was now potentially on a promise with No Name girl.

He sat back and listened to the lad's conversation, great tune, best bassist ever, Manc cunts. One looked over and caught Tom's attention. 'Eh mate,' Razor asked, 'Is it you who likes the Roses and Mondays?'

'Indeed,' Tom replied, using his beer to toast the northern sound he had so often got off his head to.

'Fucking ace, la,' Razor shouted across the pretty much empty bar, raising a stare from the two men playing darts.

'Do you wanna join us mate?'

Tom considered the move from No Name chat-up area to a table with two shifty Scousers. He got up from the bar, thanked the lads for their hospitality and joined them at their table. This could be interesting he thought, and waved to No Name girl that he'd see her in a bit.

The conversation flowed from why they were in Harwich (Tom had guessed correctly that they were on their way to Amsterdam), to music – The Stone Roses versus the Happy Mondays – to football.

'It's up for grabs now,' Tom was shouting, feeling the effects of the numerous bottles of Pils he had taken care of during the evening. He was recalling with vigour, the last game of the 1989 season when Michael Thomas scored with the last kick of the game at Anfield to win the title.

'Fuck you!' the Scousers chimed, 'fucking lucky bastards... that's all you were!'

'And who's won the title this year chaps?' Tom asked, remembering that Arsenal could have won this year's title without kicking a ball if Liverpool lost at Notts Forest before Arsenal took on Man United at Highbury in an 8 p.m. kick off. Liverpool lost to Forrest and Arsenal tonked the Manc's 3-1. Beautiful. After telling the scousers that, in effect, Liverpool had gifted it to Arsenal they were all happy to change the subject.

'Wankers.'

'Shithouses.'

'Another beer?' Paddy got up and went to the bar for more drinks.

Tom sat back, enjoying himself. These lads were sound. He even thought about going to Dam with them for a couple of days. It would be hilarious.

Paddy was on his way back from the bar, where he'd had no luck with the No Name barmaid. He sat down and passed out the beers.

Razor leant over so that his voice could only be heard by the people at the table, but because of his pissed state everyone else in the bar heard it too. 'Can you get us any Es Tom?'

'Shut your fucking noise you prick,' Paddy hissed, kicking his mate in the shins.

'I fucking whispered that, you cunt,' Razor rubbed his shins and looked at the table. 'Wanker.'

Paddy ignored the moan, and looked at Tom. 'Can you then?'

Tom looked around the bar, no one had taken any notice of the three of them, No Name girl was cleaning and the darts players had long gone. It was half nine on a Monday. Jesus, could he really be arsed? He then remembered the fourteen little fellas he had in his pocket and thought about a potential little earner.

'How many do you want if I can lads? After all it is a Monday and people tend to shut up shop till Thursday, at least round here.'

The lads looked at each other and Paddy spoke, 'Ten or so, just enough to have a little giggle. Is there anywhere to go in Harwich if you're off your nut?'

'Nowhere.'

'Who gives a fuck, if you can get them we'll have them, la, and you'll be in on the party too eh?'

'Maybe,' Tom said. 'I'll drink this and have a walk down the road. I know a lad who might have some left over from the weekend.'

A bottle of Pils was drained and Tom nodded and told the lads he would be twenty minutes or so. He walked out into the summer evening, did a left, looked over his shoulder to make sure he wasn't being followed, did another left and walked towards the shops. He reached the estate agents and sat on the wall. He looked at his watch and waited five minutes before walking back to the bar. He walked in to find a new cold bottle of Pils waiting for him. He had a bit of a buzz on now and was feeling a tad reckless. He explained to the lads that a friend down the road had had a few left over, they were OK, not Doves, but OK. Triple X's. He'd managed to scrounge fourteen, and they were thirteen quid each. He felt bad charging them so much but business was business.

'No problem, la, cheers for getting them us, after all its fucking Happy Monday!' Razor took the bag, looking like he had been given the keys to a Ferrari. Paddy went off to the toilet, counted some cash out, returned and paid the bill.

'Right, let's get on it.' He turned to Razor, who'd already got three out in his hand. They each grabbed an E and swallowed.

As time and beer passed each of them took turns to chew their lips, rub their legs, go to the toilet only to find they couldn't piss, tell each other the were REALLY enjoying themselves, shake each other's hands, rub the backs of their necks and look at their reflections in the window. They eventually found themselves in the hotel room, crushing E's on the mirror and snorting them, this was new to Tom and the heat of an E flying up his nostril made him want to sniff water next.

'Fuck me, that smarts a bit.'

'La, wait till it hits it's fucking amazing,' Razor sat holding the mirror with more powder on it ready to go the way of the others.

Tom passingly thought that this lad was a maniac. He looked across at the other bed and stared in disbelief at range of movement going with Paddy's jaw. His eyes were flickering dangerously in REM in what could be a wild dream. He looked at his watch, it was one in the morning, and in fact it was fucking Tuesday! He had to bail...

'I'm going home mate, cheers for a top night, have a good time in Amsterdam, if you're around tomorrow or when you're back give me a ring and we'll meet up for a few beers?'

Razor looked at him, gurning massively. 'Top night, la, fucking brilliant, I'm off my tiny mind. We'll ring ya.'

Tom wrote down his phone number before leaving to walk back home. *At least it was still warm.*

Razor put his hands behind his head and had a massive stretch, which gave him a huge rush. He looked across at Paddy who looked fucked. He decided he was unlikely to get much sleep that night and decided to go for a wander around the hotel. He left the room and found his way to reception. He sat looking at the parrot. The parrot stared Razor out and he got paranoid and retreated to a comfy sofa next to the phone. He sat pie-eyed wandering what to do with himself. He picked up the phone and dialled a number; it rang for a short while before someone picked up.

'Hello?'

'Hello mum, its Raymond.'

## 1.11 George – Tuesday, 4 June 1991

The black BMW was parked in front of the garage. There were three people in the car, George, and the Brothers Grim, so-called because that was how they looked. Graham and Kevin Stones had no sense of humour. They were George's self-styled henchmen. They had left school with him, and being loyal friends, had become fierce soldiers when he offered them jobs on the doors of one of the clubs he did 'security' for.

The back windows of the car were illegally tinted, much to the dismay of George, and even more disappointingly for the garage owner, who had told him it was all perfectly legal. They would definitely be the last tinted windows he would be fitting for quite some time.

The Brothers Grim held the garage owner's arms stretched out as George carried out what he called 'some touch-up work' on him for the inconvenience of having to redo the windows.

A glass shattering scream bounced off the corrugated roof of the garage as the oxy torch burnt into the flesh on the man's arm.

'You won't do that again will you, you fucking prick?' said George as he dropped the torch to the kicked it away.

Graham and Kevin looked almost disinterested as they followed the nod and let go of the man's arms.

'He fucking screamed didn't he, Kev?'

'Never smelled burning flesh before, fucking stank, real bad.'

'Awful fucking smell. Kuwait must smell like that every-fucking-where.'

George sat in the front seat, looking at the house he had just parked across the road from. This was his favourite time to catch a rat. Early in the morning, nice and simple. 'Right, I'll go in on my own. Watch out for any curtain twitchers.'

'OK.'

George got out of the car, pulled up his collar and crossed the road to the Wilkins' house thinking, as he went, through many different scenarios, all equally violent and designed to inflict pain quickly and extract information even quicker. The hairs stood up on his back and his vision narrowed. He was so fucking angry he could burst.

Mrs and Mrs Wilkins sat on the sofa, they were both slightly hung-over. Liverpudlian born and bred and well-known to all in their street, they had worked as school caretakers for years. After work every day they would visit their local off Licence, You Booze, You Snooze. They bought a bottle of rum a week and eight Stella's each night. This would see them through the mundane telly and allow them both to get a decent night's kip. They had parented just one child, Raymond.

Mr Wilkins had named him after the footballer Ray 'Butch' Wilkins. Though he couldn't remember why, as he thought Wilkins was at best an average footballer who only got into the England side because no one else played in his position.

Mr Wilkins had just put on the breakfast. Fried eggs and bacon. It was the usual. He still adored his wife and got up first each morning to make her a decent fry up. The toaster pinged and the eggs and bacon were nearly done. It was time to call Mrs Wilkins for her breakfast. They had got into the habit of calling each other Mr and Mrs Wilkins through working in the school. 'Breakfast's ready!'

He poured two cups of tea from the kettle and placed the milk at the side of Mrs Wilkins plate, as she liked to add milk herself.

'Morning, darling, thank you.'

'A pleasure Mrs Wilkins, as always.'

Mr Wilkins picked up the *Daily Mirror*. The headlines were about the IRA shootings but he turned to the sport and the European Cup final. *Robbery, Liverpool should have been in that but they were still serving their ban from Heysel. Shame he thought, a real shame.*

There was a knock on the door and Mr Wilkins stood up to answer it.

'Who's that at this time, dear?'

'I don't know love; we pay the papers at the shop and the milky on a Friday, strange.'

George Meachen stood on the doorstep and raised his hand in a friendly gesture, he stepped slightly into the hallway and placed a heavy foot in the door to prevent it from being forced closed. He looked around the place. It looked like a shit hole, full of empty Stella cans.

'Morning Mr Wilkins, Razor home?'

Mr Wilkins began to speak, but was interrupted.

'Which one is Ray's room then?'

He pushed past Mr Wilkins and made his way up the stairs looking about; he found it quickly. Mrs Wilkins had now made her way to the front of the house. Her husband was on his knees, she helped him off the floor and asked 'What's happening dear? Are you OK?'

'Yes,' he said in a panic, 'but there's someone upstairs, I think were being burgled.'

'I'm calling the police.'

George, hearing the threat, came back down stairs. He seemed to fill their hall.

'Now, now, no need to do that. I just need a quick chat with your Ray.'

'He's not here.'

'I can see that.' He felt his rage starting to build. 'Where is he? Look people, I'm a fucking friend, Ray's in trouble and I wanna help the soft lad.'

George wandered through the house into the kitchen, picked up a sausage, dipped it into some sauce and sat down. The Wilkins had followed him through and he motioned for them to sit down.

'You only have one silly no-mark of a fucking son you stupid sods. Now if you want to see him again I need to know where he.'

'That's not the way a friend would speak, and anyway, we haven't seen him since Saturday. Now tell us, who are you?' Mrs Wilkins replied.

'As I said, a friend. It seems Ray and his mate, Patrick, have been up to no good and a couple of hard noses are looking for them. I wanna help but I need to know where he is so I can.'

George could feel his hands turning white as he clenched his knuckles, his teeth started to grind. He'd had enough. He decided to change tack immediately and told them both to sit down. 'Listen, I'm gonna fucking hurt both of you if you don't tell me where your fucking cunt of a son is.'

'What?' Mr Wilkins spat out the words in shock as he stood up feeling the need to defend his wife, 'I don't know where he is!'

'How about fucking this for I don't know where he fucking is?' shouted George as he picked up a fork with half a sausage still on, bit down and ate the sausage before plunging the fork into Mr Wilkins's leg. Mr Wilkins buckled in agony and his wife started screaming.

'Shut up, both of you, fucking now! Stop fucking whining you old fucking slag. He's the cunt with the fork in his leg.'

Mr Wilkins fell on the floor, covering himself in egg and sauce, in agony he tried to remove the fork from his leg but George stood over him and smashed him over the head with the teapot, hot tea scalding him.

'You had your fucking chance, you daft pair of cunts.'

A knife emerged from a pocket and George dragged Mr Wilkins halfway upright. With the knife against Mr Wilkin's throat George says: 'Tell me or I'm gonna cut your cunt of a husband's fucking throat out and make you drink his blood before raping you with your own fucking arm.'

Mrs Wilkins dropped to her knees, pleading, 'Please, I don't know.'

'Bollocks, you lying cow.'

'Honest, please leave us alone, all, all I know is he took his passport.'

At this, George releases the man and pushed him into the floor. He walks toward Mrs Wilkins and looks menacingly into her eyes.

'If you're lying I'll fucking kill you and your son. Well to be fair, he's a fucking half-dead Zombie anyway.'

George looked around at the mess in the kitchen, 'Get your fucking house cleaned up, you pair of grubby winos. It makes me fucking sick to look at the fucking mess you live in.'

On his way out of the kitchen he picked a piece of bacon, still sizzling, out of the frying pan sitting on the hob.

He's was still eating his bacon as he passed the little phone stand and noticed a writing pad. He stopped and picked it up, reading the scribbled message written on it. A wild smile spread across his face as he ran back into the kitchen. The couple are arm in arm crying, scared and still sitting on the floor.

George stared at them, 'You fucking pair of lying cunts.'

Mr and Mrs Wilkins threw up their arms in self-defence, screaming as George lifted the boiling hot frying pan with two hands, and emptied the burning bacon fat onto them. The hissing of the fat and the screams of the couple excited him and he laughed, the laugh turning into a hideous snarl as he grabbed Mrs Wilkins' arm. Her curdling scream as George pressed the boiling hot base of the frying pan onto her forearm made Mr Wilkins sob uncontrollably.

'Just remember old man, don't ever, ever, fuck with me.'

George opened the door of the BMW and climbed in. 'We're off to Essex.'

## 1.12 Lassie

Tom Adams woke with a distinctly cagey feel. His skin felt oily, and even though he knew he would benefit from a shower, he didn't really want one... He fought his inner demons and dragged himself into the bathroom. He stood, in a kind of coma thinking about the two mad Scousers staying at the hotel. Hot water running down his body, he soaped himself and cadged a bit of Lassie's shampoo. Nice lads, generous to the point of suspicion. He stepped out and grabbed a towel. He wondered if they had left the hotel for Amsterdam yet. It didn't really matter. It was a funny evening and a nice way to forget he had to start painting fences Sunday week. As he walked into Lassie's room he wondered what had happened to the No Name barmaid last night.

'Morning Lass.'

'Fuck off Tom, unless you have some toast or a hot cup of...' At this point two arms popped from beneath the duvet and made the shape of a T.

'Who's the bird that works in the bar in the Cliff, Lass?' There was no answer so he continued with his questioning. 'Do you want toast with your tea?'

'Yes please.'

'Well fucking well answer the first part of the question, you twat.'

Lassie laboured a reply, 'Nice girl, blonde hair, early twenties?'

'That's the kiddie.'

'No fuckin idea, lad, two pieces of toast please and lots of...'

'Milk. Yeah I know.'

The kettle boiled and bread was thrown in the toaster. Tom stood in the kitchen looked at an official looking letter address to him. He took a knife and slowly cut along the top. He knew it was bad news, mainly because he never got good new through the post. No one did. Ever. He pulled the letter out and saw 'North East Essex Magistrates Court'. Fuck he thought and opened the letter. RE: Non-payment of fines.

'Fucking Jesus H cunting Christ' he shouted. 'What a bastard.'

Lassie was halfway down the stairs by now and was making all sorts of weird noises. Grunting like an old man reading a dirty magazine. 'What's up fella?'

They sat for the next half hour eating toast and discussing the situation. Tom, still on his first slice of toast and severely struggling, had forgotten to pay his fines from an earlier small indiscretion. The letter asked him to surrender himself to his local Police Station where he would be dealt with. Probably, they both agreed, by an appearance for non-payment in the local court and more fines or more community service.

'This is all I need, I want to go on holiday, son, and I need to get dressed.'

The phone rang and he went to answer it. He knew instantly who it was and he didn't really know how he felt about it.

'Eh, lad,' Paddy shot down the phone, 'You only just out of bed? Me and the Razor have been up a while, had breakfast and a walk on the beach. We wondered what you were up to today.'

Tom tried to get a word in, 'Err...'

'Well we thought we'd like to buy some new gear, jeans and that, maybe hire a car, grab the tickets to Holland, get some food, have a laugh, a few beers,' Paddy went on.

Tom considered his options. He really didn't fancy getting on it and he guessed that with these two there was always that possibility. Paddy went on, telling him they needed a guide and he was 'their man in the south'. He was flattered and said he would meet them at the hotel, being mindful not to let them know where he lived.

'What the fuck was all that about?' asked Lassie.

After more toast and tea, Lassie was laughing his head off at the scrapes his mate seemed to always end up in. 'So you're telling me that in one day, you had the lads tripping out in court, saw a girl with a Moet bottle in her fanny, met a girl you've shagged whose name you can't remember and met a pair of Scouse cowboys who made you snort E until your nose bled. Fuck me, you are one unlucky bloke...'

'You coming to meet these freaks then?'

'Nah,' said Lassie. 'Ring me if anything exciting happens though and I'll come out.'


Tom wandered along the beach, it was a nice day, sun out and no need for a jumper. His thoughts jumped around inside his head switching between the non-payment of fines letter and the community service. His thoughts then turned to the two lads, Paddy and Razor. He didn't know anything about them really. Last night was a good laugh but even when they were all off their heads something wasn't right, lots of tentative glances and pauses. It had also turned out they hadn't bought their tickets for the Dam yet, which was really weird. He glanced up and saw the two lads ahead of him, looking out over the sea.

'Alright, chaps? Just what is it that you want to do today?'

'Well, we wanna get a bit of new gear for the trip – yer know, look a bit smart for the ladies.'

'No fucking need to look smart for hookers, boys, all you need is to have the readies and the knickers come down faster than a dwarf's tent.'

The Scousers both laughed.

'Good one la, but really, we need some new gear anyway,' said Paddy. 'Like, how much are those Timberland shoes you got on there lad?'

Tom looked down at his shoes, 'A tonne.'

Razor stared at the shoes, 'Them fecking shoes, one hundred fecking pound? Fuck me. In Liverpool they would be a score and I would get to choose my colour and size, and I could order the cunts in the fucking pub!'

'Razor, if were gonna pull this off we need to look the fucking part too.'

It was this slip that Tom had bet himself would happen, something was up and he would need to be at least half-way in the loop if he was even going to consider spending any time with this pair of shysters.

'What are you trying to pull off lads? What is going on? You in trouble?' The boys were pensive, to say the least. They looked like they'd crumble on questioning from a dinner lady.... 'In your own time lads,' he ventured. 'I might even be able to help.'

Paddy said, 'You can help right now mate if you want, we wanna hire a car, have a drive about, check out a few places, and be fucking tourists!'

Tom led the lads along the seafront and down into town. They stopped at Rowe Sports and twenty minutes later both of them were decked out in new trainers where the really not so old ones went in the bin. This provided great amusement to the dreadlocked, ageing hippy, Man U supporting owner who even gave the lads a ten percent discount.

'Sound lad him,' Paddy said.

'Fucking Manc though,' Razor replied.

One word, well two actually, Shaun Ryder. He a fucking Manc.'

Razor, put his hands in the air and moaned, 'He's allowed, I know he's a Manc but the Mondays are massive, he's allowed.'

Tom butted into the conversation 'He's not a true Manc though, the lad in the shop. I remember when he was a mad Goth and into the Sisters of Mercy and The Mission. He's a good lad though. The car hire place will be open now.'

The man serving them was pleasant, if somewhat on edge about Paddy's accent. He read aloud to himself, cross-checking the names on the passport and the driving licence. 'Patrick Wherry. No convictions,' he looked at the address and back at Paddy. 'How long would you like the car for, sir?'

They pulled out of the compound in a brand new dark blue Ford Orion.

Tom asked, 'Where do you want to go then lads? Colchester or Ipswich are both OK. Colchester probably better for shopping. Chelmsford even more so but a little further.'

'What's so good about the shopping in Chelmsford then, la?'

'In all honesty there is one decent shop in Chelmsford, but it's the place to go if you two scallies wanna look the part and smell the ladies.'

The Orion blazed a trail towards Chelmsford.

Paddy turned on the radio and was quiet. What were they thinking in Liverpool? Did they know yet? His back was wet against the seat and he looked forward to buying some new clothes. He smiled at the thought of spending the money and then remembered the state of the barman, and barmaid in the Leek & Whistle. George had nearly murdered them. If Razor knew he would want to go home, he was sure of that, but he knew that they had come too far now. They either made it or they fucked it. The thing was he had to make it work; he fucking hated them and what they did. You can't hit a girl with a hammer, perhaps the lad deserved it, he didn't know what he'd done, but the girl?

'Keep on going, shag.'

Razor had nodded off in the back of the car.

'What the fuck does shag mean?'

Tom laughed, 'Don't know, mate, my Dad says it sometimes.'

51

'Do you mean keep going up the feckin road like?'

'Yup, follow the signs to Chelmsford. What's the situation then, squire? What have you done?

Paddy looked in the rear-view at Razor, sleeping like a drunken hippopotamus, and mulled over telling Tom. 'It's a feckin long story, la, and it's only just started and it's fucking scary dangerous and Razor doesn't know the half of it the poor cunt. So, if I do tell you, I'll point out the bits he doesn't need to know.'

'Will I want you to stop the car at the next railway station and get out?'

'Very feckin likely, lad, very feckin likely.

'Go for it, it sounds like you could do with getting it off your chest.'

Five minutes later the two lads were sitting in the blue Orion waiting in a queue on the A120 toward Chelmsford. Tom was almost beyond speech.

'Fuck me, mate. Jesus. £40,000, fuck.'

Paddy was happy he'd told him, he felt better, even relieved.

'Well it's not quite £40,000 now, we've spent about £800, hahahahaha!'

The three lads parked and were led to the town centre by Tom, who was trying to piece together what he had just been told while the BFG was asleep. Basically, he had managed to get himself caught up with two scallies he knew fuck all about who had robbed a family member of 40K. To compound the problem, he was now hanging out with them and at this moment was acting as their personal shopper. What the fuck?

While Tom was lost in thought, Paddy turned and quietly asked Ray about his mood.

'I'm worried, fella.'

At that point Paddy wanted to blurt out that he was shitting himself too but held back, knowing Ray would melt if he heard the truth.

'It'll all be fuckin fine, soft lad, just think sun and beaches. We can get far enough for them not to care. There's too much cash to be made at home for them to spend their time running after us. It'll be on-top for a month or so then it'll all be OK.'

Razor smiled as Paddy gave him a little punch on the arm and Tom brought the merry march to a halt outside a clothes shop that looked maybe a bit too posh for them and said, 'Fuck it, in for a penny...'

Tom led them into the shop and nodded at the two lads and the girl working there. He explained that his friends had had an accumulator come in at the bookies and want to celebrate with some new gear. An hour and fourteen minutes later, the three left the store laden with bags and headed for a pub.

Paddy had offered to buy Tom a top he had tried on, but Tom declined. He liked the lads, but 40K without any comeback? He seriously didn't think so. Something was going to happen, he could feel it in his water...

'You look like a pair of Essex casuals now – as long as you keep your mouths shut,' Tom laughed. 'Come on, we'll have a bite to eat and a beer to celebrate releasing you from your shellsuits and perms you pair of scally cunts.'

'Fuck you,' was the curt response.

He laughed, perhaps it would be OK, he'd sort out Paddy and Razor. Get them on the boat and get back to normal. No more Mushies, Hoovers or Triple X's.

## 1.13 The Brothers

The Brothers Grim were pushed back into their seats as George floored the BMW at the sight of the sign saying M1 South. Not much had been said since they left the Wilkins' house. They had stopped to collect a handful of tools and to fill the petrol tank and then were on their way.

People had to fucking know the score. His own fucking family. There was no way back for the little fucker and his old man agreed.

There was going to be a lot of pain.

## 1.13 Tuesday

Tuesday seems to be panning out OK thought Tom. The Scousers, even Razor, seemed happier, especially after their shopping trip. Tom had to admit to himself that he'd be a little fucking pensive if he was in their position. He beginning to mull over saying his goodbyes and getting shot of them.

There was a travel agent opposite the pub they were drinking in and Tom suggested they get their tickets for the ferry there; it would be easier and save time at Harwich.

'Come with us Tom?' Paddy had been thinking about this all day, it made sense. Tom seemed a nice lad and knew the ground. He wasn't a ponce and hadn't asked for a penny of the cash they had been throwing around.

'Come on,' Razor echoed, 'you're part of this now.'

Tom felt a slight twinge at this remark and stopped Ray in his tracks.

'Hang about, I am not fucking part of this crazy scheme of yours Razor, so please don't suggest that I am.'

Sensing a slight change in mood Paddy stepped in and calmed everyone down. It was agreed, especially as Tom didn't have his passport with him that he couldn't go with them, though the offer was open. A round of drinks were shared and the boys' final destination discussed in depth, with Thailand coming out tops and Vietnam a close second.

Tom listened to the boys talk; he wondered just how far the 40K would get them, and even if they would get that far without either being killed or robbed or both. How would they physically move this cash? He kept his own counsel and crossed his fingers that at the very least they would get out of England.

'Tell you what, if you make it to Thailand and get set up, I'll come out.' He then went on to suggest that the idea of setting up a motorbike hire business.

Paddy said, 'See Tom, you think beyond next week, that's what we need.'

Tom realised he'd done it again. 'Just get there first, eh, you pair of fools,' and raised a glass for good luck.

'I think I'd miss my friends, and definitely miss the football being on at the right time,' Tom said with a sigh before asking the boys "What will you two miss the most?'

Razor looked confused. 'The Football won't be on at three o'clock?'

Tom laughed, 'No! You lemon, Thailand's about six or seven hours ahead of us.'

'Oh, OK. Right.' He still looked confused.

'I'd miss my Mum too,' he then turned to Paddy who had drifted off. 'She said to say hi to you Paddy.'

Paddy looked up from the *Daily Star* he was reading, looking startled.

'Lost a bit of colour there, Paddy,' Tom said, 'You OK?'

'Did you say then that you had spoken to your Mum, Razor?'

'Yes. Why?'

Paddy lent in and asked Razor exactly what he's said in the conversation with his mother. Razor explained that he told her he was going away for a bit and that he would ring her when he got there. 'I didn't tell her where we were going though, Paddy, so we're OK on that score.'

Tom Adams felt his arse go at this point, Paddy, the brains behind the duo, looked utterly terrified. What was happening? He sensed the day was taking a turn for the worse. Paddy seemed somewhat buoyed by the last bit of information and congratulated Razor.

'I did say we were in Essex though.'

'Fuck, fuck, fuck, fuck...' Paddy got louder and louder until Tom had to tell them both to calm down. 'Come on lads,' Tom pleaded. 'It's not bad. You have loads of time, you're hours ahead, relax.'

'I wasn't talking about time, for fucks sake!' Paddy laid out the paper on the table in front of him. On page 15, a small piece in one of the smaller columns was headlined 'Old Couple Viciously Attacked in Liverpool – Police have no leads'. Razor grabbed the paper and after seeing the surname Wilkins in the first paragraph could read no further. He jumped to his feet and grabbed Paddy, arms flaying, spit and chips flying everywhere.

'This is all your fucking fault,' he screamed pushing and shoving Paddy and Tom as they attempted to calm him down, 'I fucking hate you! I fucking hate you!'

Within seconds all three were outside the pub, unceremoniously bounced out and told not to bother for a month or two. All Tom could think about now was getting rid of these two jokers as soon as humanly possible.

Razor sat down on the edge of a plant pot and began to cry. He was inconsolable. 'I have to ring them Paddy, I have to, what if they are dead or still in hospital mate. Should I go home?'

All Paddy could think about was what Paddy's parents had told George and whether he was already on his way. 'Mate,' Paddy whispered, 'You gotta concentrate now and remember exactly what you told your Ma.'

Razor said he'd just mentioned he was in Essex, he hadn't said where he was going but said it was abroad on holiday. He wanted to go home.

Someone had basically smashed Razor's parents to pieces and frankly, if they knew anything you could guarantee that the people who did it knew too. The look on Tom's face told Paddy that he thought the same thing.

Tom put a hand on Razor's shoulder and motioned to Paddy, 'Come on, let's get the fuck out of dodge.'

Back at the Orion, bags were thrown into the boot; the fun of the shopping spree with someone else's money had worn off. Paddy was low and Razor inconsolable. Paddy felt terrible. This had been his doing, his idea, and his psycho brother-in-law was his family, no one else's. Nothing to do with his bezzie mate, and now he could well have sentenced the two of them to a serious beating at the very least. And he was sure George would shoot/stab/kill Tom if he found him in their company. He knew George, he'd see this as all pre- planned with Tom as the organiser... Tom's skin to save his and Razor's? No brainer. Sorry, Tom.

'Ray, I'll find out what's happening all right? No need to do anything drastic, right? If you go back, I'm pretty sure we'll both end up in the Mersey as bait for shopping baskets and shoes. Come on, lad.'

'I want to go home Paddy,' Razor was sobbing like a child. 'I need to say sorry. This was a stupid idea.'

'We can't, la. We just can't. We've come too far. Remember what we said, Ray? An end to our lives as they were. That was only a few hours ago, this is one set back. If we go back now they'll have us dead or stitch us up with a run across that'll see us in jail on a twenty-year stretch as punishment. We have to cut the cords now Razor, and for better or worse this is us.'

Tom wanted these lads out of his own hair and away to Holland ASAP. They were becoming seriously toxic. This George bloke sounded like the Devil and he did not want to meet him. It was definitely time to go. Paddy and Razor were both still flapping so Tom offered to drive.

They pulled up at a service station so Paddy could use the payphone. He would talk to them, he said, as it may be too distressing for Razor – and he didn't trust him to keep his mouth shut. Tom and Razor watched as Paddy approached the phone box and stood waiting in the 2-man queue to use the telephone.

'So,' asked Tom, 'what's this brother-in-law like then? Doesn't seem like he should be on the streets.'

'He's a fucking maniac, Tom, and we've stolen forty grand from him.'

Razor was falling apart in front of Tom's eyes and it was giving him the willies.

'What are you going to do? You can't really go home.'

Tom felt genuinely sorry for Razor, he'd been talked into this and his parents had suffered terribly for it. Did Paddy actually give a fuck? He thought so.

'My advice is to get out of England on that boat tonight. Both of you; get to Holland. Amsterdam, or even Rotterdam or Eindhoven? Perhaps don't be too obvious? Keep your heads down, change the money to Guilders and then some into Thai Baht and get the fuck out of there. That's the way to do it.' Tom wasn't entirely convinced by this himself but it sounded good and it would get them out of his town. He checked himself – being selfish, then reminded himself of what the lad had done to Razor's parents. No time for loyalty here he thought, this was now a survival mission.

Paddy got back into the car, with some sandwiches.

'So?' Razor asked.

Will this be lies or a crock of shit? Tom thought as he listened to the outcome of the call.

'They are OK, still in hospital getting their burns treated but they should be out later this evening. I just spoke to the next-door neighbour who was round clearing up the mess. Everything will be OK Razor. We'll ring again when we're in Holland but don't do it alone. We have to make sure it's safe, OK?'

Razor seemed placated by this and they began to focus on getting to Holland.

'So, what city are you going to head for, lads?' Tom asked.

'I think it's best if you don't know, la, if you know what I mean.'

Tom instantly knew what he meant and it made his arse go again. These two do a runner, if psycho finds out where they have travelled from he could still get dragged into this mess. Jesus fucking bollocks he thought, I might have to go with them, which is not ideal at all. He tentatively suggested that they could maybe try to reconcile their differences with this George. That would, at the very least, save his own skin.

'Not a cat in hell's chance, la, we're fucking dead men, standing right in front of you if we stay.'

'Come on, let's go.' Tom turned the key in the ignition, half expecting the car to explode like a professional hit. He spared a quick glance for the white Lamborghini that was pulling into the forecourt as he drove away.

In the passenger seat next to him sat Paddy, a lad he'd known for two days, cocksure and confident. In the back of the Orion, lay Razor, deep in thought, in fact, shallow in thought he laughed to himself. The whole thing reminded him of a book he'd read at school, *Of Mice and Men*, though he wasn't sure which of these boys would be the one who squeezed the puppies to death.

## 1.14 More Travel

The BMW was making good time but George had just noticed they needed petrol. 'We'll take a quick piss break in eight miles, boys, fill the take and head on. This one's all about the getting there.'

'What's the plan from there then, fella?' Kevin asked.

'You got to remember boys, this thing is highly fucking personal to me. They must be punished severely along with anyone else they are in this with. It should be simple though. It's a matter of finding them, and hopefully before they get out of the fucking country or spend too much of my fucking money!'

As he pulled into the garage George said, 'Remember lads, be quick and best behaviour. No bother OK?'

'Fuck me!' Graham exclaimed as he got out of the BMW. 'Take a look at that fucking car!'

George ignored the excitement of the two brothers as they admired the brand new white Lamborghini that was just across the forecourt and, the blonde woman in the passenger seat. George was irritated with them, fucking unprofessional. Cunts. He could feel his anger rising and gritted his teeth as he filled the tank. 'Aye, I thought youse two were having a quick piss then we were off. When the car's fucking full, I'm paying and fucking off. You had better be in the fucking car by then, you daft cunts.'

The Stones brothers heed the warning and are back in the car by the time George returns from the kiosk and guns the ignition.

'Next stop, Harwich.'

The Lamborghini pulls away at the same time and the driver waves the BMW ahead with a smile.

'What the fucking hell are you smiling, at you cunt?'

The driver of the Lamborghini looks confused and laughs, gesturing them forward again.

George gets out of the car and walks up to the window of the Lamborghini shouting something about his tinted windows. As he walks away he runs a key down the side of the driver's door panel and cutely waves them out, before returning to the BMW.

'Take the fucking piss out of my tinted glass, you cunt?'

The brothers cast a quick glance at each other. George is in a foul mood and there may well be murders.

## 1.5 Shades

Tom Adams was nervous. He felt better that he was approaching home and hopefully would soon be sending the two lads on their merry way.

'Nice shades.' He offered the compliment, thinking that he did actually like them and may well get a pair exactly the same. It wouldn't matter as he probably wouldn't see Paddy again and so wouldn't be accused of copying someone else's style.

'Cheers, my Thailand sunnies, la,' Paddy answered gleefully.

False enthusiasm, Tom thought. He began dreaming of what he might do when he'd jettisoned the hazardous load he was transporting. A few beers with Lassie, maybe an Indian. Maybe a trip to the cinema in Colchester, a mild attempt to get his head straight.

'About 10 minutes, lads,' the relief was tangible in Tom's voice, at least to Tom.

The mild snoring that been emanating from the back seats stopped as Razor woke up, rubbed his eyes and exclaimed, 'I'm dying for a piss, la.'

Tom looked back at Razor in the rear view mirror. There was a lay-by coming up and he'd stop there and let him drain his weasel.

Paddy, meanwhile was going through the plan they had discussed earlier. They would drive to Harwich, check out of the hotel and then Tom would drive them to the ferry terminal where they would board the boat to Holland. Tom would then drop the hire car off and post the keys, everything was paid for and everyone had the right documents. They had Tom's phone number and would ring when they were settled and would send some money for Tom to come and visit them in Thailand.

'You don't have to do that lads.' Tom wasn't sure he wanted to get in any further with these two. He played along though, and after much haggling agreed that if, and when, they were set up in Thailand he would travel over and help them with their motorbike hire business.

Tom pulled over into a large trucker's layby and Razor immediately jumped out of the car and ran back up the layby toward a little path that led to some bushes that would give him a little privacy.

'Never give up the chance to take a piss my granddad always says.'

'Never waste a fucking hard-on, la, that's what my granddad always says.'

Tom and Paddy both laughed as they got out, both deciding to piss at either end of the Orion instead of following Razor into the bushes, which they both agreed, would look fucking odd to any passing motorists. Razor was done and was walking back toward the car protecting his eyes from the glare of the evening sun.

'Gis a go of your sunnies, lad.'

'You've got a pair in the fucking boot, you soft twat.' Sometimes Razor's stupidity pissed Paddy off but sometimes it just made him laugh.

Tom popped the boot and thirty seconds later he was laughing at Razor doing the Bez dance in a fucking layby. At least these boys were funny.

## 1.16 Cuts and Bruises

George's fingers drummed methodically on the steering wheel, his eyes stared dead ahead, blinking at every sign, taking them in and processing them, especially the ones showing distance to destination. Two other sets of eyes looked out into the Essex countryside, amazed at the flatness and colour of it all. It was calming and they both felt very calm considering that they could possibly be in work mode in less than an hour. George had made steady time since the departure from Liverpool and they were all thinking about what may happen when they caught up with the thieving little fuckers. The fingers drummed to an unknown beat.

George was sure that everyone back at home knew. The embarrassment of it made his piss boil, he wanted to crush their little fucking heads in vices until their little fucking skulls popped and their tiny little brains seeped out onto the floor. He had to remain calm. One was family, and family in his game was important. They would be hurt he promised himself, but the ultimate punishment he would dream up would be deserved and would also serve a purpose that would potentially open up difficult markets that he was finding it hard to crack, at least in any volume. His idea was simple. Once caught and delivered home, bruised and beaten to within an inch of their fucking useless little fucking lives they would be put to work, with the possibility of regaining trust and respect.

He would send them on a trip to Dublin. They had done it before and knew the ground. He'd set up a meet a week or so after he'd got them back, let the trip play out as normal for a while and then tip off the bizzies. The little fucking thieving no-marks would get at least three to five years for the weight they'd be carrying. It would cost him a bit but the gear would be knocked to fuck. Punishment administered and a couple of junior scag dealers in the nick to sell for him. He smiled, for the first time in a while and congratulated himself on fucking up those little cunts and still having an earner from it.

The Stones brothers had been watching George closely since the incident with the Lamborghini and had both seen the eerie smile spread across George's lips. They both knew what he was capable of and neither of them wanted a loose George, as it could end up in a bloodbath. The smile had unsettled them both.

'What's the craic, George?' Graham asked from the back seat.

'Nothing, lads, nothing at all. A little plan, but nothing flies unless we get our hands on those little cunts.'

Kevin Stones, who had been examining the road map for much of the journey, closed the book and leant back in the passenger seat. 'That shouldn't be a problem as long as they haven't left the country, boss, it can really only be Harwich they are heading for and there is fuck all there. Those two little pricks will have stuck out like a... he stumbled, like a pair of thieving little cunts with 40K in a bin bag.'

This drew a smile from all of them and George floored the BMW in a sign of approval. He would, it seemed, at least get one shot at getting his spade-like hands round the throats of those little cunts. George Meachen focused, he leant forward and fiddled with the stereo, the radio station had dropped off and the static was winding him up. He carried on hitting buttons while driving, and then began shouting at the stereo and then smashing it with the palm of one of his hands. 'Fucking, cunting, fucking, bastard fucking thing,' he shouted as he dragged the car with one hand round a bend in the road at over 100 miles per hour. The Stones brothers braced themselves, without letting George see them brace themselves. The car began to swerve as George began to brake, shouting, 'Fuck me, fuck me, fuck me.'

The car carried on swerving toward the left, confusing the Stones brothers – all they could see ahead was a layby which they were approaching at break-neck speed with George repeating 'fuck me' over and over again.

In the layby were two cars, and between the two parked cars was a young man of about twenty, dancing around in a pair of black sunglasses. He was being watched by two other lads of a similar age who were laughing. George had recognised his nephew.

The Stones brothers were confused as George cried out 'The little fucking cunt,' and could barely speak as he dragged the speeding vehicle towards the layby much too fast and largely out of control. Realising his speed, George slammed on the brakes and the car began to skid, depositing dark black lines of rubber on the concrete. George could do nothing except try to hold the car in as straight a line as possible but the BMW was going too fast. All three passengers looked towards the first parked car, it was a black Ford Sierra and just as they made that out they slammed into the back of it with a dull thud. The Sierra was then shunted into the Orion which had parked in front of the Sierra, creating another dull thud. It was essentially a three-car pile-up in a lay by.

Graham Stones, who had been observing the whole thing from the back was propelled through the middle of the two front seats, and continued forwards, smashing his face on the windscreen and rear view mirror, partially knocking himself out. There was a deathly silence, broken almost immediately by shrill screaming outside. The two front seat passengers were dazed and confused, but essentially unhurt apart from cuts and bruises.

## 1.16 The Getaway

The boys heard the screech of tyres and looked up, helpless to do anything but watch.

The black BMW lurched into the layby and Paddy saw his life flash before his eyes. He knew who it was instantly, he'd spotted the blacked out windows and, considering the speed, assumed the worst. Tom stood to the side, rooted to the spot, staring and trying to decide whether he could move or should just start crying. Razor was standing behind the Orion as the Sierra lurched forward with a sickening thud and pinned him between the two cars. He let out a deafening scream. The Orion was then shunted forward leaving Razor lying on the ground between the two cars crying and screaming for help. Tom and Paddy ran to him and saw that both his legs were clearly broken.

This was bad, really fucking bad. Tom looked at the BMW but couldn't see any movement yet. 'Are you OK Razor?' He immediately realised what a cunt he sounded, of course he wasn't all right. He looked up and pointed to the emergency phone in the layby, Paddy ran to it to get call for help.

Razor was whimpering and crying, Tom took him in his arms and said, 'Hang on, fella, help's coming. Paddy's calling an ambulance. Hang fucking in there, mate.'

Razor's was trying to feel his legs and his hands were now covered in thick blood that was pumping out of what looked to Tom like a wound you'd see on a war documentary.

'You two need to fuck off now...' Razor's voice wobbled. He was half in, half out of consciousness but was peering into Tom's face with an intensity that made Tom take notice. Tom knew he was right... "Get the fuck out of here, he'll kill both of you, I'll be OK. He thinks I'm feckin stupid."

Tom saw the driver's door on the BMW being prised open and looked up to see Paddy heading back.

'We've got to fuck off, Paddy, and fucking now. Razor will be OK. Did you dial 999?'

'Fuck it, Tom,' Paddy was almost crying, 'I can't leave him.'

The decision was made for them by the sight of George Meachen climbing free of the bent up BMW and shouting, 'You cunts have got my fucking money and I want it fucking back, now!'

Paddy looked down at Razor and told him how sorry he was and that he had to go.

'Fuck off, quick you daft cunt!' Razor shouted, before the two remaining boys, realising he was right, jumped into the Orion and turned the key, by this point Kevin Stones has also got out of the car, had retrieved a wheel jack from the boot and was approaching, luckily in a zig zag kind of manner, the passenger side door of the Orion.

'Fucking go go go go' Paddy screamed as Kevin Stones attempted to smash the Orion's window. Tom floored it, and the car leapt towards the road. It was still screaming in second as they got back on to main road, miraculously without anyone having else seen the scene they had just fled. Neither had much to say as they headed into Harwich. They just sat in silence, hearts beating at and panting like a pair of bull terriers in season.

'You OK!' Tom asked Paddy.

'Yeah, I'm OK, just fucking worried about Razor. They might fucking kill him!'

Tom could feel the fear that now coursed through his limbs. He was now under no illusions that these were serious people, and they now knew what he looked like, this made him feel sick and he had to fight the urge to pull over and throw up. Paddy seemed to have lost a bit of his balls after that incident and he really couldn't blame the lad. They were now a band of two, but he really needed it to be one as soon as possible. 'You've got to get out of here ASAP.'

'What about you?' Paddy wasn't sure about this whole thing on his own now. It was meant to be him and Razor, Tom was OK but he wasn't sure he trusted him. He was doing his bit now though so fair play to the lad, he had balls.

'I'll be fine.'

*Fuck you will*, Paddy thought, *but that's your choice. George has the bit between his teeth now and he won't let go. He'll fucking terrorise this town.*

'OK, let's get me to the port and on the boat tonight. I wanna get the fuck out of here.'

Tom parked the Orion at the side of the Cliff Hotel where the boys had stayed. They had a look at the damage. The back of the car was pretty much OK, apart from a dent where Razor had been but it was parked so it wasn't easily seen.

Paddy went in alone to collect his stuff. Tom didn't want to them to seen together. A little too late for all that, Paddy thought as he climbed the stairs to his room.

The room had been cleaned but everything was in its place. He changed into his new clothes and binned the old ones. Reminding himself not to rush, he peeled back the carpet and lifted the floorboard, he tied a knot in the bin liner and stuffed it into the holdall. He decided to leave Razor's stuff in the room. He shuddered as the door clicked shut behind him. He paced the hall to reception and paid his bill, thanking the staff for their hospitality and got a 'Goodbye and hope to see you again, Sir!'

He waved and walked down the stairs and back to the Orion.

'Sorted?' Tom asked.

Paddy patted the holdall and Tom pulled away. They drove to Parkeston Quay in silence and Tom pulled up the car at the entrance.

'Looking smart there, chief.'

'Cheers, la.' Paddy felt smart but was feeling loose and alone. Did he want Tom to come with him? Two's better than one he thought, but he'd made his mind up and Paddy wasn't going to beg.

'Straight up the stairs, left and left again. Good luck, mate and you have my phone number. Get settled and get in touch. I'll get over and have another smash up with you. It's been a wild two days!' Tom leant in and hugged Paddy, who returned the gesture.

'Cheers.'

And with that, Paddy got out of the Ford Orion, walked up the stairs and towards the booking hall for the ferry for Holland without looking back.

Tom sighed with relief, turned the car around and headed for the station to drop off the car. As he turned into Station Road he passed a Vauxhall Astra coming the other way, barely missing it. He put it down to tiredness. He was fucked and wanted to sleep this one off. He backed the Orion against the wall, posted the keys into the key bin, walked across the road, ordered a kebab and a taxi home. He was knackered and he had college tomorrow. Presently, he was lying in bed, post kebab, with a beer. What a fucking two days.

There was a knock at the door, he looked at his watch, getting late, who the fuck could this be? He wandered down stairs and turned on the light. He thought he could see two shadows and immediately thought about not opening it and calling the police. No, it can't be he thought... really? He opened the door and bam, a party popper went off in his face. Lassie was on the doorstep, pissed and stoned.

'Fuck me, Lass, you scared the fucking shit out of me!'

Lassie didn't seem fazed by Tom's negative observation on his joviality. 'Look what I've brought you, Tom,' he said, standing aside to reveal the girl with No Name from the Cliff. 'Just met her walking up the road and she said she missed you the other night, so I thought...'

Tom's eyes rolled as he let them in. Within ten minutes Lassie was asleep. Tom took hold of No Name and led her upstairs with the promise of an episode of Cracker and a Carlsberg.

'It's only a small TV though... and the Carlsberg... well... you make up your own mind, eh?'

## 1.18 Stakeout

George, Kevin, the concussed Graham and Razor were in the lay-by when an ambulance, the police and a recovery vehicle showed up. Graham's nose was clearly broken. Razor was in agony and was quietly moaning on the ground.

Before the emergency services had arrived they had agreed their story: the Sierra had been nicked by a joyrider – Razor. Razor had been dumping the car in the lay-by when he'd been caught between the two cars when the BMW's brakes failed. Razor was happy to go along with this, especially when George had stopped prodding a protruding bone with a Bic biro.

George, was furious. His BMW was undrivable; they'd had to bury all the tools but one handgun, which he insisted on hiding under the spare wheel; and he's lost the main prize.

Their statements taken, all of them were given seven days to produce their driving licenses at a police station (the local constabulary were bemused by the fact that none of them had any ID on them). Razor was cautioned and loaded into the ambulance to be taken to Colchester General, along with Graham, who had fainted while assuring the paramedics that he was fine.

George, Kevin and the BMW got a lift into Colchester in the recovery vehicle whose driver was able to arrange an out of hours hire car for them.

'Right, let's fuck off and do some re-thinking.' They followed the signs out of Colchester and towards Harwich, stopping on the way in a small business park for George to vent his anger on a parked car when he realised he'd forgotten to retrieve the Glock from the BMW. Kevin was just relived he didn't take it out on him.

They arrived in Harwich at 19.50 and drove around the streets, both men remarking what a shit hole the place was. They pulled up behind a taxi, outside a takeaway near a small station for Kevin to get some food; he was starving. He came out, food in hand, to find the car empty.

George soon climbed out of the taxi with a smile on his face. 'Cliff Hotel. Now.' He grabbed Kevin's food threw it towards a bin and pointed to where he wanted to go: 'It's up on the seafront apparently.'

'For fuck's sake, George,' Kevin began, but seeing the look in his eyes he got in and turned the car toward he seafront.

On the way, George explained that the taxi driver had picked up a couple of Scouse lads on Monday night and dropped them at the Cliff Hotel. He picked up some darts players the same evening and they'd seen the lads chatting with a local lad called Tom Adams. He later picked up the Adams lad and dropped him home. George seemed excited now, 'So, the pair of cunts must be staying at this hotel – let's fucking do this!'

Kevin took a deep breath, 'George?'

'Yes lad?'

'One thing.'

'Go on,' George could feel himself winding up. He was within touching distance again and this prick was going to put a dampener on it all.

'This is a small town, people talk. If we go in guns blazing it could bring all manner of trouble. Specially with the crash and me brother and Razor in the hospital.'

George stared at Kevin, considered punching him in the face and then calmly said, 'Good point, Kev, and we don't need to get pinched down here. We'll say err, run away cousin. Fucking good idea, lad.'

Kevin breathed a sigh of relief, he wanted it clean. In, out and home. Graham could sort Razor out. The hotel was on the seafront, high above the beach with an amazing view out to sea. The sun was going down and the horizon was a deep orange.

'Beautiful, eh, George. Really relaxing.'

'Come on, you soft cunt. We've got work to do.'

They entered the foyer of the hotel to a squawk from a huge grey parrot in a massive cage. A young girl greeted them and directed them to the manager. They explained the problem to him: their impressionable young nephew had run away and they had reason to believe that he and a friend had been staying in the hotel. The manager confirmed it.

'Superb! Can we see the room please? Let's not call them down, they might make another run for it,' George was trying his hardest but he just wanted to slap this twat, run up the stairs and batter the little cunt in his room.

The manager told them that unfortunately, the boys had already checked out.

George and took himself off to vent his fury out on the board advertising afternoon teas while Kevin thanked the manager for his time and then followed his boss outside.

'Cunt, cunt, fucking cunt. He's slipped us again. That fucking Adams bloke is helping him, and helping himself to our fucking cash probably, cunt. I'll lynch the southern cunt when I get my hands on him. Where have they gone?'

Kevin went back into the hotel and came out minutes later looking at the ferry timetable, 'They could have left for Holland tonight, George.'

'Harwich, Holland or fucking Mongolia, I'm gonna fucking grab hold of those cunts. Razor is bloody lucky that he's already be in hospital.'

At this point the friendly hotel manager came out with a full bin bag and explained that one of the boys had left some clothes behind and asked if would they like to take them. Kevin acted quickly, realising correctly that George was about to fist the innocent man, and told him to give them to a local charity.

They drove off, leaving the manager with a bemused look on his face and a bag of very expensive clothes. They followed the signs to the port only to see the huge Stena Line boat sailing out of the quay.

George decided that they'd to buy tickets for the evening crossing the next day while they were there so they parked up and headed in to the sales desk to find a long queue of people complaining about the delay.

'Hang about,' said George, 'what delay?' Looking up to the head of the queue they saw a board with a message apologising for the delayed running of the Harwich to Hook of Holland ferry. 'We may be in luck, Kev,' said George, stalking towards the departure area with a dangerous gleam in his eyes.

## 1.19 No Name

Tom opened his eyes and stared into No Name's eyes. He also felt her hand slowly rubbing his cock. He'd fallen asleep almost instantly last night – what a guest pleaser he was, eh, building an excellent reputation. No Name was still rubbing his shaft and had moved towards him, he put his arm around her and pulled her closer, mmm, still in her knickers, no bra though. He rubbed his hands across her breasts and pondered on a nipple...

Even closer, and she stopped rubbing him, gave him a light kiss on his cheek and whispered into his ear, 'Go and clean your teeth.'

Within seconds Tom was up, into some pants and in the bathroom, scrubbing his teeth, taking good care to brush inside the back ones. His mind drifted back to the last two days but he told it to fuck off, he just wanted to dive in to breakfast with No Name.

Back in bed, her kisses were a welcome sensual feeling after the mania of the last couple days. She was lovely. Just as he was settling into enjoying himself, she pulled him on top of her.

'Put it in me now Tom, *please*,' she purred. 'I'm ready.'

Wow, Tom couldn't believe it, her pussy was really wet. He was a fucking Adonis!

'Wow, you're so wet,' he couldn't help but remark, hoping to tee up an ego boosting remark in return.

'I know,' she moaned. 'I've been strumming all morning waiting for you to wake up.'

Not the reply Tom had expected, but as she pulled on his hips and he almost fell in to her, it had the same effect. He put his arm under her and pulled her tight into him.

She moaned, 'Just fuck me hard and come inside me, Tom. Fuck me hard.'

Tom didn't need much prompting and they were soon lying on their backs, hand in hand, post coitus. Wondering if all men were the same, Tom's thoughts immediately jumped to what he had to do today, while No Name just wanted to lie there and cuddle for a while.

'I can't, sorry,' Tom said, 'I have college today.' Tom leant over and grabbed his watch which told him it was 7.45! His lift to Colchester left at 8.05.

'Fuck, gotta run, baby!'

Tom rushed into the bathroom, emerging ten minutes later. He was doing OK for time. He chose his clothes for the day while No Name watched him. He could laugh college off and spend the day fucking, walking, drinking and laughing, he thought – if only he knew her fucking name. Jesus, if she knew he'd never get another sniff of that, ever! He glanced at the clock as he pushed his feet into his Timberlands, 8.01.

'One question before I go. Have done this before, baby?' Tom lent in to kiss No Name goodbye.

'No! You idiot!' You came to mine to watch *Interview with a Vampire*, fell asleep on the sofa and left at six in the morning. We did kiss a little though.'

*Embarrassing*, Tom thought as he went for the door. He laughed, smiled and told her to stay as long as she liked, grab some breakfast if there was anything to eat, and he'd get in touch when he was back.

'Write down your phone number in my little address book and I'll ring you.' He kissed her on the head and ran down the stairs. He grinned as he realised that she would have to put her name in the book with her number. Bonus he thought, as he picked up his bag and opened the door.

Tom left the house at lightning speed and bolted for the little alley that ran down the side of the house that brought him out by some shops where Bad Monkey was sitting, in his Red Seat Ibiza, waiting patiently. Tom jumped in, apologised and they sped off.

Neither of them noticed the lumbering bulk of a menacingly angry Liverpudlian bursting out of the lane.

## 1.20 It's not the Ritz

At 8:02 (according the clock on the dash board), the door of the house they were watching flew open and a lad came rushing out carrying a fucking holdall. He did a swift right turn and fled down a lane. After an initial shock, both men got out of the car and ran after the holdall.

Kevin followed their quarry down the lane. How the fuck did he clock us watching the place? Smart little cunt, Kev thought, and decided he didn't give a fuck if George snapped the little prick's neck in half. Kevin stopped running as he came out on to the road and saw the lad disappear up the road in a Red Seat Ibiza. He walked slowly back to the Astra where George stood, aghast at the mornings events so far.

'Fucking little cunt. Little fucker must have my cash in that holdall. How the fuck did he know we were here? I don't fucking get it, I just don't fucking get it.'

'Nor do I, George.'

'Ahh fuck off, Kev, I don't pay you to get it. Come on.'

They made for the door from which Tom Adams had catapulted himself just minutes earlier. At the third knock, the door was opened by a sweet looking girl in knickers and a Secret Affair t-shirt. As she began to ask if she could help them, George swept her aside and stepped into the small hallway. Scared, she tried to ask again what they wanted but this time Kevin Stones' leather-clad hand clamped across her mouth and stopped her. Petrified, she fell silent as she felt something warm running down her legs.

Kevin closed the door quietly behind them and George ushered them into the front room where Kevin sat the girl down opposite another character who was sleeping on the sofa next to some empty Strongbow cans and Supertramp's album, *Breakfast In America*, covered with tobacco papers and a bag of weed. George bent over and picked up a half-full can off the floor and proceeded to pour the warm cider over the sleeping Lassie until he was roused from his sleep.

'Wow, man, what the fuck is... who the fuck is.... Can I smell piss?'

George, also in leather gloves leant over and grabbed Lassie by the face. 'Listen, you measly little stone head fuck. I'm going to ask you some questions about your friend Tom. And you are going to concentrate on answering them to the best of your ability, because if you don't, I'm going to rape your pretty friend over there with the Wellington boot standing outside your front door, and then I'm going to instruct my friend over there, to rape her arse with a rolling pin which I'm sure we'll find in your kitchen. Understand?'

Lassie nodded and looked across the room at the now wide-eyed girl he'd met on the way home last night.

'Firstly, you have never seen me or my associate. Any contact with the law will mean we find her, not you or Tom, her. OK?'

Lassie nodded desperately trying to work out what was going on. Was it a prank of some weird sort?

'We are looking for Tom. We know he knows some lads from Liverpool. And we believe that he may have something that belongs to us. We want it back. So, young man, what I need to know where has he gone? When will he be back? And crucially, what do you know?'

'George, the girl has pissed herself, and it's all over my fucking shoes.'

'Take her into the kitchen and get her a towel or something. Oh, and maybe have a fucking look for some fucking air freshener?'

'You know, I might just fuck her myself, I bet you have some condoms laying around don't you?' He winked at Lassie who looked back, worried. He released Lassie's jaw and gestured for him to start speaking.

'Man, I know fuck all... honestly.'

'I don't believe you.'

George decided to go straight for the kill and shouted to Kevin. In no time at the sobbing girl was bent over, her hands tied to her ankles with football socks, and another sock in her mouth while Kevin brandished a rolling pin. Lassie also in tears, was pleading with George.

'I don't know anything! Leave her alone! He's been out with your friends since Monday, I don't fucking know where they are now. Tom has gone to college in Colchester. He gets a lift off a lad with ginger hair and glasses. I don't even know his name. That's fucking it man, that's fucking it!' He wanted to fucking kill these two cunts, get his football socks off No Name girl's ankles and give her a hug.

'If I find out you haven't told us everything...'

'I know, I know, you'll kill us, I've seen it in the movies...'

Seeing this as a flippant remark, George grabs Lassie by the face and punches him, then punches him again, on the third punch he is out cold. Raging, George turns to the record and CD collection and starts kicking them all over the floor. After smashing up half of Lassie's vinyl he finally calms, tells Kevin to release the girl and stands staring at her. She is petrified, sobbing, shaking and crying uncontrollably.

'Now come on love,' he whispers, mockingly, 'try not to piss yourself again, eh?' George then pulled her in close and squeezed her arse. Pressing a piece of paper into her sweating hand he said, 'Tell Tom that if he wants to live he needs to ring this number and make amends, got that?'

Barely nine o'clock in the morning and they're making progress.

As they crossed the road some muffled groans came from the car boot. George smiled but otherwise ignored the sounds as he opened the car door and stowed his jacket in the back seat. He then went round and calmly opened the boot.

'Shut the fuck up, you little thieving cunt, or you'll never see beyond the boot of this fucking car.'

Leaning in he delivered a flurry of body blows to the kidneys and ribs of the body in the boot, producing yelps and screams that were muffled as George slammed the boot of the car and climbed into the driver seat.

'Is he nice and comfortable in there?'

'It's not the Ritz, and the room service is a little fucking rough but he'll fucking live.'

In the boot, a bruised, beaten and starving Patrick Wherry felt himself going slowly mad. He was worried about Razor, but knew he was at least alive. He, on the other hand, could wind up dead. A fresh start he'd thought, a new life maybe? It had lasted barely three days and he was now staring down the barrel of his family's shotgun. He'd fucking hated Liverpool and all that went with it but he'd rather be there and breathing then dead, in the boot of a car. He'd been moments from getting on that fucking boat, moments. He'd had to think fast when they grabbed him, he'd played stupid, not as stupid as Razor but stupid enough he hoped. He shut his eyes and tried to block out the pain of the cramps he was suffering from the cable ties that were bound around his hands and ankles.

## 1.21 Bona Fide Crazies

Tom was quiet on the journey into college. This had been a mental couple of days. He thought about Razor. Would his legs be alright? The whole thing was beyond crazy and he wanted no further part in it. He'd had a laugh with a couple of lads he'd met in a pub but things had got well out of hand. Those lads were in deep and the maniacs coming after them were not fucking about! Razor could quite easily have been killed and they had been fucking lucky to get away. Jesus fuck, he thought, I just need to get a normal job, a normal life. His head fell backward onto the rest and he stared at the ceiling of the car. He decided to try to count as many of the tiny pinholes in the material that covered the inside of the roof as he possibly could before they arrived. At least Paddy got onto the boat last night. He'd be in Holland very soon and frankly Tom hoped he'd lost his phone number.

The Seat Ibiza pulled into the car park of the Institute. Tom bunged Bad Monkey a couple of quid for petrol and said he was sorry he'd been so quiet but he'd catch him at lunch. He drifted past the vocational workshops, quiet at this time of the morning, but soon to be full of day release plasterers, chippys, bricklayers and sparks. Tom had decided to some academic subjects, even though one of the vocational ones would have him earning sooner.

He drifted into the main social and canteen area. It was rammed full of lovely girls. He grabbed a coffee and a piece of toast from the friendly old girl at the counter and settled down for twenty minutes before his GCSE English class. He glanced around the room, looking for one particular girl. He hadn't met her but she was amazing to look at, with close-cropped hair. She wasn't there but his eyes carried on their tour, catching glances of leg, hair or eyes as the girls threaded their way through the room.

His class began, predictably enough, with a 'how to' exercise. Tom took out his pen and pad and began jotting down the notes from the overhead projector. Opposite him, in her regular position sat a pretty girl with lots of curly black hair and gorgeous olive skin. She had very long, slim legs and dark hypnotising eyes. Tom had only exchanged pleasantries with her but he guessed she was Middle Eastern in origin. Oh, he would, wouldn't he? Definitely. Absolutely. The little head was in charge now and he felt himself getting a riser. Jesus, he thought, get a hold of yourself. He adjusted himself in his seat and looked up to see her smiling at him. He felt himself blush, as if she could read his mind. He dived back into his notes trying to avoid her eyes in case she really could.

As he was considering looking up and catching another sly letch, the whole class looked up, like a troop of eager Meerkats. A lady holding a small piece of paper had come in.

'Morning, and sorry to interrupt your lesson. Is there a Tom Adams here today?'

Eh? He thought. Tom put up his hand and was ushered outside to be given the message that he must ring home immediately.

'You can use the office phone or there are public telephones in the foyer.'

Tom nodded his thanks and followed her down the hall and into the office where she gave him the piece of paper with the message on it.

Mum, Dad, family had been the first things that had sprung to mind. What else could it be? He looked down at the phone and at the piece of paper. He read the message and felt both relief and terror: relief because the number was not his Mum's or sister's, terror because what the fuck could be going on at home to make that stone head Lassiter get his shit together to the point that he could call the college?

After exactly half a ring the phone was answered and an agitated voice on the other end spoke through two fat and swollen lips, a broken nose and a chipped tooth.

'Tom, is that you?'

Tom put the phone down and felt a wave of nausea sweep through him. He slumped into the chair beside him and in seconds felt the hand of someone on his arm offering him a glass of water, which he took gratefully and sipped while his thoughts swirled around his head like a machine on full spin.

'Are you OK?' the lady who had brought the water asked.

'I'm fine, I'm going to have to go home though.' He had to get out of the building and gather his thoughts.

'That's completely fine, I can pass a message to your tutors for you. You get yourself off home as soon as you feel OK. Do you need a cab or anything?'

Nice lady and very helpful, he thought. 'No thanks, I'll be OK in two mins and I'll get off home.'

In a minute he was off, and frantically flipping the conversation with Lassie over and over in his head.

Fuck! What the fuck! He felt scared now. Very scared. How the fuck did they find out where he lived, and why the holy fuck did they want to talk to him? Although, he realised, that bit was clear. He was the one person who'd had contact with the boys and they would want to know where Paddy was. Jesus, he rued the fucking car crash of a day Monday had been. Fuck! He was going to be sick. He was going to have to talk to this psycho soon. What the fuck was going to happen to him? The only good news was that he'd found out No Name girl's name when Lassie had been telling him what those fuckers had done to her.

Back to Harwich ASAP was his plan. After that, fuck knew. He imagined he'd have to ring the Scousers and try to sort the whole mess out.

There was no one on the station gate so Tom breezed through the barrier. A free journey home. Some things were going OK today at least... The thought made him stop in his tracks. He walked back to the machine, selected a single to Harwich Town, paid and walked over to the platform. He needed some good karma today.

Lassie was waiting for him at the station. He looked a total mess.

'I'm so fucking sorry, man,' Tom said, giving him a hug. He really was and he didn't deserve this. What a mess, Tom thought as Lassie showed him his chipped tooth.

'What the fuck am I going to do, Lassie?'

'Well, lad, the situation, in my esteemed estimation, is not exactly ideal in any way, shape or form...'

They both smiled and managed a laugh before debunking to the Victoria Hotel for a beer to discuss what they should do.

'I have the number you have to call here, mate.'

Tom took the note and stared at it. 'Fuck, even the writing looks psychotic. What about Jodie?'

Lassie considered that less was more in the circumstances. 'She's OK. Shaken. She had a shower and I lent her a top so she could get home. She'll be fine. We can ring her later.'

Tom thought he couldn't even begin to say how sorry he was or make up for the mess he had dragged her into.

'First things first, you have to ring them and find out the lay of the land. They might just want to thank you for looking after the lads and that will be it.'

'Fuck off Lassie.'

'You never fucking know,' Lassie pointed to the quaint little phone booth in the pub, one of the oldest, most run down in the whole town. 'Come on, this won't go away and those two mad bastards could be anywhere.'

Tom stood up, felt in his jeans for change, nodded at Lassie and walked over to the payphone. Lassie watched as he put in some money and dialled the number. Tension gripped him as he heard the money drop, signalling that Tom was through. Inside ten seconds Tom was waving his arm and calling for a pen. Lassie got one from the bar and gave it to Tom who wrote down another number. The receiver down, Tom sat back down next to Lassie.

'That was another psycho. I had to give him the number of that phone. We have to wait here. I don't like it at all. I feel sick to the fucking core.'

Lassie could see Tom wobbling and put a Laphroaig in front of him with two ice cubes in it.

'Sip that mate and we'll have a think. Clearly the boys have a pager and he's going to page the one down here and then he'll ring the number. You can talk and we can sort this out. Though if it doesn't ring in ten minutes lets bail and ring from somewhere else eh? Keep ahead of them?'

Tom wanted to cry. He had to muster all his strength not to let it out and he took the whisky in one, the peaty taste snapping his senses. He hadn't eaten at all and needed to. He went to the bar and bought two rolls, a few bags of crisps, a whisky for Lassie and an Appletiser for himself. He was going to need a clear head, he was sure of that.

The rolls were released from their Clingfilm prison and devoured, the Quavers and Frazzles were opened, poured into the same bag and split on the table between them. As they shared the crisps the phone rang. They exchanged glances and Tom walked towards it, counting the rings.

He picked up the receiver. 'Hello,' Tom said.

'Is that Tom?' said the voice on the end of the phone.

'It is.'

The voice was almost upbeat, which made Tom immediately uneasy. 'Alright, la, it's Paddy.'

Tom was speechless, what the fuck was going on? 'Err, alright, Paddy. What the fuck is going on? I thought you were in Holland?'

'Yeah, long story like, but I kinda didn't get on the boat. Decided against it. Rang home to make amends.'

Tom wanted to ask what the fuck he was ringing him for? If they had him and Razor, why hadn't they just fucked off back up to Liverpool to sort out their own shit and live happily ever after? He was about to ask all this when the reason for the call became apparent.

'See the thing is, la, I need that money I lent yer back.'

Tom felt his knees buckle. Had he just heard that right! Was that dirty little northern weasel stitching him up? 'What fucking money?' Tom screamed done the phone. 'You barely bought me a fucking drink, you fucking cockroach!'

Tom could hear other voices talking in the background at the other end of the phone, but through his rage he could hear what could only be Paddy saying to someone 'I knew he'd be like that, cunning lad him.'

A different voice came on the line, calmer but with a tone that made part of Tom's roll come back up and sit at the bottom of his throat, bursting to get out all over the phone.

OK, Mr Tom fucking Adams of 11 Park Ridings, fucking Harwich, fucking Essex... You, it seems, are a slippery little toe-rag gipsy throwback thieving cunt.'

All Tom could do at this point was listen in stunned silence. He felt like he was floating and in court again, only this time he was not guilty, had been found guilty and was awaiting the judge's decision on punishment.

George Meachen continued delivering his verdict. One he had been rehearsing since grabbing Paddy out of the queue for the ferry, the ferry that had to wait while another ferry left port that evening. Dragging him like a naughty school boy back out into the car park and into the boot of the car.

'OK cunt, our Patrick tells us you took the boys on a right merry spend up. A spend up that happened to be with my money. Now since myself, my nephew and his divvy side-kick have been reunited, I have had a chance to have a decent chat with them and it has come to light, that with a few Es inside them you managed to persuade them to lend you £5,000 to do a little score. A score, you told Patrick, that you could turn around in two days with a profit of a tidy £500 a day. I was impressed, to say the least, you little fucking thieving cunt. Very impressed. Now, I am going to be kind, for the grace of God and all that. I am going to give you til tomorrow, that's two and a half days by the way, to turn this around, I will also be taking half the profit on your end and I am charging you 500 fucking pounds expenses. All in all, Tom fucking Adams that makes £6000 you are going to give to me by midday tomorrow. You may be considering what will happen if you fail to pay. In response to this I can only say that very bad things will happen, probably to people you know and most definitely to you. You hear me?' I said, 'Do you fucking hear me?'

Tom was speechless. He managed to get his voice to work and rasped down the phone, 'You do realise that this is a total load of bullshit?'

'Lad, I really don't give a fuck, either way, I just want getting my money back plus interest. I'll ring this number at eleven tomorrow to arrange the meet."

It was true that George didn't really believe a word of what Paddy had told him, but he was family man, after all.

'Done?' Kevin asked as George got back in the car.

'Pretty much, let's find a hotel. We can pick up and go home tomorrow.'

Kevin Stones turned the car around and out of the Colchester Institute car park, heading into the town centre.

'There, that'll do us,' George said, pointing at a sign. 'The George Hotel. It has secure parking too, that'll do us fine.'

'What about the boy?'

'I think he'll be absolutely fucking fine where he is.' Meachen turned and shouted at the boot, 'You'll be fucking fine won't you, Paddy?' There was no response. 'See? no fucking problem whatsoever, Kev.'

'You've been well and truly fucked, mate,' said Lassie.

'Mmm.'

'Any ideas? What about the Police?'

'No way, mate, they wouldn't or couldn't help us anyway. I, my friend, am fucked. I have to find 6K by lunchtime tomorrow, end of.'

Lassie could see Tom was shaken and he couldn't help thinking that he'd got off lucky in his brush with those two. He tongued his broken incisor and felt his nose as he spoke, 'What a cunt that Paddy is, eh? A proper cunt!'

'I can't even get angry about it, Lassie, it's unbelievable. Where did the 6k even go in the first place? Did they count it wrong? Or is that psycho just making it up? Either way, I'm in it up to my neck.'

Staring into space, Tom started laughing. Not in any way a huge laugh, but definitely a laugh,

'It's madness, Lass, but madness that isn't going to go away. We are.'

'Hey Adams, I love you man, but I'm not with you on this one.'

'I need a wingman, Lass, nothing dangerous will happen, just someone to bounce ideas off of and get a bit of counsel, a second pair of eyes you know?'

'Well that bit sounds OK,' said Lassie. 'But what about the psychopaths?'

Tom realised that Lassie wasn't up for it, but he really needed someone with him. He hadn't quite thought everything through but he needed Lassie, if only to keep him company. 'Come on, Lass,' Tom urged him with a dig in the ribs. 'All expenses paid... it'll be a laugh.'

In the back of his mind Tom also realised that this was his only real chance to save his legs from being broken, or worse. He wasn't enjoying this new situation.

'I promise you, with hand on heart, Lassie, that we will keep these loons at arms-length until we, sorry I, have the cash.'

Lassie thanked him for his timely correction in relation to the 6K, shook his head, looked at his pal and said, I'm' willing to listen, Mr Adams, but if I don't like the sound of it I'm walking.'

'OK,' Tom said. 'This is what I have so far...' He realised his opening line didn't really inspire much confidence but it was early doors and he was somewhat desperate.

Tom's pride & joy, his SAAB V4 stick shift would have to go, unfortunately it was only worth around 500 quid. He did, however, have the bank of sock. Which was in fact just a sock with his savings in it. Much to Lassie's amazement this totalled around 2k. Flogging his Stereo and some clothes would fetch another 1k. This left him 2.5k to find. This, he explained to Lassie, he would try to borrow in town. Everything he had scrapped for would have to go, just because he'd gone to the pub on Monday and met those two lads, who had now left him destitute through absolutely no fault of his own. This would cripple him and leave him without any options or independence. No stereo, no car and a thinned-out wardrobe, just for going out on a Monday. Fuck, he thought. Fucking hell. His next thought, however, sobered him... it could be a lot worse. As long as he could carry on with college he thought, he'd be happy.

'Tom, your miles away mate, come back to reality.' Lassie nudged him on the leg and waved an empty glass at him, all expenses paid remember?'

'You in then lad?'

Lassie smiled and nodded, despite feeling somewhat apprehensive.

Tom felt the relief course through him and was smiling he approached the bar for a celebratory drink. At the bar, his frown deepened as he thought about what he was actually proposing and how he was going to get the other 2.5K.

## 1.22 Gary Sparks

George and Kevin were sitting quietly in the bar of the hotel, both having ordered a full English breakfast with a side of onion rings. Outside, in the boot of the hire car, a heavily sedated Paddy passed in and out of consciousness. And when conscious, wished he was dead.

'Gary Sparks is on his way down,' George said. 'He'll meet us at the hospital when we go to collect your brother.' George put his hands into his pockets, pulled out a bunch of black cable ties and pass them to Kevin. 'Look after these, please.'

Kevin pocketed them.

'You and Graham can take that cunt Paddy home and Gary and I'll concentrate on the southern thief.'

'Do you honestly think he's got it?'

'He might have, he might not, Kev. It's not my fucking problem. If Paddy has stitched him up, he fucking well deserves it. What would you do if a pair of grubby Scousers rocked up with 40K of someone else's money? I'd walk the other fuckin way, lad, the other fuckin way.'

George looked up and smiled as the food arrived. 'Thank you,' he said, and gave her a fiver for her trouble. 'Sweet girl', he remarked as she walked off with her tip.

The two sat and ate their food in silence until a friendly tourist at another table tried to strike up a conversation. Speaking confident, but broken English he said, 'Hello, are you here for the festival? We are, we come every year.'

George replied, 'There is an old English saying. Never interrupt an Englishman while he is eating his breakfast.'

He leant forward and smiled at the group, lowering his voice to a whisper he added, 'Now fuck off and leave us alone.'

At this the other man blushed and, embarrassed, turned away, trying to fathom what was going on.

George and Kevin soon finished and headed for the door.

'Fucking hell, can't a man have a breakfast in peace nowadays?'

They made for the hotel car park, where George opened the boot and pulled up Paddy's head. His eyes are a dull yellow and the smell coming from the boot is foul. Using the boot lid as cover, George opened Paddy's mouth, pushed in two more tablets and made him swallow them with water. He then dropped him back into the boot and smiled at Kevin. 'He's having a fucking wonderful time in there, Kev, and he sends his best.' This cracked him up and acted as a cue for Kevin to join him, which he dutifully did.

'Come on, we're off.' George pulled out of the car park and followed the road toward Harwich until he reached a filling station. 'Just gotta make a couple of calls.'

Thirteen minutes and forty seconds passed before the car door opened and George returned to the driver's seat. 'All fine at home,' he said.

'I didn't hear a squeak from the boot, even with the engine turned off, should we check on Paddy, George?'

George Meachen ignored this observation and continued, 'Sparksy'll be there for two.'

The woman at the hospital reception desk sat filing her nails and ignoring the phone. She glanced up to see a well-built, short, stocky chap striding towards her. Not good-looking but not ugly either. He had the look of a boxer with a rather large losing tally, a flat nose, and fallen eye sockets. And she had never before seen a man in a full shiny shell-suit before. She decided she definitely wouldn't shag him. She couldn't understand his broad Liverpudlian accent and was relieved when she finally managed to direct him towards the ward holding his friends.

'I hate that fucking accent,' she mumbled to her colleague as she watched the shell-suited character shuffle off down the hall.

When Graham had first come around, he had forgotten to ask about Razor. When he did remember to ask how the 'joy-rider' was he was told that Raymond was in quite a bad way. He had sustained some horrific injuries, had lost one leg, and had already been into theatre twice. Looking upset for Razor hadn't been easy but he was sure he had managed it. The little toe-rag deserved all he got, and worse was probably to come.

He now sat up in bed laughing to himself at the comic he was reading. It was the Beano. He looked like a panda thanks to his bruises and had been nick-named Chi-Chi by the nurses. He had been heavily concussed when he'd been admitted and had spent most of the last twenty-four hours asleep. His head was sore but he was definitely enjoying the attention from the nurses. Especially the Irish girl with tits to match her arse and a forehead that was coming in a close third as the most prominent feature on her body.

At this point he saw the shell-suited Gary Sparks walk through the ward doors, speak to a nurse and then walk towards him smiling.

'Fuck me Gaza,' Graham laughed, 'You look like the silver surfer!'

The ward was momentarily filled with Scouse laughter as the two men exchanged unpleasantaries and generally slagged each other off.

Gary told Graham they were meeting George and Kevin at two, but he'd arrived early. Graham called the ward nurse and explained that he needed to check himself out of the hospital. He glanced up at the ward clock, he had about an hour to get things sorted. Should be easy.

'That's fine, Sir,' the nurse said. 'Home rest would probably best for you now. However, the police have called and would like to talk to you before you leave.'

Graham replied, 'OK, well... my brother's coming at two. Can I do the formalities with you, wait for my brother and then talk to the police. Does that sound OK?'

'That's fine, I'll start the paperwork.' The nurse smiled, retreated to the nurse station and picked up the phone.

At exactly two o'clock, George and Kevin pulled into the hospital car park. Waiting outside for them were Graham, now fully dressed and bandaged, and Gary.

'Any news on Razor?' asked George.

Graham replied, 'He's lost a leg and he's having surgery to try to save the other one. He isn't walking out of there any time soon.'

'OK,' George said, 'he'll keep. This is what we'll do. We put our passenger into Gary's car with Kevin and Graham to take back to Liverpool. I'll change the Astra for another hire car and Gary and I will chase up the Adams boy and clear up the mess in Harwich. Given no major grief we should all be back in Liverpool by Thursday evening.'

Kevin brought Gary Sparks' car around to where he and George had parked the Astra.

'Will it be OK to do this here George?' Kevin asked.

'Fuck it, just do it,' he said.

When they opened the boot the smell was powerful – his stay in the boot had included no toilet breaks. Paddy can't open his eyes as he has been in darkness for hours and is mumbling, crying.

Kevin Stones is visibly taken aback at Paddy's state, 'George, we need to clean him up, he's fucked.'

'Not as fucked as he's gonna be, Kev. Now grab the smelly little thieving cunt and put him in the back of Gary's car. When you get home, cable-tie the cunt to something solid in the shed. If you wanna wash him down then you can, after all, you're gonna torture the little shite and you might not want to get all shitty, eh?' George laughed at his own humour as Kev pulled Paddy's dishevelled, stinking body into the boot of Gary's car, momentarily he feels like apologising and leans in

88

to speak to the boy but is thrown back by the smell of human excrement. He slams the boot shut and leans on it, breathing heavily.

'Done, let's go home.' He doesn't know whether he is talking to himself, to the others or to the youngster in the boot of the car. Whichever, he gets into the car next to his brother, shuts the door and waits for the others to get ready.

George walks over to the car, slaps a hand on the roof with a loud bang and leans into the window. 'Good work lads, see you in a couple of days.'

He bangs his hand again on the roof of the car and nods to Gary to get into the Astra. 'Let's do this.'

# 2 How to get?

## 2.1 Taff

'Any ideas who you can borrow 2.5K from, squire? That's a lot of cash.' Lassie knew of one person who might be able to do it, but wasn't going to be the one to make the suggestion.

Tom smiled. 'I think we both know only one person who would entertain such a ludicrous idea, my friend, and that's Taff.'

Lassie nodded in agreement, 'I think it's hilarious that Taff is the only person we know that can potentially save your bacon. How fucking ironic...'

The two boys smiled a rueful smile as they peered into the bottom of their glasses and drained their pints. They stood, gathered their thoughts, left the Victoria and crossed the road to the taxi office. Tom made a call from the phone box outside and they then went in to get a cab. The office smelt musty and of stale kebabs. Behind the desk was a huge man who looked like a moose and smelt like an elk. The boys looked at each other and both raised one eyebrow, something they had spent months practising. They called this the 'SRM' or 'single Roger Moore'. This show of surprise wasn't as serious as raising both eyebrows, indicated by the 'DRM' or 'double Roger Moore'. They opted to wait for their cab outside.

The cab skirted along the coastline and made its way into the older part of Harwich, where the narrow streets were lined with overhanging houses.

A middle-aged man sat waiting for them in an old wicker chair on a patio to the side of a house. One hand held a scotch and the other a huge reefer. He was dressed in an old pair of jeans and a shabby fisherman's pullover, and wore unmatched flip flips on his feet, one black, and one electric blue. An Essex County Cricket Club hat sat a jaunty angle on his frizzy grey hair. He leant forward, about to speak and stopped, looking at his watch. 'Morn... Oh, good afternoon boys,' he mumbled, wondering where the day had gone.

Tom leant in and shook the offered hand. 'Hello Taff – fuck me, that cricket hat used to be white, didn't it?"

Taff's reply is quick, dry, sincere, is finished off with the draining of his glass, and has all three laughing and instantly at ease.

'Catch me givin' a fuck, boyo? Drink?' The offer duly accepted, shortly all three were sitting in the warm June sun, sipping whisky.

'Got to have a patio boys... too dark otherwise.'

The boys agree with fervent nods.

'However,' Taff continued, 'I don't imagine you're here to discuss the importance of outside space or the greatness of my fucking whisky are you? Especially when taking into consideration the state of your fucking face...'

Over the next twenty minutes, Tom Adams retold the story of his week. Taff sat there throughout, attentively listening and nodding, occasionally muttering 'Jesus wept' or 'bloody hell'. As Tom finished Taff began shaking his head and staring into his whisky. He could obviously tell where he would come into the story.

'These seem like serious people, boys. Very serious. I wouldn't touch them with a barge pole.'

'Neither would I if I had the fucking chance again,' Tom answered.

'Aye, but you have, Tom, and you've dragged young Lassie into the fray too, you fucking idiot.'

Tom looked at Lassie and gave him a single Roger Moore, almost in apology.

'I know, I know, it really was just bad luck though, and now we, sorry, I need help.' Tom could feel the pleading in his voice and told himself to stop begging. It would be the end of it if Taff felt he wasn't in control.

Taff looked up from his glass and stared into Tom's face. 'Thing is, Tom, you've lost control of this situation haven't you, you silly bastard?'

'I admit,' Tom offered, knowing Taff had the measure of him, 'that I'm not fully in control of the situation. But, with a little help from you, it is retrievable.' Tom felt his Adam's apple nearly in his mouth.

Taff fell silent and looked at the floor. He was sharp and smooth operator despite his projected image and persona, and was clearly why he was well known to one of the top men around in terms of underworld contacts and general naughtiness. He was a man to be respected and a very handy man to know, especially as he was also a brilliant painter and decorator.

'You're two and a half grand short Tom, two and a half grand, not 500 quid. Two and a half grand! And if you think I am going to lend you 2.5k you are fucking mad. It's not because I don't like you, you're a nice lad, but how the fuck you could pay that back is beyond me. You've already said you'll have to take gifts at the weekends and they don't come cheap. You'll be working it off for years and no one wants that liability. And what if something happens to you in the meantime? What then with my money? What happens if the psycho wants to tap you again in future? You know what these fuckers are like, leeches! You know how we operate down here boy... quietly, under the radar. Like fucking ghosts... now you've shattered that in three days and there are people running round town waving guns about!'

Taff sighed, finished his drink and looked at Tom.

'Sorry, boyo, you're on your own.'

Tom listened to the words fall from Taff's mouth. He felt like he had a baby elephant sitting on his chest, he stood up and tried to take in a deep breath. He couldn't and felt dizzy as he began to sway in the early afternoon heat. He was well and truly fucked. He felt himself leaning over and then went very light as Lassie's arms grabbed around his chest. Lassie and Taff sat him down in a chair, Taff went inside and got some water and returned with a wet dishcloth. Tom came around and sat quietly, staring at the reality of the situation.

After five minutes of silence, with Lassie and Taff watching over him, Tom spoke. 'Totally understand, Taff. I totally get it. It's massive. Sorry for asking. You too, Lass, sorry for getting you into this, you've got to distance yourself from me straight away. This bollocks is mine to deal with.'

'I've got your back, mate. I'd be a cunt if I didn't.'

'This is a bridge too far.' Tom looked at his best mate and took his head, 'This is well beyond my expectations of a mate, and you've got to leave it.'

Taff sat and watched the scene unfold, he was struck by the maturity of young Tom Adams, he'd clearly bitten off more than a rabid hippo could chew but was doing his best to deal with it.

Tom stood up and offered his hand to Taff.

'Cheers, Taff, it needed saying. Don't know what the fuck to do still but I needed to hear that. Thanks, mate.'

Lassie nodded and stood up, shook hands with Taff and the boys walked toward the stairs.

'Hang on,' Taff said, scratching his head. 'I might have an idea.'

The two boys turned round and faced Taff with a look of confusion, trepidation and mild hope in their faces. Taff was busy pouring them all another whisky.

## 2.2 Wilhire

Safely behind the counter and a secure door the sales assistant and the manager of Wilhire's Harwich branch looked at the car paperwork, at the two characters standing in reception behind the two-way mirror, and at each other.

'Have you checked the car thoroughly?' The manager asked the sales assistant.

'Yes, I have. There's no damage, apart from the horrendous smell.'

'What type of smell?'

'Err, it's like human faeces.'

'Shit you mean?'

'Yes,' the sales assistant confirms, 'shit.'

'And it's almost overpowering?'

'Yes.'

'Is that why they want another car?'

'Well, yes…'

Both men fall silent and look out through the safety glass at the menacing George Meachen and the shape of Gary Sparks.

"Yes", the sales assistant replies.

'So, it's just the problem of an overpowering smell of shit that is permeating throughout the whole vehicle that is the problem here?'

'Yes.'

The Manger looked through the two-way mirror once more, fumbling with his name tag, took a step toward the door put his hand on the door knob, waited and then allowed his hand to drop away.

'Fuck it, give them a new car and put the valets on double time. Life's just too short.'

'Thank you,' the sales assistant chirps at his manager, the relief almost tangible.

Twenty minutes later a white Vauxhall Astra pulled away from Wilhire's Dovercourt branch. Inside it two broad Liverpudlian men were much happier than they had been an hour earlier.

'That fucking car is a write-off George, they'll never be able to get that smell out of it. It's fucking ingrained in it. It's like a part of its fucking DNA, they'll have to rename it the Vauxhall Shitstra.'

'I get the fucking idea, Gary, now shut the fuck up.'

George wanted to keep tabs on this Adams toe rag. He didn't trust him. First they drove back to his house and waited outside to see if there were any signs of movement. It was a cul-de-sac though and they couldn't be seen to be hovering. Especially if the lad who took a whack in the face had called the old Bill. They drove by a couple of times but nothing stirred. He waved a hand to Gary Sparks that he'd had enough. He'd turn up. The town was too small. They'd eat, have a few beers and if needed tap up the taxi drivers again for information. It was simple enough stuff and frankly, he felt pretty confident that Adams would come up with most, if not all of the cash. Which would come in handy for his Xmas in the sun. He smiled to himself and rubbed his belly.

'Let's take in the sights of this unholy cunt of a town and then get something to eat, eh, Gary?"

*You're the boss*, Gary thought, nodding his agreement to George.

They drove around Harwich, past the docks and along down the sea front past old lighthouses, tired amusement arcades, decrepit beach huts and a wind battered roller skating rink. A yellow-turfed putting green almost screamed for help and beyond that a throng of Cockney holidays makers shoved chips into their already overweight offspring.

'This place is fucking depressing, George, it's worse than fucking Southport!'

'Calm down there, Sparksy, I fucking like Southport, this is a true blot on the cuntscape.'

Gary Sparks turned the Astra around and headed back into town.

'I'm sure a saw a Chinese restaurant that was open in town, George, fancy it?'

'OK, but if it's crap you're gonna get a kick in the bollocks.'

## 2.3 The Plan

Taff sat back in his chair smiling.

'That, my friend is pretty much that.'

Lassie had a question, 'Why not just out them here? It's a massive risk moving them abroad isn't it?'

'It is, but it's all come a bit on top here, and someone in the Low Countries has offered to take them a job lot, if my associates can deliver. Even if we lose this one, we aren't down. We're still actually in mild profit. This will be a huge bonus all round.'

'So,' Tom said, 'basic gist is this... you want me to smuggle 50k of forged UK bank notes into Holland, drop them off in a locker in Amsterdam, for which you will pay me... in fake fucking notes?'

At this, Taff smiles. 'Yes, that is it, you ungrateful cunt. It's the best I can do.'

'Getting paid in fake notes? I'll have to gamble on getting them changed and everything. It could take me a week, maybe more to do it. I could end up with nothing!'

'You could,' Taff laughs and sips his drink. 'But the beauty of it is that I could afford to pay you 3k in forged, rather than 500 in bona fide notes. You can have a look at the notes, they are pretty much spot on. So what do you think? Solve a problem or what you little monkey?'

Tom looked across at Lassie, who was, sporting the biggest DRM he had ever seen him produce. There was no need for words at this point. This could potentially solve all his problems, put Lassie out of danger and even make a few quid! He returned the DRM and turned to Taff.

'You could be on tonight's boat, boyo,' he said, sipping his Laphroaig. 'And yes, before you ask, I'll give you 500 quid expenses and I'll even throw in a fare for your trusty sidekick!'

Tom glanced at Lassie, 'Fancy a trip to the orange country, my friend?'

'Why the fuck not?' came the brisk reply.

By five o'clock all was pretty much done. The boat was booked and the boys were in a taxi home to pack a bag. While at Taff's, Tom had written a note explaining that he was going to Holland to collect the money George wanted. They stopped at the Victoria to give the note to Big Eared John the barman to read out when they rang again at eleven o'clock the next day. A score had helped smooth over this favour. As they approached home, Lassie seemed more nervous than Tom.

'We have to make sure they're not around again, Tom.'

'It'll be alright, Lass, just relax. I can't see anything dodgy... Things will work out and in reality, it's my only option.'

'I think you should ring the number you have in Liverpool and explain you're not doing a runner, Tom.'

'If I did that, we'd never make the boat. They'd hunt us... sorry, me, down and fucking shoot me! It has to be this way. Perhaps I'll ring them when we're in Holland, deal?'

'OK, mate.' This seemed to appease Lassie.

Tom went into his room and put on some tunes and started to pack. It was clearly a Smiths day. *Strangeways Here We Come* side A. He hummed as he tried to digest the last three days. It was fucking mental. He had been well and truly stitched up by those Scouse fuckers and he still couldn't work out where 6K had gone. Just a random number he assumed, to bleed him for. He placed some carefully folded tops into his bag. Everything had to look natural he had decided, no 'special' bag, or suitcase. It had to look as though they were on a regular beano to Holland. Just with 50k wrapped up in a towel in the bottom of the bag. It had to fucking work. End of. He locked his windows, turned off the heating and headed down stairs.

'You ready Lass?'

The kitchen door opened. 'Ready ten minutes ago, knobhead. I've been stood here listening to you talking to yourself, you fruitloop!'

The Taxi arrived and they threw their bags into the boot and made their way to Taff's, ordering another cab to the port for nine that evening. Taff greeted them with cheese on toast. After consuming an impressive amount Taff pulled out the 50k and passed it to Tom.

'Look after it, lad, and don't get any funny ideas.'

Tom did a DRM 'Fuck me, Taff, as if I've got the inclination or the energy to do anything like that!'

'Just saying, boyo.'

Taff then gave Tom his 3k, which Tom inspected very closely before handing it to Lassie.

'What do you think, Lass, doable?'

It looks good to me, feels OK, even got a strange, if somewhat paraplegic watermark,' Lassie said, holding a note up to the light in the kitchen.

Neither knew anything about forged banknotes except that it was a huge gamble. But they did look OK.

Tom carefully wrapped his big purple towel around the notes and put them back in his bag. It made the bag heavier but he didn't think it looked odd. Lassie agreed, it was a goer and Taff concurred. Tom seemed happy, although the thought of kiting 3k of forged UK banknotes did give him a squirty ring. It was, as had been pointed out to him earlier, totally out of his control. The reality was, he thought, that Taff was doing him a huge favour. One he wouldn't forget it either.

They then sat down and listened to the plan for the drop off. There was to be no contact between the parties involved in Holland. In the car park just along from Amsterdam Central Station would be an old red Ford Capri. On the back left arch of the Capri would be a key for a locker inside the station. They would need to find the Capri, take the key, find the locker and place the bag with the cash in the locker and then return the key. Their time was then their own. There would be no further contact.

There was a steely look in Taff's eyes as he finished with, 'If and when you make it back, pop round and say hi, but both of you must forget about the whole thing. I don't want any discussion. OK?'

Tom and Lassie both nodded in agreement.

'Finally,' Taff said, 'you both understand that, if caught, you're fucked. And, of course I know you wouldn't, but if you did, my friends will know whose mouth opened and will also be able to make sure it's filled with something I imagine you'd rather not have in your mouth when you touch down in the nick.'

Nods all round and not a sight of a Roger Moore suggested to Taff that the boys fully understood the gravity of the situation.

The taxi and Tom and Lassie made their way downstairs and got into the cab.

'Parkeston Quay please, mate.'

Sitting proudly in the middle of the dash was a lime green digital clock showing the time was 20:59.

## 2.4 An Alarm Call

George Meachen grinned as he got out of the Astra. He was hungry but getting this shitty situation sorted was more important. 'Let's eat. Then a few bars, see who knows what, back to Colchester for a decent kip and we'll see what tomorrow holds, eh?'

'Bars?' Gary Sparks laughed. *Bars?* he thought... *bars of draw maybe in this shithole. Fuck all else.*

Inside the restaurant two employees were watching the men's approach. They nudged each and smiled. With one looking like Arthur Daly and the other like Terry McCann, it was, they laughed, 'Minder' for the nineties!

George and Gary went into the Shanghai Chinese Restaurant fully prepared for a big feed, but stood aghast at what they saw in front of them.

'What, in whoever is listening's name, the fuck is this?'

In front of them were two employees, one very fat, one very skinny. One had a bald head, one had very straight, slightly oily hair. One grinned like a maniac, one smiled with a deep sincerity. One wore Fred Perry, top button done up. One wore a shabby polo with a snooker cue embroidered on the left tit. One wore a trilby hat. The other wore nothing on his head. Both looked slightly drowsy, both grinned like they were stoned and both, to his total disbelief, were stone cold Englishmen. Fucking Harwich he thought, full of freaks and nutters!

Gary Sparks recovered first, 'Can we have a table for two please lads?'

'Of course, chaps,' the skinnier one of the two answered. 'Follow me please...'

Shortly, both men were sitting down with a beer in front of them. Gary had quickly ordered the set menu for two, the most expensive one. George was out of sorts about the lack of pure ethnicity in the restaurant. 'English lads, working for Chinks? It's just plain wrong.'

'Works work, boss,' Gary replied, as began to say a private prayer for everyone in the restaurant.

George began to get used to having English people serving him Chinese food when the food arrived and by the end of the meal had mellowed to the point of being able to order a chaser and offer a drink to each of the waiters.

As always, there was an angle.

'So boys,' George asked, 'do you know a lad called Tom Adams?'

Both took their time, then, without looking at each other replied with a negative.

George tired and full of food decided to cut to the chase. 'Listen lads, my mate here is a nasty cunt. We're interested in this Adams lad, and as you can tell, we're not from these parts. So, if you want me to call off my shell-suited Staffordshire bull terrier I suggest you come across with some information. I ask because if the women at the Hilltop Bakery know him, I'm sure you two little cunts are bound to know him too.'

The two waiters, visibly perplexed threw a wild glance and then both said at once, 'Try the Victoria.'

'And where the fuck is that?' enquired George Meachen impatiently.

The skinny one replied instantly, obviously trying to please, 'Just down the road, opposite the taxi office.'

'Thank you,' George replied. 'Can we have the bill please?'

'No problem, Sir,' the Skinny waiter replied, thinking *fuck off, you great big fat cunt.*

The bill paid George called them to the door, 'Just down here on the left then chaps?' he asked, making it abundantly clear that if they fucked him about he would be back to push nails into their eyes.

'Yup. Just down there, Sir, on the right.'

Inside the Victoria there was the usual bunch of waifs and strays, the disenfranchised, the disaffected and the lost. Ex-forces and benefit cheats a plenty. They gambled, they cheated, they bought and sold, whored and stored at and in the Victoria. So, when two strangers entered their domain, questions were asked without a word being spoken.

1 0 0

George broke the deadlock with the slightest of movements. Gary Sparks spoke first, 'Two brandies please, no ice.'

The cloth-eared barman dutifully obliged and shortly the drinks were on the bar. Transaction complete, the two men stood, sniffing brandy and slyly surveying the room.

George beckoned Gary Sparks into the snug. 'I'm a bit pissed Gary, I'm almost enjoying myself, but I can smell that little cunt in here. They know him. Let's get it sorted and get the fuck back to the hotel, I need a shit.'

Gary Sparks walked away with the green light. Following the signs for the gents, he entered the toilets. He headed for the stalls, sat down and took off both his socks and then put his trainers back on. He then carefully balled the socks into one, dropped them into the toilet, pushed them down with a naked hand and flushed the cistern until the toilet began to flood. With a few millimetres of water spread across the whole of the toilet floor he returned to the bar, where George joined him. With a flick of his head he called over the barman.

'How can I help?' He didn't like the look of these two, but then that's a pub.

George Meachen replied. 'We're trying to locate a friend of ours.'

The barman instantly felt uncomfortable and took a glass cloth and began cleaning wine glasses from the store above his head.

'He's a young lad called Tom Adams, tall lad, bit of a skinny bean pole. Do you know him by any chance?'

'I don't really know anyone by name. I've only just moved here myself, sorry.'

He put the clean glass back on the shelf took another glass down and began to push the glass cloth into it.

As an afterthought he added, 'Do you have a picture of him?'

'Unfortunately not,' George Meachen replied. 'Are you sure you don't know him?' George had a feeling that everybody knew everybody in this town. Even if they were sitting on different tables and didn't like each other, everyone knew everyone else's business.

'Sorry, I don't know the name.' The barman went back to cleaning his glasses.

'OK,' George said quietly.

Gary Sparks had been busily picking apart a beermat while quietly listening to the proceedings. Big Ears seemed sincere but he was sure there was more. 'By the way, fella, your WC's blocked.' Gary Sparks smiled, trying to look helpful and trustworthy.

A call for drinks took the barman away from the uncomfortable conversation he was having, but he habitually left on a positive note, 'OK, I'll take a look shortly, thank you.'

The two men stood against the bar, quietly sipping their brandy. George was convinced the barman knew more than he was letting on. He was tired though and they had to think about getting back to the hotel. The lad had nowhere to go really and despite anything he came up with, he would still have to take a hiding from Sparksy, but all in all he was happy to go back to Liverpool tomorrow evening. So long as these people knew not to take the piss he was happy.

He looked at his watch. It was ten o'clock. George raised his glass and finished his brandy. He looked at Gary in his shell-suit and felt the urge to set light to it. He resisted though and put his glass down on the bar. 'Well, time flies when you're enjoying yourself.'

At this point the barman wandered past them with mop and bucket on his way to the gents. Gary finished his drink too, nodded at George and followed the baggy eared barman. George couldn't help but notice that Gary wasn't wearing any socks.

In the toilet the barman stood looking at the wet floor trying to work out where the excess water was coming from. Bemused he wandered into the cubicle and looked into the bowl. In the bottom of the pan he could see something that looked like a ball of wool, as he leant over to further inspect the foreign body in the WC he heard movement behind him and he turned around to find the quieter one of the two from the bar standing in the doorway of the cubicle.

'Well, I think I've found the source of the leak, or rather flood,' the barman said. He walked forward and motioned to get by saying, 'Excuse me, please.'

Gary Sparks stood firm and pushed the barman back into the toilet, the surprise of this assault led the barman to lose his balance and end up sitting on the toilet.

'What, is going on?' the barman said shakily. He looked towards Gary Sparks and became even more confused as the man in front of him grinned and pulled up his grey, shiny shell-suit trousers to reveal a pair of sockless ankles. The next thought that came into his mind was that he was in danger because this bloke was clearly mad. The thought after became a cry of anguished pain. He screamed as a thumb was pressed into his eye, the rest of the huge hand gloving the side of his head. In between his screams he managed to string together a sentence designed to help save his mangled eye. 'What the fuck do you want for fucks sake, please leave me alone!'

Gary Sparks stood over the crumpled mess of the barman on the toilet, his thumb at least 2cm into his eye socket. He wiped his forehead with the grey sleeve of his favourite shell-suit, lent over and whispered, 'Tell me about that little fucker Adams, or I'll take your fucking eye out you cloth-eared fucking throw-back.'

Minutes later Gary walked back into the bar, strode up to George and spat out 'Cheeky little fucker!' passing George a crumpled note in the process.

George took the note, steadied himself against the bar, and began to digest what the note said. George turned to the nearest person in the bar and asked about the ferries to Holland from Harwich. He could feel his blood starting to boil. The white heat, the need to smash everything in sight was in danger of overwhelming him. Gary Sparks saw this happening, considered the fact that there was no barman as he was still crying in the toilet and suggested to George that it was probably best if they leave. Unable to speak, George walked out of the pub and stood in the warm late summer evening, there was a slight breeze. Gary got into the car and waited, knowing the right thing to do was to allow George time to calm down. He turned on the radio and began to nervously hum, the last thing they needed was George going nuclear. He also really didn't fancy chasing this Adams no-mark about in Holland but he knew how George worked. The door opened and George got into the car. They sat in silence for a short while before George spoke. 'I need to make a phone call, Gary.'

Gary started the engine and moved away from the pub, he drove approximately 20 metres before stopping alongside an old red phone box. George stepped out and into the call box. Gary turned on the radio, 'I Wanna Sex You Up' oozed out of the radio, and he instantly turned it off. Sexing anything up wasn't what he felt like at the moment. He watched as George Meachen finished his call and then stood still, in the phone box, with his eyes closed. He remained like that for thirty or so seconds before returning to the car.

'We need to go to the port, Gary.'

'No problems boss,' Gary replied and drove back through the town following the signs for Harwich Parkeston Quay. They had seen the boats and freight routes as they entered the town earlier and soon they were in the car park looking across at the dockside where the huge ferry was tied up. Lorries, cars and motorbikes could be seen snaking their way over a colossal concrete ramp system they fed them into the hull of the ferry, Gary was impressed and stood watching the drama unfold like a child watching a big wheel at the funfair. George, meanwhile had drifted away and was deep in conversation with a member of staff in the car park kiosk. He returned to his mesmerised, shell-suited sidekick and placed his hand on his shoulder. He felt calmer and wondered if being by the sea helped his mood. It felt nice being able to look out to sea and see nothing, not even the horizon.

Gary Sparks was surprised at George's change in mood.

'Well, Gary, we'll have to call it a night. We couldn't get on now anyway if we wanted too, boarding has finished and it leaves in thirty minutes.'

'Is he on there then boss? Gary enquired.

'Yeah, I'm pretty certain he is. What for, I don't know, but he's on there. Strange thing is he says in his note he is coming back, and he's coming back to pay us our money. Whether I believe him is another question, as the little cunt has already lied to us once. Fuck knows what he's up to.'

Gary shrugged, 'Well, I haven't got a fucking clue what the cunt's up to, boss.'

With a sarcastic smile, George replied, 'I didn't expect you to, lad.'

They got back into the car and George told Gary to head back to the hotel in Colchester. They'd ask the night porter to book them on to the ferry the next morning with the car.

'We're going after them then? Fuck...' Gary began to moan. Thankfully George was still mellow and a look reminded Gary that he wasn't part of the decision making process.

'Yes we are, Gary. Do you want to know why?'

Without waiting for a reply George carried on. He explained that by taking matters into his own hands, this little fucker Adams had tried to take control of the situation. This, in George's view, was unacceptable and therefore would require some form of retribution. This was where Gary came in. He was also unsure of Tom Adam's intentions and it was necessary to find out what they were, especially as he owed them 6k and the debt would be due at eleven tomorrow morning. He also explained to Gary that he thought this little fucker Adams could be up to something in Holland. It had to be Amsterdam and if they could get their hands on him there may be other spoils to be had from this little trip.

'Fair enough, George, but how do we find him in Amsterdam, I bet it's massive?'

'I spoke to a fella while you were dribbling, you daft cunt. He said the boat docks at the Hoek Van Holland on the other side. Trains then take foot passengers to Amsterdam and beyond, but ninety-nine percent of foot passengers head for the capital. We'll take the car and cut out all the waiting around shit, and catch up with him. He'll be six hours ahead but we can shave two hours off of that by taking the car. Anything doing, we'll get a sniff. And anyway Gary, I've never been to Amsterdam!'

Gary looked shocked. Was that a smile he just saw on George face? Nah, he thought, it must have been a shadow. He turned the car around and pointed it towards Colchester. Both men remained silent, for different reasons, all the way back to the hotel. Both had a large brandy and both made calls back home, for various reasons.

'OK, Gary, I'm off to sleep.' This was obviously a cue and Gary finished his drink and headed for bed too.

## 2.5 Duty Free

The two boys thanked the driver, tipped him handsomely with Taff's money and waved goodbye.

'Ready mate?' asked Tom, adding 'remember, Lass, you're a legend. I love you, and if anything happens you know nothing. It's all on me, OK?'

'All cool here, squire, love you too you big fucking fruit. I hope this all works out OK.'

Lassie was feeling especially relaxed as they had basically been drinking steadily all day and he had smoked a huge reefer before they left. He stank of the Joop! Tom had sprayed on him to mask the reek of the green before they left.

They picked up their bags and wandered into the departures hall. Doing his best to hide it, Tom could feel himself sweating, and not just his armpits, crutch and forehead. He was convinced his liver, kidneys, heart and bones were perspiring at a rate that would justify a small towel...

Twenty minutes later, after a quick stop in their cabin and the bar, they were standing on the port side of the boat looking back towards the tip of Harwich and the Angel Inn pub, sipping an ice cold pint of Heineken.

'Cheers Tom, I'm not gonna jinx anything but –'

'Fucking don't then, Lass!' Tom said, interrupting as fast as he could. 'This is barely out of the woods my friend.'

He didn't want to alarm his wingman, but when they had first come outside and were looking down at the final cars coming on and the car park and the quay below, he'd noticed a Vauxhall Astra parked near the entrance to the car park. Just to the left of the car he had just made out the shape of a bloke staring at the ferry. He had watched this bloke, who didn't move for minutes. Then, another man joined him and they both got into the car and drove off. The second man, he was sure, was the psychopath that he had seen in the car on the way home to Harwich on Tuesday when they had lost Razor. He was fucking convinced of it. That was the man he had spoken to on the phone, the man that evidently must know they had got on the boat. Clearly, Jon at the Victoria had either actively found these men or they had actively found him and he had then been bled for the note that he had left with Jon to explain the situation tomorrow morning when they were due to speak. He could feel himself begin to shiver. At least they were safe tonight though. He thanked god for small mercies, called himself a fucking hypocrite again and decided that Lassie didn't really need to know about this as he deserved a good night's rest before it really did all kick off.

'Fair enough, I'm feeling your pain,' Lassie smiled and raised his glass. Let's have the craic tonight lad, it could be our last supper.'

'Cut out the Catholic bullshit please, Lass,' Tom pleaded.

'It's the guilt, lad, it's the guilt.'

Tom laughed, "You've been a terrible Catholic since you were ten, you've barely had your cock out of your hand since then, you serial wanker!' They both fell about laughing.

They wandered back inside to the bar area which was alongside a little dance floor. Both boys enjoyed the size and style of Dutch beer, and the way bar staff whipped off the bottle tops with their little beer knives. The events of the past three days eroded away like a sand dune in the wind with each drink. They were relaxed and beginning to enjoy themselves.

Lassie stood up and had a look about, 'I'm off for a piss and a look in Duty Free.'

'Too much information, but cheers, I'll be here.'

Tom got a couple of beers in, one for Lassie on his return and then leant back in the chair and thinking that if this boat never docked he would be fine and dandy forever. Presently he saw Lassie smiling in the distance as he sauntered through the crowd. Under his arm was the biggest Toblerone Tom had ever seen.

'What the fuck is that?'

'It's my lucky Toblerone, mate,' Lassie replied, grinning.

'Really, Lass?'

Lassie picked up his drink, had a look around and carefully handed Tom a small pill.

'Just bumped into Egg. Top man. Took me off to his cabin, we had a quick spliff and he gave us an E each for the journey. He sends his regards, he'll try to come say hello later, top man, eh?'

All Tom could do was agree.

As the E started to kick in the bloke in the DJ booth brought in a new tune with a drag back. The hair on the back of Tom's neck stood up; he leant over to shake Lassie and pointed into the air and touched his ear at the sound of 'I wanna give you devotion'. Both boys scrambled for the tiny dance floor and started applauding the DJ, who instantly cranked up the volume for them. The horns looped and the boys were flying. The dance floor was empty aside from two steppers but began gradually filling up with ravers from all over Europe who were equally going nuts. The DJ took his chance as the record began its descent to the finish. Over the top of the fading tune the boys heard 'I can move any mountain' get underway. The whole dance floor was moving as one to the Shamen and Mr C.

The boys jumped around mouthing Mr C's rap. Both of them had forgotten the strife that they'd managed to tie themselves up in and were jumping round hugging, off their fucking tits. Lassie, bent over, motioned to Tom that he needed a rest and they headed back to their seats.

'Beautiful', said Tom as he picked up a still ice cold Heineken and took a gulp.

Lassie too, had grabbed a lager and they laid back in their seats and listened to the music and watched people dance. The tunes went a bit Euro pop but he was still playing some decent stuff. The boys were enjoying themselves, especially watching two girls who were dancing not too far away from them.

Tom was sure one of the girls kept smiling at him. He looked over at Lassie, whose eyes were on dip and dazzle. He nudged him.

'Hold it together, Lass, I reckon we could have a crack at these two birds.' He flicked his head in the girls' direction.

'I can't fucking see, Tom, I'm battered.' Lassie grinned and swallowed some lager. He squinted, through his nutted eyes, 'Oh yeah, I've got 'em. Nice.'

They discussed their quarry, while having an undeclared competition to see which of them could use every single facial muscle.

The girls clearly loved Impedance's 'Tainted Love' as much as the boys did and were putting on such a show that Lassie asked Tom if he thought they might be lesbians.

'No idea,' Tom replied. 'I'm not too hot on Euro culture!' And fell about laughing.

The janglers we're starting to wear off now and their face contortions were beginning to subside. They'd been good thought and the boys wondered whether they should hunt down the Egg and grab some more. They had agreed that this was an excellent plan and then another option arrived. Completely out of leftfield, the two girls who had been dancing appeared at their table and asked if they could join them.

'Of course,' both boys replied simultaneously and the girls sat down.

They looked very similar Tom thought, not unlike Lisa Stansfield, except that one had short dark hair and one had long dark hair. Shorty spoke first and said that she and her sister had seen them jumping around earlier and had thought they seemed like fun and they had in fact planned to come over earlier. 'But you were looking a bit off your heads,' Shorty said.

Shorty was called Pascale and her sister was Abi. They all shook hands. Pascale went on to say that Abi was deaf but she signed, which was probably useless to them but she could also lip-read very well if you were looking straight at her. Both boys nodded and turned to Abi and said hello.

'You speak perfect English, and your sister can lip read in English as well as Dutch. That's amazing,' said Tom.

Abi began signing to her sister. She says, 'It's normal, it's you lot that are fucking backwards…! And what the hell has happened to his face? He looks like he's been in a fight with a dog?'

'I know a little German,' Tom said, suddenly embarrassed at his lack of a second language whilst ignoring the reference to Lassie's injuries.

'Just in case you get invaded, eh?' Came Pascale's razor sharp reply.

They laughed and the boys offered the girls a drink. Before long another round was needed, which the girls insisted on buying. Lassie's explanation of falling down the stairs was heartily laughed away from both girls with a knowing look and was put on the back burner as the drinks flowed and the rushes from the pills became more distant in memory.

The girls came from Amsterdam and had been in the UK visiting friends in London. Tom said that they were just on a bit of a jolly to Amsterdam to take in a bit of culture, maybe a few cafes and maybe a few clubs.

'I know many great clubs in Amsterdam, Tom,' Pascale said, placing her hand on his leg. 'You must let us take you out and show you around?'

She was gorgeous, thought Tom, a cracker. He looked across at Lassie, who seemed to be doing equally well with Abi, they were chatting, obviously at a slower pace due to her lip reading but they seemed to have made a connection.

'We'd love that,' Tom said. 'We have to, uh, meet some friends in the morning. Perhaps we could meet up tomorrow evening, Thursday, that is?'

Pascale's gaze had left Tom's face, he followed where she was looking and saw  Abi and Lassie were snogging each other's faces off.

'Jesus,' Tom said, 'it must be the Ecstasy.'

'Well,' Pascale answered, 'my sister's a bit of a... how do you say it... man-eater?'

'That's the one,' Tom laughed, hoping the trait ran in the family...

They sat and drank, listening to the DJ bash out some half decent tunes for an hour or so more before Tom became tired and began to think about the morning. He was just drunk now and melancholy circled around him, trying to settle in for the night.

Lassie and Abi had been enjoying each other's company and now Abi got her sisters' attention and began a sign conversation. Tom could see what could only be described as a Dutch version of a Double Roger Moore appear on Pascale's face but she shrugged her shoulders and signed what could have only been OK. She turned to Tom.

'My sister has asked if I could sleep in your cabin so she and your friend can carry on in our cabin. Are you OK with that?'

Tom considered this change of arrangements for about half a second before replying, 'Sounds fine to me.'

Almost instantly, Abi took Lassie by the hand and towed him off into the night.

'Oi, Lass, you got your cabin card with you?'

Lass turned around and nodded at Tom before disappearing down the stairs toward the cabins, with a huge smile on his face.

'Are you tired too, Tom?' Pascale asked. 'I don't mind  if we stay here for a bit.' She nodded towards the half-drunk jug of beer and a brace of warming vodka, lime and sodas.

'Let's try and finish these then, eh?' Tom said, and they settled down and began to chat. It seemed that the girls were quite well off and rented a nice apartment from their parents on the cheap. Her dad worked for ABN Ambro, a Dutch bank. She was 23, her sister was 24 and had been deaf since birth. Both girls were at university doing part time Masters degrees and worked in an Italian restaurant near Amsterdam central station. Clearly, they were very close. And Pascale was amazing.

'Shall we go to bed, sorry, she blushed... to our, I mean your... cabin now, Tom?'

Tom couldn't help wondering, was he in here? Was he? He didn't know. The cabin was a tiny space for people who knew each other, let alone people who had only met four hours ago. Pascale grabbed his face and began kissing him, tongues and all. The erection was instant and he nearly came in his pants it was so sensuous. He was returning in kind when she brought the proceedings to a halt, gave him a peck and stood looking at him.

'I like you Tom, but I'm not fucking you. Or at least not tonight.' And she winked at him.

Trying to find the right words, Tom finally said, "OK, would you like to use the bathroom first? Oh, what bunk would you like?'

She laughed and replied 'I like it on top. And thank you.'

The bathroom door closed and Tom sat on the bottom bunk, dazed and confused. He hoped Lassie was faring better!

When she had finished, Tom used the bathroom and returned to find the lights off apart from the little reading lamp in his bunk, he thanked Pascale for this and undressed and got into bed in his pants, the front of which were a tad fizzy, but he didn't want to change them in case he exploded in the night. After all, how could he not dream about this?

They chatted a little longer, and Pascale even offered them a place to stay.

'Goodnight, Tom. It was really nice to meet you both. I had a fun evening.'

'Me too,' Tom replied. 'Goodnight.'

Tom laid in his bunk thinking. Thinking about Lassie's chipped tooth and bent nose. Thinking about Razor and his leg, thinking about George Meachen and whoever that other bloke with him was. He was sure they would be on the boat tomorrow morning and that they would be looking for them as soon as. Jesus. It was all still quite a mess. Tonight had been good though. He'd had that feeling of safety as the boat pulled away. He ruffled the pillow and tried to close his eyes. He was only dozing when he heard some movement from the top bunk, Pascale was muttering something about having lost an earring. She climbed down and began searching the floor.

'Put the light on,' Tom said, 'it can't have gone far.'

'It's OK, I'll be able to feel it. Get some rest.'

'OK,' he said and lay there listening to her rub the floor.

'It might have dropped onto your bed,' she said and started rubbing over his duvet. Within seconds her hand had slipped under the duvet and had found his rock-hard cock. 'Thought so,' she said. 'I can't leave you like that, it would be unfair.'

Her hand began to glide up and down him, her thumbs massaging the fizzy bit and using it to lube his shaft, all it took was nine or ten soft strokes before he exploded with a grunt into the front of his Jockeys.

'There you go, you'll sleep well now.' Pascale climbed back into her bunk, peered over the side and whispered, 'See, I told you I wouldn't be fucking you.'

As much as he has enjoyed it, Tom couldn't help feeling like he had just been sexually assaulted... he'd sleep it off though he assured himself and wouldn't be pressing charges. He pulled off his blown Jockeys, rolled over and drifted off to sleep, happily disturbed...

## 2.6 Morphine

Razor, eyes still shut but wide awake, lay trying to quell the moaning that had been going on inside his head for most of the night. The same ideas had been coursing through his head since he had seen Gary Sparks in the ward. If that evil bastard was around things had clearly gone a bit wonky. Where was Paddy? Was he with that Tom lad? What had happened to him? He imagined George and the others would be back for him. In fact, he knew they would be back for him. If Paddy had got away then he would have to carry the can for the debt owed by the both of them. The thought of what he might have to do made him fear for his life and contemplate the worst sin of all in his Mum's eyes. The idea that suicide might be the easiest option scared him. He tried to feel his legs but couldn't. He was pretty sure he wouldn't be running anywhere soon. How were his Mum and Dad? Were they alive even? He felt utterly helpless, he couldn't even remember what he had told the nurses. Name, address, telephone number. He needed to get out of there but how? And where could he go? He had watched the nurse drift along the ward with the drugs trolley. If he could get his hands on that he could solve all his problems. Dead he would owe no one anything.

He listened as the nurse went about her work. He sensed the rush and realised she'd given him a little early morning boost of morphine. He felt his resistance erode and he began to mutter loose words.

## 2.7 Karma and cable ties

The Stones brothers sat quietly, slowly devouring the food in front of them. The car was parked in a quiet spot at the end of the car park. They had considered the lorry park but Kevin had pointed out that HGV drivers were more on the ball which could lead to unneeded and unwanted 'work'.

Graham finished his burger and did a massive fart. 'Better out than in.'

'That's a burp, Graham,' Kevin said.

'I feel bad, brother. That lad has been in the back of a car for over 24 hours now. He stinks, he's covered in his own mess, and out of his tree on pills. We're fucking gangsters, Graham, not fucking torturers. He could fucking die in there before we hit the city limits. Fuck, I'd rather shoot him now wouldn't you?'

Graham peered up from chasing a cold chip around his brown plastic tray pointed at his older brother. 'No fucking way.'

'Be a fucking human, Graham, eh? He's not going anywhere.'

'And where do you want him to go Kevin? Fuck right off, Kev. Right fucking off...'

Kevin had been troubled by the inhumanity of this latest mission. He saw himself as a stand-up guy, an American gangster type. Honour-driven and righteous. Fuck George and fuck Graham...

'It's my call, George, and I've got an idea.' Kevin got up and walked off to the WHSmith directly opposite the restaurant they had just finished eating in.

Graham grudgingly shifted his bulk out of the static seating and followed his brother. He didn't enter the shop though, he wasn't interested in Kevin's idea.

Ten minutes later Graham was still swearing and telling Kevin he wouldn't have any part in his idea. 'Humanitarian bollocks!'

'George,' Kevin refused to plead, 'I'm in charge and I want no part in torture unless I'm doing it. Die with dignity I reckon, don't you?'

Graham gave his brother the finger, opened the door of the car and got in.

Thirty minutes later Graham stood watching as his brother led Paddy towards a small secluded lake the brothers had once fished in with their uncle. It was surrounded by trees and offered a privacy that was demanded of the current situation. George was amazed Kevin even remembered it until Kevin had admitted he had buried some guns there a few months back. Kevin stood watching Paddy as he undressed.

Paddy was a mess, bruised, cut and stinking. Paddy was George Meachen's brother-in-law. Kevin couldn't quite get his head around how cruel George was being to his own family. He truly felt sorry for him. He stepped forward and pushed Paddy to the edge of the lake and spoke quietly to him. 'Look Pat, get washed and sorted. All I could get as clean clothes was this stupid Spiderman suit but it's better than the boot covered in shit, eh? Against orders so no fucking about or I'll top you myself. OK?

Paddy smiled, then cried. He couldn't speak. The tranquilisers had ruined him and his eyes squinted at the light. He winced as Kevin Stones cut the cable ties and he stepped into the lake and squatted so the cold water reached his shoulders. He slowly washed himself while continuing to cry. He hoped Razor was OK, and Razor's Mum and Dad. This was all his fault and he sensed this was only the start of George's retribution.

'He's not sitting in the back, Kev,' George shouted down to the now dressed Spiderman and his brother. 'He could do all sorts in the back.'

'He'll have to ride up top with me. I've got more cable ties. It'll be fine.'

Re-tied and dressed as his favourite Marvel superhero Paddy was unceremoniously sat in the front seat of the car. Graham sat on the diagonal in the back, watching him. Kevin then took up his position in the driver's seat and signalled the all clear.

'Thank you.' Paddy struggled to get the words out through dried and chapped lips.

'Just no fucking about, eh?' Kevin started the car and edged it back up the lane towards the main road. 'Probably two more hours and home, boys.'

Paddy drifted off into a tranquillised dream state. He was, at that point, quite comfortable and grateful to be out of the boot. His thoughts began to wander and he felt pangs of guilt about the mess he had landed everyone in, even Tom, the poor cunt. Tom had helped them and got shafted for his troubles. Perhaps this was his comeuppance. If Jesus was watching he'd be shouting at him, *do unto others as you would have them do unto you...* Fuck, what was it called again... Karma. He looked across at Kevin and then down at his cable-tied hands. Could he just yank the steering wheel and run the car off the road? Did he have the strength? Probably not. He flinched as he saw the signs for the M62, they were close. He wondered how long he had until George turned up, or was he already there, hammer in hand? He looked again at the steering wheel and then his hands. He suddenly lurched forward towards the wheel, opening his arms and trying wrap them over the wheel.

His sudden movement was met with a crack as Kevin's elbow hit his nose. The crunch and pain, followed by the warm feeling of blood running down his face made it clear to Paddy that his attempt at self-destruction had failed, miserably.

'Little fucking cunt tried to kill us all, Kev! Little fucker eh?'

Kevin was angry and felt betrayed. "My mistake, Graham, and the little shit is going to pay for it too... clean Spidey up, brother.'

Graham leant across to clean up Spiderman in the front seat as Paddy began to struggle. Blood splattered onto the driver's side window and the dash, Graham was failing to control Paddy and both brothers began to shout at Paddy, as Graham began punching him in the side of the face from the back seat. Paddy tried to protect himself, raising cable-tied arms to shield his face and head.

None of this escaped the attention of the Firearms Officers travelling in an unmarked police car at it pulled alongside them. Kevin's mouth dropped as he saw the four officers staring into the car watching his brother pummelling a young boy who was cable tied at the wrists and dressed in a Spiderman costume that was clearly too small for him. The blues and twos came on, accompanied by a magnetic blue light that the passenger had just plonked on the roof.

'Graham,' Kevin shouted, 'stop punching that twat, we're all fucked.'

With that, Kevin floored the accelerator, happy that Gary drove a BMW M3.

## 2.8 Sleep

George Meachen was standing in the foyer of the hotel sorting out the bill. It was 4.45 and they had to be in Harwich ASAP to get on the ferry. He suddenly tuned in as he heard a story on the radio which grabbed his attention:

*'There was a fatal car crash on the M62 into Liverpool yesterday evening, involving a BMW M3. Three people were confirmed dead at the scene. Only one of the victims has been identified, as a man who had been discharged from a hospital in Essex yesterday afternoon. One of the victims appears to have been in the car under duress. It is believed that the car had been involved in a high-speed pursuit and left the road just outside of Liverpool. Police are appealing for witnesses and any information to help them with their inquiries.'*

'Can I use your phone please?' George asked the receptionist.

George replaced the receiver, thanked the receptionist, picked up his bag and walked out with Gary behind him. Gary was worried. He was sure he'd just seen a tear in George's eye.

In the car, George told Gary what he had heard on the radio.

'I think it was the Stones and Wherry, Gaz. I can feel it.'

Both sat in stunned silence. Fuck thought Gary. What now?

'Do we go back, George?'

'Fuck no, we carry on as agreed. I don't give a fuck that they're dead, it's the game you play. The thing I do give a fuck about is WHERE IS THE FUCKING MONEY!'

'And where is it, George? We gave it to Kev to run it back, you reckon the old bill have it?'

'The Stones were meant to drop it before they got back, so hopefully the bin liner full of my fucking money wasn't in the fucking car. Fuck, fuck, faaaack!'

'What are we gonna do then, George?'

'Well, Gary, first, someone has to pay their debts. And then if I find out the old bill have had a summer bonus we are going to fucking war my friend!'

George glared ahead and Gary, sensing the mood, floored the Astra in the direction of the ferry in Harwich making a mental note not to trivialise the deaths by moaning about his pride and joy that was clearly now in a breakers yard somewhere near Warrington. He sighed and pointed the car east.

The men boarded and ate a quiet breakfast.

'What if he's not in Amsterdam, George?'

'Then we'll have a nice fucking holiday, Gary, I feel like I fucking need one. Anyway, he'll be there. He's on a mission so it has to be Amsterdam, and I have a feeling these Harwich boys have probably done this before and may well even have contacts there. We'll see eh? I've got a cabin down there, you're next to me. I'm going to catch up on some sleep.'

## 2.9 The Ship

Tom awoke to the sound of someone having a shower, quickly followed by the ship's tannoy system announcing that breakfast was being served and disembarkation would begin in thirty minutes. The thought of Pascale in the shower made him smile and he lay back on his bunk, hoping to catch a glance as she exited. The door opened and Lassie stepped out, rubbing his balls with a towel.

'Morning. You were out cold when I came back. Pascale said to say bye and she'd see you soon hopefully'

Rude, Tom thought. Just rude.

'So, how did you get on?' Lassie enquired with a big grin on his face, clearly itching to unload his story as soon as humanly possible.

'I'm not that type of...'

'Balls,' screamed Lassie. 'Spill it you slag!'

Tom told him there'd been a bit of snogging and then a sly hand-job, with the promise of more if they saw each other again.

'How odd,' said Lassie. 'Pretty much exactly the same happened to me, apart from the fact that we snogged to the point where she had stubble rash on her top and bottom lip! Magic though, she even had a pencil and pad in her bag so she could write things down. She's brilliant!'

'Oh no, in love...?'

Lassie dismissed that, but said it was true that he liked her. She'd made him laugh despite being deaf – brilliance in his book. And she was as fit as a butcher's dog.

'Right, let's find these girls, get off this boat and make it to Amsterdam. Do you know where their cabin is?' Tom grabbed his bag, had a quick glance to make sure hadn't left anything and burst out of the cabin. 'Come on, you daft cunt, let's chip.'

Their cabin was empty. In a controlled panic, they ran up the stairs and started looking around at the passengers waiting to disembark, the sisters were nowhere to be seen.

With Lassie's face covered in bruises, albeit subsiding, and him covered in sweat induced by the thought of getting through the formalities, they would be an obvious flag for customs. He had obviously enjoyed the girls' company and wanted to see them again, but they may well help to ease the transit through customs, too. For a second Tom contemplated rushing up to the deck and throwing his bag over the side and maybe himself too. 'We could do without this, Lass.'

Then, from close by they heard a voice. 'Ahh, look, they've come to say goodbye...'

The sisters were sitting down on their bags having a coffee. Tom made a mental note that Pascale looked even better when he was not off his face.

'Well, you did disappear, we thought we might escort you off the ship like gentlemen from England should do. After all, you've both been so kind to us.'

The girls giggled and Abi signed to Pascale and both boys looked on waiting for the translation. 'She said, "Chill, it was only a snog and a handjob!"'

At this point an elderly couple got up and decided to wait elsewhere. Which amused the Dutch and embarrassed the English.

Disembarkation was announced and the four wandered together toward passport control. As they approached the desk, Pascale slipped her arm into Tom's which he thought was a great idea. Their passports having been checked and stamped they made their way to customs. Tom could feel a bead of sweat trickling down the side of his forehead and he turned and smiled at Pascale as they funnelled through, Abi and Lassie breezed through. Then a hand came out and stopped Pascale and Tom.

'Step to the side please, Sir,' the Dutch Customs Officer said. 'What is the purpose of your journey?'

'Tourism,' Tom replied, 'and I also have recently acquired a Dutch girlfriend.' His attempt at humour failed as the Officer looked at Pascale as though she was some kind of traitor.

He was fucked he thought, this truly was the end, importing forged currency, he'd rot in a Dutch jail for years. He could feel himself breaking. He'd also just dragged an innocent Pascale into all this too.

'Is this your bag, Sir, and did you pack it yourself?'

He couldn't look, he gathered himself together and stared at the man, go out proud he thought. *Fuck you all...*

'Yes and Yes,' Tom replied, staring at him.

He heard the bag unzip and the officer begin to rummage around in it. Tom kept his eyes fixed ahead. The officer then stood back and said, 'Is this yours, Sir?'

Tom looked down to see the Customs Officer holding a copy of *Fiesta*.

'Err, Yes,' Tom replied, grasping what had just happened.

'Then your new Dutch girlfriend may well have some important questions to ask herself,' he said, as he smiled, zipped up the bag and wished them a nice stay in Holland.

Tom smiled and said thank you. As they left he saw Lassie, the relief on his face indescribable. Tom glared a 'keep it together' look and gave his mate a hug.

'Jesus you lemon, you picked up my bag, I nearly got done for having a copy of *Fiesta* in there you fucking pervert!'

Pascale, taking instructions from Abi interrupted, 'Abi says Dutch porn is far superior to your English jazz mags.'

The boys DRM'd and they all walked off in the direction of a café.

In the café, Tom excused himself, went to the toilets and stood starring into the mirror. He then leant over and bathed his face in cold water. He stared into the mirror for a couple more moments before turning to the cubicle, running in and throwing up. Had Lassie swapped bags on purpose? If so the man was a fucking legend, and if not someone was looking down on him. Either way, it was another step toward the ultimate goal.

'Feeling better?'

'Loads, mate. Amsterdam here we come!'

The girls' Dad had organised a lift for them from the Hook to Amsterdam and invited the boys to join them so they could save themselves the train journey and fare. This sounded ideal but needed Tom some time to think, so he told them that he really loved trains and wanted to go on a Dutch one. This worked. Both girls thought that was very English and very cute.

The girls did insist on escorting them to the train station and showed them how to purchase their tickets and told them where to change for Amsterdam. Kisses were exchanged and Tom said they would ring them later in the day. They said their goodbyes and they watched as the girls jumped into a big black Mercedes and sped off towards the motorway.

'Looks like their mum and dad aren't short of a few bob, eh?

Tom breathed a sigh of relief. He needed some headspace and the constant lying had been making his brain ache. They stood on the platform across from the ferry and spotted a pub called the Harwich Bar. Tom considered sitting in it all day if it was open, but he knew they couldn't. The train pulled in and they boarded. When they were settled, and their bags safely stowed Tom looked Lassie in the eye and asked him to tell the truth, 'Did you take my bag on purpose, Lass?'

Lassie looked right back and said, 'You'll never know, fella, because either way you'll call me a fucking idiot so I'll suffer in silence eh? We made it, and that's all that matters. Let's just get this done and then go for a pizza, if you catch my drift.'

Tom smiled 'Thank you, whichever one it was. You saved my life. I hope I can do the same for you one day.'

Lassie snorted, 'I fucking hope not!'

The train shunted forward as it took on more carriages and five minutes later they pulled away from the port. They had a change at Schiedam for the Amsterdam train and would arrive just before 9 a.m. local time. Both boys fell asleep until thankfully, a Dutchman woke them, telling them they had to change if they were going to Amsterdam. They thanked him and got onto the other train without incident.

Lassie again crashed straight away but Tom stayed awake as they approached Amsterdam, impressed by the graffiti and street art he saw on the buildings they travelled past. It was all very simple now. Get there, find the Capri, deposit the cash and do their own thing. It was easy to say it, much more difficult to deliver. The train tannoy spoke to him, first in Dutch and then English, announcing that they were now approaching their destination. Tom leant over and shook Lassie.

'We're here. Let's get our shit together.'

'I've been dreaming of deaf girls,' Lassie said, smiling.

'Pardon?'

'Fuck off, cunt.'

They both laughed as they grabbed their bags.

They walked out of the station and into the morning air. Tom followed the yellow and blue signs until they found themselves outside a huge car park.

The trick, Lassie suggested, was to walk like you meant it. Like they had a car in there. Not to look vague.

'Fucking do it then, Robert Downey Junior,' Tom said. 'I'll look after the fucking bags!'

'OK,' said Lassie, 'you wait here,' and off he sauntered into the car park. Not long after he walked back out smiling. Tom couldn't help but admire his mate. He had balls the size of Wales.

'Sorted,' he said. 'Let's find a café.'

They found a little coffee shop nearly opposite the lockers in the station and surveyed the scene. It seemed simple. In his hand Tom held the key to locker number 1601. He had to open that locker, take the 100k in forged notes out of his bag and deposit them in the locker. And walk away. It seemed easy enough but he kept working angles for himself. Do the Dutch police monitor the lockers for drug traffickers? Do they use that new Closed Circuit TV that they keep banging on about on Crimewatch? Is there an angle for Taff stitching him up?

Lassie sat watching him.

'Fuck it, Tom, lots of different things could happen, we've got to just do it. I've got your back, remember?'

Tom agreed, told Lassie to wait and watch, picked up his bag and walked over. There were signs with numbers on the sides of the lockers and he soon worked out where 1601 was. He took a deep breath and stepped forward confidently. Instantly he was grabbed on the arm, which made him recoil and consider screaming. He spun round to confront the aggressor, praying that it wasn't the police. Hanging on to his arm was a young lad with a small dog.

'Need a locker, friend? I can help you.'

No thanks, I've got one cheers.'

'Where is it friend? Can I help you find it?'

Tom needed this kid to fuck off. The last thing he wanted was someone looking over his shoulder.

He took out a ten guilder note and showed it to the kid. He then leant over to him and whispered into his ear, 'I need you to fuck off now, mate.'

The kid took his cue as if that was his whole blag. He'd probably seen loads of similar stuff going on if he was here every day. The locker was on the bottom row in the middle of a bank of about five rows, he placed the key in the slot and turned it. The door popped open and he couldn't help but look over his shoulder. No one seemed to taking any notice of him so he unzipped his bag. He put in hand into it and felt for the carrier bag that held the cash. In one swift movement he took the bag from his holdall and got it into the locker. He quickly closed the door and zipped up his own bag.

Suddenly he felt a hand on his shoulder, and froze. 'Bang to rights' they call it he remembered. 'Honey trap' also careered across his brain. He turned to see who it was.

'Have you finished with this locker?' a female voice said innocently.

He struggled for air as he looked into the face of the young backpacker. 'Sorry, I'm still using it,' he gasped

Minutes later he slumped back down back in the café, his heart pounding.

'What did she say?' Lassie asked.

Tom couldn't even speak. He needed a lie down.

'Give me the locker key,' Lassie said. 'I'll drop it back where I found it. You wait here. Have a rest.' Lassie headed off to the car park. Tom sat in solitary silence. He rubbed his eyes as if to make sure it was all real, *fuck me* he thought, *it's not even the weekend...*

## 2.10 Battered

Gary Sparks couldn't sleep and he fancied a beer. He contemplated knocking on the George's cabin door but he decided to leave him snoring and have a wander around the ship and see what was going on. Things had been a little quiet since hearing about the crash on the radio. It seemed George was even more hell-bent on revenge now. The bar was open and so he thought he might as well have a pint as he had to drive later so the sooner he got pissed the better. After a brief reccy around the entertainment deck he settled in the livelier part of the boat and stood waiting for service. No sooner had the first been placed on the bar than he was ordering a second. He had a third and then a fourth, all in the space of twenty minutes. He was feeling a lot more relaxed.

He was glad to have gotten away from George Meachen for a while. The man was intense as fuck. He fancied a change of scenery and decided to have another walk about. On his second walk through the Duty Free shop he stumbled upon what he thought must be the biggest Toblerone he had ever seen. He thought about buying one but then thought what the fuck would he do with a Toblerone that big? He imagined trying to kill someone with a Toblerone and decided that with that thing it was probably possible. He found himself in the rear bar, where there were a few more people and a bit of music playing. He stood at the bar waiting to be served and became hypnotised by the machine in front of him. Hotdogs, on spikes, swirled around a glass case. Round and round they went, it was making his mouth water and when he left the bar with a pint, he also had two Dutch hotdogs, smothered in mustard and ketchup. The fifth beer came and went, along with the hotdogs. The seventh and eighth were not long after. He could feel it by the time the ninth went down and by his tenth he felt perfectly relaxed. It was at this point that he joined a Hen party travelling from Harwich for a long weekend.

He introduced himself with a round of drinks, and was duly entered into a game of spoof. The loser of which had to down a shot or take a forfeit. The Hens sat around, calling the total number of coins in all hands and slowly, by the process of elimination the game was reduced to two players, of which Gary became a regular fixture. After losing [or rather being cheated out of winning] for the fifth time he began to feel quite nauseous. He held up one of his big fighting mitts and declared he would take a forfeit. The girls hooted with laughter, rubbing his head and putting their arms around him. The forfeit arrived in the form of a pair of knickers and a bra. Luckily one of the Hens was on the large side and he thought he might actually get into them. He wandered off to the gents and returned five minutes later to reveal his new lingerie, to the screams of laughter from the Hens and other punters in the bar.

The game continued, with the loser now necking a shot of the winner's choice. He was feeling a little better after avoiding the play-offs for a couple of games and thought he may well have got a second wind. He then lost again, stood up and called the girls a bunch of cheating cunts.

'OK, OK, darling, calm down, calm down. We won't play anymore and we'll just sit and chat. Eh, girls?'

The girls cheered their approval; the poor fella was smashed after all and was beginning to get arsey. However, one insisted that Gary must honour his final forfeit. He accepted, tore down the shot banged the glass down and exclaimed, 'Who wants to take my knickers off with her teeth?'

There were no takers. Some suggested they were going for a fag, others to sleep it off, and others for something to eat.

'OK,' he said, 'Fuck you all then!' and sat on his own, legless in the back bar. He began to doze and then began to feel a bit funny. He managed to order another pint at the bar where a little check in the mirror confirmed that he had been spiked and was chewing his face off. He went back to his seat swearing that he would fucking kill them if he saw them again. He necked his lager and decided to try to sleep through it, but that wasn't going to be easy.

George woke from a formidable sleeping session. He got down from the top bunk and grabbed a plastic glass and filled it from the sink. He'd had a decent kip and hoped Gary had too. Though he imagined he'd be in the bar, probably too pissed to drive.

He wasn't surprised that he didn't feel much sorrow for Kevin and Graham; he'd seen too many go to be that bothered. But what had happened to the money? If John Law had retrieved it his chances of getting it back were fair. He had countless coppers in his back pocket. Everyone had a weakness, and he was the best at finding those weaknesses and pushing those buttons. An even better result would be if they had met their grisly end after dropping off the cash before heading into the city.

He showered and shaved as he mulled over his thoughts. He dried his armpits and balls with the handy hair dryer, taking his time. He then plucked some unsightly hair from his nose and cut his nails. He put on his last clean top, thinking that he'd have to go shopping and get the rest washed. Goodness knew what Sparksy would do, he wasn't even sure he had a change of clothes with him. The announcement came that they would be docking shortly and that there were light snacks and a full breakfast available in the restaurant. George felt hungry but there was still no sign of Gary so he decided to grab a bite to eat. He made his way to the restaurant where he tucked into a full English and a cup of tea, just what he needed. He bought a bottle of water to take in the car. He felt good. He guessed, by the lack of contact, that Gary Sparks didn't.

He decided to walk anti clockwise around the deck with the bars, shops and eateries. He passed the Duty Free, the arcade and shop and finally got to the bar area at the back of the boat. There, in front of him, was a cleaner gamely trying to rouse what resembled Gary Sparks from what looked like a self-induced coma.

'Fuck me,' George said. He gathered his pace, waved off the little cleaner, undid the top of his bottle of water and began to pour it over Gary Sparks' head. He woke startled, jumped up and put up his fists.

'What the fuck is going on?' he said, spitting water out of his mouth.

'You fucking tell me,' George said.

George marched Gary down to his cabin and said 'Right, you fucking idiot, you have fifteen minutes to get in there, sort yourself out, get back out here and off this fucking boat. I imagine I'm going to have to fucking drive too, eh?'

'Sorry, George –'

'Don't even start with that shit, just fucking get on with it!'

They made their way down the endless stairs towards the car deck, Gary feeling faint at every turn. They soon passed through immigration and had navigated themselves onto the road to Amsterdam.

'Have a kip, you useless cunt,' said George, putting his foot down. The Astra responded like a mobility scooter. 'For fuck's sake,' he moaned to himself.

## 2.11 Amsterdam

Tom and Lassie walked out into the mid-morning Amsterdam sun. Tom had called the UK, all concerned were happy, and as they stood looking at the trams, an old beaten up Red Ford Capri drove past and gave them a beep.

'They must have been watching us all the time, Lass. Fucking hell, it might have even been them who spoke to me?'

'Who cares? Everybody's happy. Now our, sorry, your, work begins.'

'I need a fucking rest, Lass,' Tom pleaded.

Lassie already had the Amsterdam city guide out and had bent a couple of corners. 'Let's find a hotel, eh? Then we'll see. We'll go to Rembrandt Square, I've stayed there before, it's OK and near a nice little area away from the madness. Well, nearly.' Lassie recalled the pub he had fallen out of years ago caked on acid. It wasn't a good memory, although he was convinced he had entertained a madding crowd...

'What if they don't have a room?' Tom didn't think he could cope with the prospect of not having a bed to lie on within the hour.

Lassie said there were loads of hotels in that area and it would just be a process of elimination until they found one. They hailed a cab, knowing full well they would get their arse felt hailing a cab outside the main station in any city, anywhere in the world. They felt ready for it though and grinned as a cab pulled up, the driver clearly thinking this was the only fare he'd need that day.

The taxi crept slowly through the narrow canal-side streets. The townhouses stretched high into the morning clouds, looking coy about the second use most of the basement and first floor windows were put to as dusk settled in and the tourists came out in force.

The Taxi soon pulled into the square and stopped outside the Old Bell. Tom handed the driver a twenty guilder note, thanked him and told him to keep the change.

They headed for the entrance to a small hotel next to the pub to enquire about a room.

'A twin will do us won't it, fella? Anything we get up to we won't be bringing back here eh?'

'Whatever,' Lassie he agreed.

They were in luck. A twin room with a view of the square was available. Room 401 was quite small and up in the gods but clean enough. They put their bags down and flopped on their beds. It had been a fraught and emotional journey so far, to say the least.

'I'm gonna have a shower, Lass, then let's grab a burger somewhere and plan what the fuck we're going to do with three grand worth of forged twenty pound notes, eh?'

Tom realised he was talking to himself as Lassie had crashed out the moment his head had touched the pillow. Tom then grabbed his wash bag and headed to the bathroom. The shower was warm and he considered beasting himself, but he thought it would be rude, as Lassie would probably want to use the room immediately after him. He wondered what the girls were up to. Probably forgotten them by now he thought, though Abi seemed to quite fancy Lassie. They could ring them later, after he'd got his head round this whole forgery thing. He stepped out of the shower and wrapped a towel around himself. Opened the door and called to Lassie to wake up.

'It's all yours. squire! Just try not to slip on my man oyster eh?'

Lassie rubbed his eyes and made a gagging sound. 'You didn't, did you? You dirty bastard.'

Tom laughed, 'I considered it, but decided it just wasn't tennis, young man.'

'Good fucking job.' Lassie stood up and retrieved his wash bag from his holdall.

'I'm gonna fucking check before I put my fucking feet anywhere.'

Tom laughed. 'You've got twenty minutes.'

'I've got as long as I need,' Lassie said before locking the bathroom door and turning on the shower.

Tom sat down on the bed, opened his bag and took out the forgeries. He wondered how this part was going to turn out. He wasn't even sure how good they were, and where he was going to try to change them. The whole thing was mental he told himself, and he'd had it, no more after this. If he could get out of this there would be no more stupid ideas, no more

130

dealing, no more dodgy friends, no staying out all weekend. Things would change.

Lassie exited the bathroom wrapped in a towel, still cleaning his teeth. He'd been thinking along the same lines as Tom.

'What's the plan with the notes then, mate? I've got absolutely no idea, not my thing if it's not green and smokable. We don't even know how good they are do we?' He looked at Tom, who looked desperate, like a man on the edge. He considered a funny one liner about it not being the end of the world but then remembered the whack on the nose he'd taken from those psychotic arseholes who were probably looking for them as they spoke.

'I suppose it has to be the Bureau de Change then, lad?'

'Mmm.' The reply was curt and suggested that Tom had already had arrived at that conclusion.

'Just trying to help.'

'Sorry mate, I know you're just trying to help, I was just thinking. We can't use our own ID because when it comes up bent the money will be traced back to us through our passports.' Tom had felt his heart drop when he had realised this as Lassie showered. He was dead again. He'd escaped the Scousers, thought he'd had a touch and had now been mugged off again. He should have known or at least considered they would need ID to change any money. Now they were stuck in fucking Holland with enough cash for 2 days and tickets back to Harwich in three days. He felt like someone had dropped a waterlogged blanket on him, his shoulders dropped and he felt himself physically shrink.

Lassie saw Tom's eyes begin to well-up and said, 'Get it together, Tom, we can sort this out, we'll find a way. Hey, don't hotels usually change cash?'

'Hotels take an imprint of your passport too, Lass.'

'Sorry mate, wasn't thinking...' Lassie decided he would have to do something to save Tom, he could see him sliding towards defeat and that wasn't like him at all. It had been a fucked-up week though, and if he were Tom he would probably feel like every man and his dog was trying to fuck him with a lamp-post. 'Let's find a bar, get a beer and have a think.'

## 2.12 Jamaica

Smokies was dark and very smoky, with little corners like caves dug into the walls to afford the punters a little privacy. Bob Marley wailed out tunes and various Rasta flags and scarves reminded them of Jah and the drug of choice for the practicing Rastafarians. Neon signs advertising Amstel, Heineken, Grolsch and Budweiser lit up the bar area and lit the way to the toilets. Tom and Lassie ordered two Amstel, with which they retreated into the darkness to discuss their impending fate. Two more beers came and went and they had made no headway. If fact both were feeling a little drowsy from the passive intake of the smoke that was drifting around the bar.

'No real need to buy anything to smoke, eh, Tomo?' Lassie smiled.

'Indeed not, Tom answered, In fact, I feel a little hungry.' They both laughed for the first time in what seemed ages to both of them.

'I'll go and get some more beers.'

While ordering the beers Lassie spied a British looking lad eating a huge plate of nachos. The lad nodded at the nachos and put both thumbs up with a big smile. Lassie decided to order some for him and Tom.

'Cheers for the heads up, fella,' Lassie said the lad as he headed back to where Tom was sitting. As he sat down and gave Tom his beer he realised that the lad had followed him back the table and was directly behind him.

'Hi,' he said. 'Mind if I join up for a bit? I'm a bit bored with sitting on my own.'

'No problem,' both replied and Tom gestured to a chair.

He introduced himself as Aky. He was a self-confessed 'massive stoner' and regularly came over to Holland from Tollesbury.

Tom wasn't sure if he wanted to spend any of his afternoon with this bloke. He was clearly off his nut and probably flying solo and looking to hitch a ride with them, which he could do without. 'Yeah, I know Tollesbury, nice little place on the way to Maldon. So, are you over with some mates?'

'Well, this is it chaps, you wouldn't fucking believe this!'

'I imagine we won't,' Lassie laughed. Tom nodded in agreement.

'Go on then, what happened?'

They sat back, beer in hand and listened to Aky explain why he was on his own at the moment.

'Well, a friend was giving us a lift from Tollesbury to Harwich and we stopped on the way for a few beers and a smoke and so on. Everything was fine and she dropped us off at Harwich and we finished of everything in the car park before we got on the boat.' He stopped for a mouthful of beer as Tom and Lassie's nachos turned up. They both tucked in as he began again.

'We were all off our fucking heads by this point and were trying very hard to keep it together. We got into the departures hall and ordered a beer and a shot to try and level us out. It was still early so we had a few more beers and shots until some wanker said they wouldn't let us on board if we carried on drinking, so we stopped and queued up. We managed to get onto the boat but that's when it all got a bit trippy. Those fucking corridors with the cabins on all look the fucking same, don't they?'

Tom and Lassie nodded in total agreement at this.

'So, I was floating about looking for my cabin. Some bloke tried to help me but I was fucking hammered so he just pointed me in the right direction and off I toddled. Twenty minutes later I ended up in this lounge full of truckers. I don't know how and I'd be fucked if I could find it again! Anyway, I was battered and sat down next to this fella, a big Dutch guy who offered me a drink.'

'Oi oi!' said both Tom and Lassie.

'Nothing like that lads, just a nice fella, anyway, we ended up on deck smoking a massive doobie before going back into the lounge This thing wiped the floor with me and I was all over the place. I said I was so fucked I was just gonna crash in the lounge and he said that if I wanted, I could have a lift to Amsterdam in the morning. Turned out he drove a fucking huge flower lorry. So, he gave me a lift, dropped me off at Leidsplein Tram Station and sorted me out with this –' Aky produced something that resembled a dung beetle's creation and rolled it to Tom who immediately gestured to Lassie.

'He's the smoker in this outfit!'

'That's Nepalese Temple Ball that is, what some?'

'Lassie gave the ball back and replied, 'I've got Nachos to eat here, but thanks.'

'What a fucking legend, eh?'

Tom nodded and said, 'Absolutely, a total legend. Why are you on Rembrandtplein then?'

'Ahh, that's where we are staying, at a hostel just around the corner.'

Tom and Lassie watched as Aky built a substantial spliff.

'Fuck me, you feeding the five thousand with that bad boy?'

Impressed by the size of the spliff and the quantity of Temple Ball it contained Lassie motioned to Aky to pass it over for inspection. Aky followed it with a lighter and the offer that Lassie could sparked it up.

Lassie felt a kick in the shins as he began to raise the spliff towards his mouth. Tom was staring at him across the table with a mouthful of nachos...

'Not a good idea mate... things to do.'

'These must be important things you have to do my friends. After all, this here doobie *is* Nepalese Temple Ball. The stuff of legend my friends!'

Tom explained they had met some lovely girls on the boat and they had arranged to meet them later, so wanted to remain on an even keel, at least until they could all get shot away together.

Aky had lit up while listening to Tom's excuse and had concluded that they were probably a bit scared of the Temple Ball. He spoke from behind a huge cloud of white smoke.

'Good plan, dudes, good plan. You don't want to be wasted if you've already pulled. Great work. Essex rules!'

Tom and Lassie watched Aky's high-speed deterioration in awe. In no time at all he had turned into a bumbling mess who was struggling to get himself to the toilet. As he finally disappeared behind the curtain they laughed at his demise.

'That is what the Dam can do to a man,' Tom spoke in a rough Jamaican patois, laughed and looked toward Lassie for agreement, which he didn't. Lassie was holding a wallet and staring at it.

'I wonder,' he said out loud, 'I wonder.'

'You wonder what Lass?'

Lassie worked quickly, without even asking Tom what he thought. He glanced up at the curtain, which concealed the entrance to the toilets. Seeing nothing stirring, he opened the wallet, sifted through it and with a smile, pulled out a driving license.

Tom wasn't sure about taking the lad's license and Lassie sensed it. 'Listen, Tom, you're desperate, mate, and we'll make sure the lad gets his license back. We can post it to him. It's just that I've got an idea.'

Tom realised that desperate times led to desperate measures! It was too late to back out now anyway, he realized, as the lad had just swept the curtain aside and was zig zagging his way back towards the table. Aky reached the table and slumped into his seat. Instantly both boys turned their noses up at the smell coming off the lad from Tollesbury.

'Is that piss I can smell, Lass?'

Lassie nodded in agreement. 'Yup, he's had an accident!'

They grinned at each other.

'We've got to help him, Lass, let's try and get him back to his hostel, shall we?'

Aky couldn't speak but he'd had the sense to put a card from the hostel he was staying in into his wallet and the barman was able to tell them where it was. Tom and Lassie hoisted Aky up between them and began the 300-metre journey to the Happy Hostel where Aky was due to meet his friends. Half-way up the road they found themselves having their picture taken by a group of other pissed up Brits. All they could do was smile and carry on, embarrassed to be seen carrying a man who had a big wet patch on the front of his jeans at lunchtime in a packed tourist square in one of the most fashionable capital cities in Europe. They found the hostel which had a nice little patio area outside.

'He goes there, I'm not carrying this fucking mess into the hostel, they'll probably ring the law...'

Lassie agreed and helped Tom guide Aky through the little picket gate where they lay him down on a wooden bench. They had begun to retreat when Tom had a change of heart. 'We can't leave him there, Lass, we have to let someone know he is there, don't we?' Tom found a scruffy looking character who was sitting at a small desk with an old PC and an even older phone on it. He explained that he had parked a drug casualty on a bench outside the hostel and he was leaving the fella to it.

'I feel better for that, we couldn't have left him there, especially given the circumstances, eh?'

Lassie smiled, 'Of course not, lad, after all, that young man has potentially been an enormous help.'

## 2.13 Kerching!

They stopped at the top of the road. It was early afternoon and they could see Rembrandt Square beginning to come to life. In the middle of the square was a small fair with rides and stalls, the music was starting to pump and small groups of Dutch youths in wild coloured European issue Nike and Adidas trainer, tight jeans and gilets were starting to mill around. They found a bench in the square, sat down and began to plan their afternoon.

The plan they came up with was simple. They would approach the money exchange outlets and attempt to change some money without any ID at all. If asked for some ID they would offer the driving license, and explain that their passport, was safe in the hotel. If the license wasn't accepted as ID they wouldn't push the situation. They'd just shrug and say, no worries, thank you and off to the next. They would also try to change odd numbers of notes, like £120 or £90. Anything up to, and including £190. He tossed a coin for who would go first, Lassie lost.

'OK,' he said to Tom, smiling. 'Let's see if this is a goer, eh?'

Tom shifted in his seat. Lassie had already saved his sorry arse too many times this trip. In fact he would probably be six foot under if he weren't with him today. He put out his arm and grabbed Lassie. 'No, Lass, this is a stretch too far, this is my coffin mate. I'm gonna do the first pitch.'

Lassie shrugged and nodded. It was Tom's thing, but he was in the fucking thing up to his neck too. It didn't really matter anymore... 'Your call, Mr. Adams.'

Lassie sat back on the bench and looked up into the warm Amsterdam afternoon sun. This was it. Do or die. He couldn't help but search around in the pocket of his jeans for the remnants of a spliff.

Tom walked off, leaving Lassie to relax on the bench. They agreed that he would try to stay in eye contact, just in case anything happened. Tom saw the *bureau de change* in front of him and gulped. Behind the glass screen sat a calm bloke who didn't look much older than Tom himself. Beside him was the display with the price of the currencies available.

He couldn't help but be surprised by how calm he was. He realised that this was, essentially, a piece of cake after the week he'd had. The worst that could happen was that the guy would say was sorry and he would require some more ID. Surely it was a matter of just plugging away until someone either trusted his face or didn't give a shit? He was pleased there was no queue as he approached the window.

'Good afternoon, mate,' Tom said, looking interested in what the signs were telling him and looking as bona fide as he possibly could. 'Do you speak English?'

'Of course, Sir,' he replied, 'this is the Netherlands.'

'Of course, you lot are amazing!' Tom stepped forward confidently and leant forward with one arm resting on the chrome shelf in front of him. 'Can I get some guilders please, fella?' Tom didn't wait for an answer, he just carried on talking. 'Only been here three days and I've done all the guilders I brought with me. You know what it's like. I'd like to change the rest of the English money I have with me and hope it bloody lasts five minutes!'

'This is no problem, Sir, how much would you like?'

Tom had prepared a crumpled wad of 190 GBP, which he removed from his wallet and placed onto the counter in front of him. 'Cheers.'

The cashier took the English money and dragged it onto the counter below where Tom couldn't see what he was doing. He smiled and looked up at Tom. Tom was attempting to remain calm but he could feel the inside of his legs sweating. He reminded himself that at the very least he could probably do a runner. He could feel the heat of the early afternoon sun on his back. He could do with a hat, he thought.

The cashier smiled and spoke to Tom, 'That will be fine, Sir. It will be 360 Dutch guilders. Do you have any identification to support your transaction?'

Tom tried to look natural as he took his wallet out again and said 'Err... I've just realised my passport is back at the hotel, but I have my driving licence, would that be OK?'

'That should be fine, Sir.' He began to process the transaction, with Tom looking on. Tom had begun to feel better when the cashier leant forward and pushed a piece of paper through the screen and asked Tom to sign the receipt. Thank fuck Lassie had insisted that he should practice the signature on the driving license. He took the pen and, as confidently as he could, signed the name. He returned the pen with a smile. The signature was inspected with a glancing look and the transaction finalised. A minute later Tom was walking back into the square where he winked at Lassie and nodded at him to follow as he turned the corner away from the kiosk.

It was like taking sweets from a baby Tom assured Lassie. They toured central Amsterdam carefully selecting the *cambios* with staff who looked young, friendly, or even stoned. Which, to their amazement and joy, they found in abundance. They really couldn't believe how easy it all was. Each time Tom played out the same ruse, looked a little desperate, acted a little stupid and made it clear he was getting robbed by this wonderful, picturesque and friendly city. In the course of the afternoon only one cashier insisted on the need for a passport.

They stopped at the hotel and deposited a fair quantity of crisp Dutch guilders in their room. Lassie carefully stashed the cash in different pairs of socks which, he insisted, would fool any robbers who decided to try it on. 'After all, lad,' he said, 'who in his right mind would steal someone else's fucking socks?'

They then made their way towards Anne Frank's house, which they both knew of from school and were both interested to see. Money changed on the way, they moved on to the Sex Museum, which they both thought was a bit leftfield after the bleakness of Anne Frank's house, but it also had lots of *cambios* nearby. A double back toward the Bulldog cafe and the red light district gave them access to a new raft of *bureau de change* and presently they found themselves just outside a smokers' paradise of a shop called Old Man Head Supplies.

Tom was exhausted, happy and relieved. He grabbed hold of Lassie and gave him a hug. 'We've only got to do one more Lass, one more and we've gone and done three grand in a day.'

They had done fourteen *cambios* in just under four hours. They sat down outside a café and presently a nice young girl came out, took their order and returned shortly with two coffees and two slices of apple pie with cream. They both steamed into the pie without hesitation and then laid back in their chairs, taking in the early evening ambience of the Dutch capital.

Tom looked at Lassie, put his hand in his pocket and passed over the driving license and a small wad of purple notes. 'There you go, lad, you fancied it earlier, you can do the last one and you can keep the guilders you get.'

Lassie, laughing, pushed the ID and cash back into Tom Adams hands, melted back into his chair and took a sip of his coffee. 'No way, mate, you're on a roll. It would be a stupid man who broke such a winning streak, and anyway, I like being the wingman. I don't wanna go confusing my job role so late in the day.'

Tom vigorously shook Lassie's hand and reminded his best mate that this wouldn't have been possible without him.

'Come on mate, I'll buy you dinner.' Tom stood up, leaving a twenty guilder note on the table and nodding to the waitress.

Lassie pointed to a *cambio* sign across the road, 'Last one my friend?' and then at another sign further along for Burger King. 'I'm a cheap date.'

Tom pondered the *cambio*, then turned to Lassie, 'I'm gonna laugh off the last one, Lass. Quit when I'm ahead.' As he said this he put his hand in his pocket and gave the beggar sitting on the floor next to them a crisp twenty-pound note. 'It's British, mate,' he said.

The reply was in English too, 'I know,' said the happy beggar as he scuttled of into the night.

Lassie smiled, 'You soft twat.'

'Only because he was wearing an Arsenal beanie, Lass. Come on.' Tom opened the door of the restaurant and they went in and lined up for a burger.

## 2.14 Vanessa Paradis

They got their meal and sat down opposite two girls.

'I honestly don't think it could have gone any better, Lass, we've had a right result. That's why I decided to laugh off the last one.'

At this he took out the remaining British notes. 'Thought I'd quit while I was ahead! Now all we've got to do is have a good time with the girls. We're bound to be in there and Pascale even said we could stay with them.'

'Fuck yeah, we've had it right off. Well pleased for you, Tom,' said Lassie vaguely.

Tom realized that Lassie was looking over his shoulder and nodding towards the two. One had clearly seen the cash Tom had been brandishing earlier and was smiling sweetly towards him. When she both boys were looking she slowly opened her legs a fraction and pushed her toes together, while biting her bottom lip.

The boys were transfixed.

'She looks like Vanessa Paradis,' Lassie whispered to Tom.

In a soft voice with a light Dutch accent the girl said, 'I can hear you... and yes, my friends say that too.'

At that point her friend chimed in with, 'And she'll give you the best blow job you've ever had for 50 guilders.'

Tom and Lassie were both mesmerised but Tom knew instantly what he wanted to do. 'Where?' He stuttered like a fifteen-year-old school boy.

'In the toilet, upstairs,' the friend said nodding the way.

'Do you take English money?'

The girls both laughed and nodded.

Tom then mustered all the backbone he could, reached into his trouser pocket and took out £60. He beckoned to Vanessa Paradis and said 'I'll give you all of this if you make it truly amazing.'

She giggled and smiled, opening her big wide eyes. 'I'll try my hardest,' she said.

At this, regretting it even as he did it, he turned to Lassie, handed him the £60 and said, 'Go on, Lass. You deserve it!'

It took a few seconds for Lassie to register what Tom had said, but when he had he didn't hesitate. 'Cheers, mate!' he said as he got up and followed Vanessa upstairs.

On the way upstairs she explained they would have to both stand outside the toilets, under the pretense of needing to use them. She would wait in in the Women's until there was no one about and then she would beckon him in. She had clearly done this before. Barely two minutes passed until the door opened and she pulled him in to the toilet cubicle and told him to stand. She was sitting on the toilet and within seconds had unzipped him and was going up and down his shaft like a

piston on a John Deere combine harvester. He was in heaven. She had beautiful long hair she had swept to one side and he stroked the soft skin of her neck that was usually covered by her hair while trying to think about cricket, or Margaret Thatcher, anything to prolong his enjoyment. Unfortunately, watching her work was far too much for Lassie and it wasn't long before he could feel himself swelling up for a controlled explosion.

'Where do you want it?' he said desperately.

She just carried on going, clearly giving him the OK, and his back arched as his pelvis bucked and he lost himself in Vanessa Paradis. She greedily took it all and nonchalantly took a piece of toilet paper to wipe both him and her mouth. He felt quite faint and could only muster a thank you, as she stood up and motioned that they should leave discreetly. Lassie let her leave first, mainly because his legs had turned to jelly.

He finally got his shit together and went into the Men's to sort himself out and presently went back downstairs. Tom looked at him and gave him a double Roger Moore which he returned. Tom felt insanely jealous. While Lassie was upstairs he pondered getting her number and having a go himself before they left, especially as it was essentially free with dodgy UK currency.

Before Tom had a chance to ask, a middle aged couple approached. Tom thought it was a bit odd as the restaurant had lots of seats but they were making a bee line for the girls' table.

The man spoke first, not to Tom or Lassie, but to the girls. Tom wondered what he was saying as they clearly knew each other.

Vanessa Paradis replied in English 'Please, we are learning English, please speak in English.'

The man slid into the seat next to one girl and put his arm around her and patted the hand of the other. Lassie and Tom immediately assumed that he was her pimp and braced themselves for some kind of extra payment demand.

Instead, the man smiled, and said, 'Hello, my little Princesses,' and how was your studying today?'

Tom began to grin and Lassie nearly spat his burger out. He felt Lassie kick him under the table and he returned the favour.

Vanessa Paradis gave both boys a sly look as her Mum and Dad carried on the conversation in Dutch. She smiled, picked up her milkshake and sucked hard on the straw. 'Mmm,' she said. 'This tastes funny.' She laughed and took another big slurp, grinning as she pushed her lips all the way down the straw to the base of the cup and back up again, strawberry milkshake now on both lips.

'Err, it was nice to talk to you both,' Lassie said, getting up from the table. 'Come on, Tom, we have to get back to the hotel.'

Tom followed Lassie outside, where they both fell about laughing.

'Can you fucking believe that? Can you fucking believe that?'

'I really can't,' Tom replied. 'The one time you get a decent result it turns out you've had your knob polished by a school girl!'

## 2.15 The English Spirit

Gary Sparks sat astride a huge motorbike as a group of girls cheered and screamed his name. He got off the bike and smiled to the baying crowd before realising he had his helmet on. He raised his hands to his chinstrap and began to remove his lid to show the girls his dashing good looks... He squealed and jumped, hitting his head on the roof of the car... his eyes were open and his hand was painful, to say the least.

George Meachen calmly dispatched the cigar he had been smoking out of the open window, the same cigar he had just stubbed out on Gary's hand.

'What the fuck? I was fucking asleep then!'

'You cheeky fucking cunt,' George mumbled, and then more loudly, 'I've got a good mind to throw your fucking no-mark arse out of this car and do the job myself.'

Now wide awake, Gary remembered who he was with, 'Sorry, George, I'm really fucking sorry, Boss.'

He hoped the boss bit would calm George down. George liked people to know he was the Guvnor.

For a while neither of them spoke, and then George finally said, 'We're going round in fucking circles here, Gary.'

Gary grabbed his chance. 'Nah, we're OK boss. Pull over here and I'll grab a map.'

While George waited for Gary he considered their next move. He needed a hotel, a bath, a whiskey and a meal. Then they would have a trawl around. He was convinced those Harwich throwbacks would be here; trying to drum up some useless little scheme to save their raggedy little Essex arses. It stank of them. He could feel it in his blood, he smiled to himself as he considered how fucking easy it would be to top someone here, *they must be pulling them out of the canals everyday* he thought, smiling to himself as Gary knocked on the door of the car. He considered not opening it and driving off but thought better of it, even if the bloke was a complete waste of space.

'OK,' Gary said, 'I've got a half decent map and there's a hotel not far from here.'

Twenty minutes later they were still driving round looking for the hotel when George slammed on the brakes. 'Get out of the car with your fucking stupid little fucking cunt of a map and go and show a taxi driver. Then ask him to drive to the hotel, we'll follow the fucker. Do it now, before I explode, Gary, I'm at fucking breaking point!'

Gary didn't need any prompting. He leapt out of the car and found a taxi driver, who nodded and waved at George in the Astra. George followed for about twenty metres before the taxi-driver stopped and waved his hand at the sign pointing out the hotel with a broad grin.

'For fucks sake... you can fucking pay him,' George said, 'and give him a decent tip too, you fucking maggot.'

A concierge waived them into a parking space.

'Fucking pay him up fucking front, Gary, I don't' give a fuck how much it is!' George growled as he grabbed his bag and walked into the hotel.

They checked in and George went straight to the bar for a settler. He sat brooding in silence for a while and then said, 'I'm going to have a bath and lie down. I'll be up for five o' clock. Do you think you can manage to be ready then, eh, Sparksy?'

Gary took his cue, grabbed his stuff and headed for the lifts. 'See you at five, George.'

George requested a wakeup call for five and made his way up the grandiose staircase to his room. His bags were neatly placed on the bench at the end of a large bed. The window gave a view of a canal and the streets where those little fuckers were probably wandering about right now. He found there was a TV over the bath so he settled himself in for a soak with the BBC World news and a miniature Glenlivet from the mini-bar.

In the room across the hall, Gary Sparks lay on his bed. He imagined that his room, nice as it was, wasn't as good as George's. Still, he was the boss and things hadn't exactly gone well so far. He needed to put on a good show from here on in if he wanted his reputation to remain intact.

At five, George was sitting with a whisky in a quiet spot in the hotel garden. His back was to the wall and he faced the door, giving him 360-degree view of the area. At 5.01 he was frowning at his watch wondering where Gary was. When he looked up he saw the concierge pointing Gary towards him.

'What are the plans then, George?'

'Firstly, Gary, don't talk to that nosey cunt of a concierge. Let's be as low key as possible here, don't talk to anyone we don't have to. Accents, faces, they're all memorable.'

This brought a nod of agreement from Gary, along with an internal wince. *Who did he think he was kidding? A fucking great big Scouser, dressed like a gangster. Keep it low key? Fucking lunatic.*

George continued, 'Secondly, we go out and have some dinner. Maybe Italian. Then we'll go for a wander and see if we can spot our two young friends. If we do, we follow them.

We can't fucking hijack them off the street in Amsterdam with nowhere to put them unless we're going to out them and I want that cash, it's a matter of principle. We need to get them back to the UK and then we'll drag the cunts home and take it from there.'

Again, Gary nodded in agreement. He had decided he wasn't going to disagree with him at any point.

'Come on then, let's go and get something to eat.' With this, George downed the last his Scotch and headed toward the door. They passed the concierge, who politely bid them a nice evening. Gary followed George's lead in ignoring him and they walked out into the warm Amsterdam evening. Their search for a decent looking restaurant took them down thin cobbled streets. They walked alongside narrow canals toward the main train station, both reluctant to ask anyone for a recommendation and neither picking up any leaflets for fear of looking, as George had said 'like a fucking tourist.'

Gary slowed as George stopped outside an Italian restaurant.

'Here we go Gary, this'll do us, Ginos. Like Dexy's Midnight Runners. This'll do.'

A waiter approached them and after a quick conversation they were seated at a quiet table away from the heat of the oven, as George had requested. There wasn't much conversation as they worked their way through their pizzas. Gary was relieved to see George had switched to drinking lager. He had seen the destruction George could wage after a session on the Scotch and didn't really want a repeat while he was alone with him, abroad and out of his comfort zone.

They finished their meal, paid the bill and began walking back up the road towards the hotel.

'Try to remember this road name, Gary,' George said. 'Have a good scan of the area, and how to get out of here in the car.'

'It's on the hotel cards,' Gary showed George the one he'd picked up as they left the hotel earlier.

'Still, get your bearings though, eh?'

'Course.'

As they walked up the street a young man, scruffily dressed but with clean trainers and an Arsenal hat intercepted them, 'Now, there's a couple of true English gents if I ever did see them.' The accent was Dutch but the English was perfect. 'Don't suppose you can change an English twenty-pound note?'

'It's a bit warm for a hat isn't it, la?' Gary said, immediately checking himself for letting his accent surface.

The youth shrugged, 'I love the Arsenal, they are so fucking boring! Fucking English football, all you want to do is fight.'

At this George laughed, 'You cheeky fucker, go on then, I'll give you fifty guilders for it!'

'Thank you so much Sir, I truly love the English spirit, such lovely people. I have met lovely English people all day!'

George paused, thought about it, laughed and gave him the guilders. Wasn't worth asking, there must be thousands of English around. He pocketed the note, shook the youth's hand, instantly regretting it, and walked them back up the main street to where there was a row of bars all advertised with neon signs. He chose one that had a table in the window with a good view both up the street and across the canal and sent Gary to the bar.

Gary returned with Amstel's and two shot glasses.

'What in fucking hells name is that?'

'It's something called a B52 and it's free. The bird behind the bar has just learnt to make them and offered them to me for free. I stood and watched her do it, nothing underhand. Just a friendly bird.'

Without a word, George picked up the shot, raised the glass and sank it.

'Nice,' he said looking at the shot glass before putting it down. 'Let's have another?'

Gary was soon back with two more B52s and two more beers.

'What now, boss?'

'We look, we watch and we wait my friend.'

Gary nodded and gazed out across the canal, wondering what he was meant to be looking at.

'What do they look like, George?'

George realised that Gary hadn't seen them before. He looked over at Gary Sparks with a twisted grin. 'Don't worry, I'll point them out to you as soon as I see them.'

George's mood was unsettling and Gary felt the need to scratch his arse – he hoped to God his piles weren't going to start playing up.

George sat looking out of the window.

For the next half an hour the two men watched the ebb and flow of people. During that time, they were twice propositioned and drugs were offered to them constantly. Both men were warming to Amsterdam.

'Come on,' said George as he finished the last of his Amstel, 'We're going to another bar.'

The city was livening up and there were increasing numbers of messed up folk lining the streets they went along. As they walked, George scanned the crowd and the bars drooling for business alongside the canals, he spotted a bar he had overheard a Hen party talking about earlier, if these two were anywhere, here would be a good place to start. Once inside the Bulldog, they mounted some stools in the corner by the bar. Beers ordered, George looked about the place. It was much bigger on the inside and seemed to have more than one floor. George tapped Gary on the arm; he didn't want to shout over the music

'Go have a walk about, lad, have a look. One of them is tall, short cropped hair and the other, shorter with slightly longer hair. Typical British, southern casual.'

Gary was more than happy to have a wander, the place was rammed full of birds, and most of them were either partially or totally off their heads. It was like a fucking sweet shop. He glided aimlessly through the bar area, and smiled at a couple of girls sitting rolling a huge spliff from tens of separate Rizla. He found the stairs and climbed to the first floor where there was a group of Geordie lads who were smashed out of their faces, all with girls sitting on their laps. He suddenly felt a little stoned and light headed so he made his way back down to George who was still sitting at the bar.

'I feel wasted George, stoned… I've got to get outside in the fresh air."' He went outside and sat at on a bench. George joined him and said, 'You fucking lightweight, Sparksy. You OK?'

Gary thought about the question for a bit. 'Err, I don't think I am George. I feel all over the place.'

George looked at his watch; it was just past seven in the evening. Clearly the beer and shots, along with some powerful passive smoking had got to Gary, the fucking lemon. He didn't mind too much though. He actually quite fancied a little walk about on his own. 'Why don't you go back to the hotel, Gary? Have a lie down, get your head together. I'll pick you up about nine, nine thirty.'

'You sure George?' Gary really fancied the idea but didn't want to rouse any anger that would ruin the next few days or even leave him being blamed for a mission failure.

'Sure, I'm sure. I need you fighting fit.'

George pointed Gary in the direction of the hotel and then wandered off on his own into the mêlée of Amsterdam, with a grin growing on his face.

## 2.16 He Wanted Out

Razor sat staring at the TV at the end of his bed. It wasn't on. On his bedside table was a selection of books that had been donated to the hospital or been left by people who had been on the ward, but he hadn't read a book in years, unless you counted the *Shoot Annual* from 1987. He looked down at his legs, he'd had two operations in the last three days to try to save the left one. He clearly wasn't going anywhere soon. This worried him, especially as his bullshit lying was clearly waving a red flag over the question of his identity. He had to do something but he didn't have a clue what. And he was worried about Paddy. He hoped he was away somewhere but he had a horrible feeling, especially as George and his mob had got to Essex so fast, that he was in trouble. He needed to call his parents too, but any call he made would blow his cover and he needed to get out of this hospital as soon as possible and try to get things sorted. He knew he was in trouble wherever he ended up but he thought he'd take his chances with George, after all, his legs had already been broken, wasn't that punishment enough?

'Morning,' the nurse said. 'Just going to change your dressings and check your legs, OK?'

Razor smiled and the nurse went about her business. He leant back and dozed, looking at the ceiling. He felt pain as the nurse adjusted his bed. The painkillers he had been given were being reduced in strength and he was beginning to have the occasional panic attack. What he heard next didn't calm his mood.

'Well now, you're all nice and clean and ready for your visitors, eh?' She patted the bed and wandered off, leaving him to fall into a blind panic as to who was coming to see him. He started rubbing his head and looking about frantically. Was it the Stones brothers? Or George himself? Were they going to kill him or kidnap him? He rolled over and tried to open his cabinet to see if his clothes were clean, perhaps he could attempt an escape?

When it was two policemen who walked onto the ward he was no less alarmed. His bollocks retreat into his groin so fast they winded him. He was speechless and more importantly had nowhere to go. It wasn't as if he could get on his toes and get out of there. He had to lie there and take whatever was going to happen. He couldn't help but think it was a losing battle from the start, he wasn't like Paddy Wherry, they'd trick him and make him say stuff he didn't want to. He decided to say nothing and continue looking at the ceiling.

The policemen drew up to his bed, pulled the curtains round it and one of them asked if it was OK if they sat down. He ignored them.

They silently watched him for what seemed to Razor like ages, he didn't know what to think.

Eventually one of them said, 'Well, Raymond, do you want to go first, or shall I?'

Razor scratched the inside of his leg, trying not to make direct eye contact with either of them and again looked at the ceiling. He felt confident looking at the strip lighting, it calmed him. This sense of wellbeing didn't last long...

'OK, have it your way. You are Raymond Wilkins. You live at... Your date of birth is... Your address is... Nickname, Razor...'

He listened intently as his particulars were read out to him; they seemed to have it all. Where the fuck was it all coming from? He wasn't interested he told himself. It wouldn't work. He just had to stay on the ceiling...

'I'll call you Razor. Is that OK, Razor?'

The ceiling was melting now and his eyes were welling up, the enormity of what had happened to him had hit home with the realisation that whoever came to get him he was fucked. He couldn't help but think what a fucking stupid idea it had all been. But that realisation was a bit too late, wasn't it?

'Well, Razor, I'll take your silence as agreement. I know the answers to most of the questions I'm going to ask you, Razor, but we'll follow procedure. Have you spoken to your mother lately, Razor?'

Silence from Razor.

'Do you know a Patrick Wherry?'

More of the same.

'Or the Stones brothers?'

The strip lighting was beginning to make Razor's eyes sore so he decided to close them and again, remain silent.

The chief questioner took a rest and leant back in the plastic chair which creaked with the weight. He nodded to his number two who got up and headed toward the nurses' station. Razor couldn't work out what was going on. Within seconds he saw him returning with the telephone cart. He was smiling broadly and parked it alongside Razor.

'Would you like to talk to your Mum and Dad, Raymond, sorry, Razor? He offered the yellow receiver to Razor and placed a stack of twenty pence pieces on the trolley. 'Thing is, mate, even if you wanted to you couldn't. Don't worry, they

aren't dead, but unfortunately your mum can't speak as she
has a broken jaw, severe burns to her entire body and is, in a
very bad way. And so is your dad.'

Razor wanted to jump up and scream. Surely this was all
lies?

'Fuck off.'

He'd bitten and the cops knew it, though worse was to
follow as one of them stood up and began to lay out pictures
of his mum and dad, all of which were horrific and soon
instigated a tide of bodily fluid into a hastily gathered pillow.
Razor had known he was fucked, but Mum and Dad? What
the fuck was going on?

'George Meachen was seen leaving your Mum and Dad's on
either Monday or Tuesday morning, the witness was unsure
which. Your dad has confirmed it was him. We also have
reason to believe that your friend, Patrick Wherry, is dead.'

Razor felt numb. Number than both his legs had all week.
Mum and Dad? Paddy? They'd killed him? He fought with
everything he had to remind himself that they had surely
played all their cards now and were waiting for him for break.
All he wanted to do was see his parents, and of course find out
the truth about what the fuck was going on. He took a deep
breath and mustered all the courage he had, looked up and
spoke. 'Are you charging me with anything?'

'No, Razor, nothing at all, yet.'

'Well, I'm tired, so can you leave me alone?'

'Let's speak soon Razor,' one of the policeman said as he
laid his card on the cupboard beside the bed.

Razor's gaze followed the backs of the departing policemen
as far as was possible before refocusing on the ward around
him and down towards his smashed and broken legs. He was
trapped, helpless and wanted more information. He looked at
the card, was instantly sick again. He groped around, found
and hit the button for assistance, some painkillers and some
clean sheets. While waiting for the nurse to arrive he began
to sob.

By the time the nurse got to his bed Razor needed the support of another nurse who then rang for the Chaplain. Razor was inconsolable and crying uncontrollably. He could hear them talking about the possibility of sedating him but he couldn't stop crying. He wanted out...

## 2.17 This Twisted City

The day had gone well for Tom and Lassie, but there was still the itching terror of what that bloke could do to them. He had the cash pretty much covered, which was honestly more than he thought they'd have achieved by now. He wasn't yet in a hole in the ground in Liverpool, and he had to keep reminding himself that it must be possible to get out of this with perhaps a severe hiding. They just had to remain out of the clutches of the two psychos he had seen missing the boat Harwich. They would have caught the next one and so could conceivably be in Amsterdam now, looking for them. He had considered getting off straight away to Rotterdam or Eindhoven, guessing that his knowledge of Holland was better than theirs. Meeting the girls had changed that though and even though he realised that his little head was now ruling his big head they were going to stay, for at least for another day... They would spend it with the girls, and ask them to show them the 'off the beaten track' Amsterdam.

Tom did wonder how they would get the cash to them The last thing he wanted was to get fucking kidnapped and dragged back up north, or even smashed up and left for dead in a ditch somewhere outside Leighton Buzzard. It would have to be proper cloak and dagger stuff when he got back, and he was pretty sure that if they wanted to find him again it would be easy, unless he disappeared from Harwich forever, which he wasn't quite prepared to do just yet. If he could get the cash to them safely they might decide they had had a little holiday, made a little earner, got their big money back and just fuck off home leaving him and Lassie to get on with their lives. That was maybe a pipe dream but that's all he had the moment.

They were soon back in their hotel room, Lassie sitting on the bed and Tom on an easy chair looking out of the window across the square. Tom told Lassie about seeing the two Scousers at Harwich and that they were probably in Amsterdam now.

'Fuck this. We should go to Rotterdam, Tom, it's the sensible thing to do. If we get caught here anything could happen!'

'I disagree, Lass, Amsterdam is fucking huge. We will be with the girls and I honestly don't think they've thought it through. What will happen if they try anything here? There are plain clothes Tourist Police all over the place. We'll be OK, trust me. We'll get back to Harwich and sort it out there. We'll be on our own turf then too and have a better view of the whole thing, don't you think?'

'I think you're fucking mad, mate. I mean, if they weren't serious why the fuck would they bother chasing us over here, just for a fucking mini- break? Get a fucking grip...'

'Come on, Lass, trust me. The girls are switched on and we'll just chill with them, in safety. If we did decide to move they could be watching the train station or the airport, don't you think? I'm sure we're better off in the eye of the storm.'

He could tell Lassie wasn't even slightly convinced.

'Let's just get dressed, phone Pascale and arrange to meet them later and see how we go, eh? We've done the main thing – we have the cash. We just need to relax, have a bit of fun and work out our next move when we get back.'

Lassie stood, grabbed his wash bag and walked toward the bathroom. 'Your move next, Tom. But I retire on arrival at Parkeston Quay.' He smiled, closed the bathroom door and turned on the shower.

Tom began to rifle through his bag for something to wear tonight. It seemed odd with all that had gone on over that week that they were now going on a fucking date! He laughed to himself, imagining Cilla saying, 'here's our Graham with a quick reminder', and then went cold at the thought of the Scouse accent.

On the bedside table was the phone number the girls had given them when they had split earlier. They'd ring them in a bit, it was barely seven in the evening and he knew that the evening was still very young indeed. The sound of the shower dying spurred him into action and he grabbed a towel from the bed and waited for Lassie to exit. Lassie walked out rubbing his hair, exclaiming how much better he felt and Tom hoped for the same outcome as he turned the shower back on. It took seconds to reheat and he was soon under the hot water, scrubbing away the day. He was enjoying the shower until he heard the door of the room bang shut on its mechanism. The room went quiet.

'Lass?' he shouted. 'Lassie?' There was no answer and he immediately panicked. He left the shower running and as quietly as he could have slipped out, put a towel around himself, put his T-shirt back on over his wet top half and crept toward the door. At the door he stood and listened. There wasn't a sound. He could feel his heart rate increasing as his ears strained for any sound of movement. He took a deep breath and jumped out into the room...

'Lassie?' There was no one in the room and he felt enormous relief as he realised the fact. This, however, was short lived as he then realised that neither Lassie nor any of his stuff was in the room. His heart began to race again. He hadn't heard any scuffles or shouting. All he could think was he'd had enough and fucked off somewhere, maybe even home? Tom sat on the end of the bed. He was gutted. He got up and checked his bag, the cash was still there, as he'd thought it would be, Lassie wouldn't do anything like that to him, and he found it hard to blame him for wanting out. The bang and scream sent Tom's heart racing and towel flying as he frantically reached out for something, anything, to use as a weapon, as Lassie jumped at him out of the wardrobe...

'You fucking cunt,' was all Tom Adams could squeeze out of his mouth as he collapsed back onto the bed. 'You fucking cunt!'

Lassie was in pissing himself with laughter on the floor; Tom was still trying to get his breath back, his chest heaving.

'What the fuck made you think that was a good idea, Lass?' he wheezed through his tight chest.

'Thought it would cheer you up, mate,' Lassie answered. 'You looked like you needed it!'

'You gave me a mild fucking heart attack, you fucking prick.'

'Come on, you lemon, turn of the shower and get yourself sorted. I'll go and ring the girls if you like. I'm into it now.'

Still panting, Tom wrapped his towel back around himself. 'You've changed your fucking tune, lad.'

Lassie shrugged, picked up the piece of paper and waved it at Tom. A nod told him he had the right one. He also grabbed the city map as he went through the hotel foyer. Directly opposite the hotel was a small nest of phone boxes. It took him three attempts before he worked out how to use it, but then, 'Hello?' A familiar voice said.

Lassie and Pascale talked for a few minutes and planned a meeting, Lassie referring to the map he had taken with him to make sure he knew where to go. He'd told her they wanted somewhere you wouldn't see many Brits or tourists and she'd agreed. She said that two unhinged Brits was more than enough to contend with. As he walked back to the hotel Lassie felt happy at the thought of seeing the girls again, but edgy at the possibility of being kidnapped at any moment by those two psychopaths who were hunting them, well Tom, down. He allowed himself the hope of not getting a battering to enter his mind, but the image of Razor between the two cars and his feel of his own chipped tooth soon put paid to that.

He found Tom sitting on the bed, doing up his trainers.

'Alright mate, all good?'

'I Spoke to Pascale. We're meeting them in a bar called Feelgoods in Leidsplein in about an hour. She said it was more of a Dutch place and there were little bars all around it where we could sit and relax and then head out later.'

'Sounds good, Lass.'

They decided to walk to the bar, relying on Lassie's tourist map for directions. The June evening sun was still high in the sky and it felt warm.

Tom squinted in the sunlight and found himself stepping on the back the heels of the man in front of him. As he looked around at tom the giant in question cast a huge shadow over the boys. Tom looked up to apologise but only managed a stuttered, 'Fuck. Oh Jesus fuck!'

Lassie had stopped too but was quicker to recover. He stepped in next to Tom, pulled out his city map and said, in his best English, 'Michael Jordan! Could I possibly have your autograph please?'

## 2.18 Fifty guilders

With Gary Sparks safely tucked up in bed George wandered back along the canal. It was a beautiful summer evening and he fancied a bit of time to consider the whole situation. He chose a small bar and sat outside. A petite, blonde girl in a little apron approached and asked him if he would like anything, he couldn't help but wonder whether everything in Amsterdam had a suggestive edge to it. The girl, probably in her late twenties, had a lovely set of tits on her and a beautifully pretty face. George didn't like to talk about his age, but was happy to let people guess at anything around the early fifties. He still looked good though, he thought, and was always well turned out. He looked her slowly up and down, taking in the full pleasure of her knowing what he was thinking about. Even better then, when he noticed her slight blush as his eyes reached her face. 'I'll have one of your blondes please.'

She looked at him with what he was sure was a pitiful look at his suggestive line about the beer, touched her own blonde hair and asked, 'A large blonde beer, sir, or a small?'

Obviously rebuffed, he instantly felt like punching her in the face and throwing her in the canal. The cheeky little flirting cunt. Probably just after a tip. He felt himself simmering over and told himself to calm down. Clearly this was just her job, and there wasn't exactly a shortage of slags about.

'I'll have a large please,' he said smiling as he gave her a large note and told her to keep the change.

Calmer with a beer inside him, George leant back in his chair and relaxed. He sat and watched the world go by while he finished his beer. The people here were truly, to a man, off their heads. No one seemed to give a fuck either. And it struck him that it wasn't just the tourists that were having a good time, the locals seemed to be enjoying themselves even more. And why not? They lived in a twenty-four-hour party zone that was also a very nice earner.

He smiled. He was really enjoying himself for the first time in years! It was a beautiful city too. He sat and watched as numerous tourist boats cut through the city on the canals, some it seemed, had bars on them. Some, he thought were probably floating whorehouses. The place was rife with it. This thought stirred him into action and, thanking the lesbian who had served him, he left the bar and went out to explore. It didn't take very long for something to grab his attention. The street-level windows, which earlier had had their curtains pulled in a show of non-working unity, were now fully open for business, and some of the girls were truly magnificent. His pace slowed and his heart rate quickened as he looked into each window as he passed. At some he had to use his height advantage to peer over little groups of adoring crowds peering lustfully into the window at the smiling females. The women sat on little chairs, they were on display exactly as though they were in a shop window. And they were all for sale. George decided that he would jump in straight away if he saw something he particularly liked. After all, leaving it may well allow some dirty pervert to muddy the waters and he didn't like the idea of stirring someone else's porridge. He wandered on up the street and then off to his right he saw a small alleyway that men and boys were pouring in and out of like a busy colony of ants. Some were drunk already; some were in groups. One, he thought looked like he had high blood pressure and was about to keel over, he'd obviously just lost his dirty water George thought and laughed to himself. He squeezed into the alleyway and found himself in whore paradise. The windows were only a metre or so across at some points and there were male 'ants' running in and out, some stopping or negotiating on the doorstep. Easy prey, George thought, as he watched the packs of sixteen and seventeen-year-old boys. Most would work themselves into such a frenzy that once inside a crafty handjob, a little kiss on the end and a couple of strokes would see off most of them. A decent pro would be able to make a barrow load of cash on a good night with these teenage virgins. He wandered on, the voyeur in him lapping up the spectacle of seeing the human butcher's shop open for business. His gaze was caught by one girl who met it with an innocent smile that almost had him, she'd practiced that he thought, and although she was gorgeous he wasn't looking for a beauty. No, he was looking for something different tonight. Something to satisfy the hidden pleasures that he kept in his locker. He smiled and walked on. He came to the end of the alleyway. There was a bar on his right and a kind of sex arcade directly in front of him. He steered to the left and kept on walking. The pedestrianised road was wider but still had interesting little alleys drawing the punters in and out. The road bent round and as he looked towards where it was taking him he heard a tap, tap, tap on the window. He turned toward the direction of the noise and saw, sitting in a doorway, a woman beckoning him to come closer. She waved again, and again and motioned for him to approach her doorway. She was probably early forties George thought, with a South East Asian look about her, maybe Thai. She sat half on, half off her chair and out of one side of her mouth hung a lit cigarette. He walked up to her and she started talking. George was surprised to hear that she she he had the voice of miner who had been feasting on gravel alone, and she accentuated the rasping sound of her voice by talking exclusively out of the side of her mouth so that she didn't have to remove the cigarette, which hung out of the other side. It was not very attractive.

'You are coming in then?' She said, dropping ash on the floor in front of him. 'It's early. You can do whatever you want for fifty guilders.'

George was repulsed by the thing in front of him but intrigued too. The thought of doing anything with the thing in front of him made his cock recoil in horror into his groin. This horrible, dirty, disgusting old filthy slag thing was up for anything. He stepped in closer to the window and spoke to her.

'Anything?'

'Tits, arse, face, hair, mouth. Anywhere you want, baby.'

She opened the door for George to step in but he remained outside looking into his wallet. He looked back at her with the fifty guilders in his hand. He then slowly screwed up the note and threw it into the doorway.

'Get a bath, you fucking manky old slag,' he said through gritted teeth.

He heard her shouting obscenities at him as he walked off. She looked on the way out. The money he'd thrown at her would probably be best spent on an overdose. He carried on walking and found that the road bent around and brought him back onto the main street by the canal. He repeated the circuit, this time going into some of the alleys he'd missed on his first walk round.

A young black girl caught his eye and he stopped to have a more lingering look. A look that unfortunately lasted a little too long, and before he knew it he was inside the small room, the curtain pulled across, his jacket on a hook and his cock in the small sink, being gently washed by the attentive ebony beauty. They agreed the price and that there was no kissing or anal, before he was told to lie down on the bed. Hands lightly dosed with some sort of lube she began to massage around his balls before sliding a condom on him. She continued to massage his shaft and then sunk his cock into her mouth as he began to rise to the occasion. She was a fine practitioner of her profession and he was soon standing to full attention. She deftly spun around and offered herself to him from behind. Thinking he'd probably explode if he went in from that angle, he pulled her back round and lay her on her back before edging himself to her front door. At this point he stopped, looked her in the eyes and then plunged in right up to the balls. She gasped with what he thought were great acting skills and made out she was enjoying herself, which he was pleased about. He had no illusions about what was happening, it was a physical contract that would be over after he had blown his muck into the top of the cock balloon, which didn't take him long.

'You OK, baby?' she asked, as she replaced the used towels and began to take quick glances in the mirror, considering what she may have to touch up before her next customer.

'Good, thanks,' George replied, and it was true. He felt relieved. She was pretty too. His itch wasn't completely scratched though, and after he had put his jacket back on he took a step toward the girl and spoke softly to her, which immediately made her cower away and move towards the back door into the main house where she knew there would be help if punters got aggressive.

'Don't be afraid, darling, I just want to ask you for a favour.'

'OK,' she said.

'I like, uh, certain things, and I hoped you might be able to help me. You were great but I like my girls, well, to be frank, on their period.' She looked at him quizzically, but he carried on regardless and without embarrassment. 'Really heavy if possible, and I was hoping that you might know a girl who could help me? I'd pay double the going rate.'

She could tell he was serious, if a little bit fucked up but she had seen it all before. She looked at her watch, and then at the clock on the wall.

'Wait here.' She left him in the small room with the curtain still pulled, and walked out the back door into the main building. A few minutes later she returned.

'Yes, I can help you. There is a girl, but she is not working. I will send her a message. Come back every hour, she will be here at some point for you.'

George thanked her and gave her a large note of some description that she seemed to be happy with before pulling back the curtain and making his way out. He saw an Irish Bar in the distance and set his sights on a stiff whiskey. The whole place seemed to be alive now. He felt comfortable as he entered the Irish Bar and was met with a typical nod and a greeting in 'Dutch English', which he thought was basically English but with S's on the end of the words.

He ordered a pint of Guinness and sat down close to the large front window. He was convinced he'd see the boys at some point. He was sure the little cunts were here. Doing what? He couldn't work it out. Probably just shitting themselves and hoping it would all blow over. He laughed to himself at the idea.

## 2.19 Abi Asks...

Waves of paranoia coursed through Tom's body on the way to meet the girls. He started using shop windows and other reflective surfaces to try to see whether anyone was following them or had taken any kind of interest in them.

He gave a start when Lassie suddenly came to a stop in front of him. 'Welcome to Leidsplein.' Lassie took a bow and folded away his map. 'Don't want to look like tourists now, do we?'

Tom shook his head, 'Of course not, lad. We want to blend in with our European brothers and sisters as much as possible!'

They looked at each other and laughed.

'Come on, let's find the bar and get a drink.'

The sun was beginning to set and the neon signs were now jostling for position in the evening sky. They soon spotted the sign for Feelgoods Bar under a flashing 8 ball pool sign and headed towards it. Tom felt especially pleased at the thought of getting off the street. He kept imagining the Scousers coming up behind them...

At that instant, Tom felt a hand grab his arm and pull him back sharply. His first reaction, as he pulled away, was to shout to Lassie; his second was to chin the cunt who had just grabbed him. He spun around trying to just that, and was successful in breaking the grip on his left arm. He began to back away into the road.

'Fuck me, boys, you're a bit jumpy – you been eating those fucking mushies?'

It was Aky, the Tollesbury stoner they had met earlier and who's driving license they were still in possession of.

'Listen, lads, I owe you a fucking drink. I was fucking totaled earlier and the guy at the hostel said two lads brought me back. I guessed it could only be you two so thank you, muchly appreciated! I needed a fucking rest. Small world, eh?'

Smiling, and now much calmer, Tom said, 'Cool. Yeah, it was us. We had to, you were fucking mashed! How are you feeling now?'

Aky toasted them with a pint of what looked like water, 'I feel a little better, though my piss is like warm, hot Lucozade! How the fuck has your day been panning out, boys?'

Tom and Lassie laughed at the mental image they had just been sold...

'Drinking the good old H2O, then?' Lassie asked.

'Fuck no, Vodka lime and soda without the trimmings! Listen, join us for a drink? Let's all get mangled.'

At this Aky began to introduce the other lads he was with, who all seemed to be from different places and weren't the people he'd actually come to Amsterdam with. His mates were somewhere else and were meeting him later.

The boys cried off, explaining that they were on their way to meet up with some girls. They made vague promises to meet up later for a few beers and other indulgences.

'Nice one,' said Aky as Tom and Lassie retreated in the direction of Feelgoods, but the taking the precaution of walking past and then ducking in without any of the other crowd noticing.

'We don't really need that, Lass. We need to keep below the radar.'

Lassie agreed and then said, 'Can you see the girls?'

There was no need to answer the question, as there were the two girls, holding pool cues and waving at them from across the bar. Kisses and hugs were exchanged as though they were old friends and Tom felt instantly relaxed – as if any preying eyes looking for two English boys would be instantly averted at the sight of two couples who obviously knew each other out on a double date playing pool...

Abi signed to her sister who then spoke to Tom and Lassie, 'Abi wants to know what you boys would like to drink?'

'Whatever you're having,' Tom replied. Lassie chimed in with a nod and thanked Abi with a wink. Pascale was soon back from the bar with four beers and four shots of vodka. 'Keeping it simple,' she exclaimed and handed out the shots which were downed and chased with cold Amstel. "'OK, teams? And who's going to break?'

## 2.20 Take her home

George stared into the foam at the bottom of his glass and then looked around the room. He decided he liked Amsterdam; it was his kind of place. Anything goes here he thought to himself as he stood up and walked to the door. He nodded as he left and was thanked for his custom in perfect English. Yes, he was very impressed with what he'd seen so far and made a mental note to return, next time on a more leisurely trip. He strode purposefully through the now busy streets of the red light district, his imposing size leaving groups of stags and hens and Asian tourists in no doubt that they should give way to him. He reached the doorway he was aiming for and saw the curtain was drawn, clearly the girl was busy inside plying her trade. He waited and it wasn't long before a stringy teenager came out, blushed red and smiling to a chorus of well-dones from his waiting crowd of friends who, it became apparent from the overheard conversation had paid for him to lose his virginity.

George smiled to himself and approached the window. The girl inside recognised him, put on a dressing gown and approached the door. She said she'd been able to get in touch with the other girl who was willing and would be in later. She went on to say that he was welcome to use her room but he would have to pay her for the room hire and pay the other girl for her time.

George said, 'So I have to pay twice?'

The girl smiled and told him that basically yes, he had to pay twice, but it was actually her doing him a favour as she would be out of pocket as she would not be earning while he was enjoying himself. 'That's the deal, mister, you want it or not?'

George internally applauded her business sense and agreed, happy with the deal. He had a special one in the bag and nobody else would be slaughtering it before he got there later which made him feel slightly better about the money. He thanked her for helping him and turned on his heels to get Gary Sparks up and out.

George knocked on the door of Gary's room and waited for a response. Nothing stirred for over thirty seconds. He knocked again and this time heard shuffling. Gary soon opened the door, dressed in a clean top, pants and one sock. George pushed the door open and walked in. He waited for it to close before speaking to Gary.

'You dirty little bastard, Gary.' George laughed.

'What the fuck are you on about, George?' Gary grabbed his jeans and began to put them on.

'You... you dirty little cunt,' George laughed as he pointed at Gary's naked foot. 'You've been choking the Bishop!'

Gary laughed, 'Fuck it, you got me,' and flipped his sock into the bin to join the other one. He grabbed a new pair from his bag and sat on the bed to put them on.

'You been shopping, Gary?' George asked in surprise.

'Just a few things. Give me two minutes', boss, and I'll be with you.

Gary finished dressing and the two men went downstairs and out onto the street. They decided to wander about and watch the crowds.

After a while they came to a huge neon sign offering 'live shows with audience participation.'

'Fancy it, Gaz?'

Gary shrugged.

'Come on then,'

They took their place in a queue of about twenty people. The queue began to erode as it slid into the small red double doors of the club. It was dark in the foyer with low ceilings and a small bar area with toilets to one side. They paid the entrance fee and Gary Sparks sourced two large single malts with two ice and handed one to George, hoping he was calm enough to handle it. The walls were plain dark red, the door into the main room was also red and clearly marked with Entrance and Exit lights and draped with heavy curtains with red and gold velvet tassels.

'Looks like a fucking porn abattoir don't you think, George?'

'Very fucking much so, Gary, very fucking much so.' George felt like a porn gladiator and he was ready for battle.

Neither man got very far before stopping and turning to each other. Gary spoke first and made sure he didn't give away any emotional response as he needed to know what George thought first, 'Well... Thoughts?'

George looked as though he had just climbed into a doll's house. He was a big man and frankly he could probably touch the ceiling if he stood on one of the chairs. He nearly laughed, this was definitely amusing.

He turned to Gary, who relaxed when he saw the look on George's face.

'It's a bit fucking intimate isn't it, Gary?' George put his hand on Gary's shoulder and finished his whisky as a little bell sounded and a dwarf dressed top to toe in leather and a gimp mask climbed up onto the little stage and announced the show would start in five minutes. He also said that any members of the public who wanted to appear after the main event should register with the front door staff. 'Couples, singles or groups are welcome. Anything goes.' He exited stage left to the applause of the twenty or so punters in the tiny theatre.

They sat down on the end of a row of bench like seats covered in easy-clean faux leather. A man and a woman soon sat down next to Gary and smiled at him.

Clearly hired for the weekend, Sparksy,' George whispered into Gary's ear. 'Wonder how much it costs by the day?'

Gary thought George was about to ask but fortunately he just leant forward to take off his jacket.

'It's fucking hot in here, eh?'

Gary Sparks nodded in agreement, while staring at the beautiful arse on the girl sitting next to him. The punter had his arms draped around her and was busily caressing her left tit whilst kissing her neck. Gary couldn't tell if she was enjoying this but he told himself she clearly wasn't and she would be better off with him, he'd show her a much better time! He was staring at her arse again and admiring the hot pants that were barely holding her in, when he glanced up and saw the punter was looking directly at him. He gave Gary a little wink and carried on, almost popping her tit out of her top and attempting to pull her on top of him. Gary heard her tell him to watch the show and he slid her off and took his drink from the little ledge which ran along the back of the seats. He leant over to speak to Gary, 'She fucking loves it, the slag, they all do!'

Gary felt sorry for the girl. She clearly had to put up with wankers like that most of the time. Gary smiled briefly and raised his hand and ordered two Amstel, still trying to keep George off the scotch.

For the next half hour, they were treated to naked dwarf sex, doggy style sex and a girl blowing ping-pong balls out of her fanny, for her finale she scored 180 on an oversize dartboard by blowing darts out of a piece of grey gutter piping inserted into her vagina. The whole room clapped and the curtains came down for the interval. They ordered more drinks and, Gary saw, to his surprise, that next to him the man had released his little beauty from her hot pants. She was now sitting astride him in her knickers and pouring lager into his mouth. He then began nibbling and biting her breasts, telling her that she fucking loved it and was a dirty little whore. He turned again to Gary as he pushed her off and got up to go to the toilet.

Gary looked her almost apologetically and sipped his lager. She leant over and spoke quietly to him, 'I don't fucking love it at all, especially with fucking arseholes like him,' with which she winked at him, took his beer and drank a mouthful.

Gary just smiled and hoped she hadn't been sucking the arseholes cock earlier as she had just touched the top of his glass.

The arsehole returned and took his seat, again winking at Gary as he went straight in for the tit and began sucking on it greedily. He pulled her around to massage the other breast and again, gave Gary Sparks a beautiful view of her arse and pretty much everything else.

The lights came down and the show started. This time it was a girl and a dildo on stage doing her thing to some Dire Straits tune. Both men sat mesmerised by the girl on stage and Gary could feel himself starting to get a little fizzy. He sank his lager and ordered some more. As he lowered his arm his hand brushed against the girl next to him. He thought nothing of it as he watched out of the corner of his eye as the arsehole groped her. She didn't seem to mind. The drinks arrived and he passed one to George who was totally engrossed. Gary leant back in his seat and sat watching the show until he felt someone touch his hand. He looked down and saw it was the hand of the girl sitting next to him, she took his hand and led him to her arse, placed his hand on it and left it there. The room was totally dark now and the punter was still groping her tits and kissing her neck. Gary began slowly stroking her arse, rubbing her cheeks and arse crack. She responded with a low moan of appreciation, which encouraged both men to continue doing what they were doing, though only one of them was having any effect. Gary continued rubbing her and slid one, then two fingers into her as she began pushing back onto him moaning ever so lightly. The punter, meanwhile, clearly thought he was Hugh Heffner and continued telling her that 'she loved it' in her ear. Gary Sparks couldn't believe his luck as he sat there, in the dark fingering the girl next to him. He wanted to tell George but didn't want to make a scene. His cock was nearly busting out of his jeans and it took all his concentration not to fizz up into the front of his shorts. The show continued and as the girl on stage writhed and approached her own, natural conclusion, the girl next to him – now soaking wet – was moaning in unison.

On stage the girl's back arched and her belly twitched as she reached her climax, or not, George thought. She could just be a bloody good actor.

Next to him Gary, with almost his whole hand inside the girl next to him, came in his pants for the first time since secondary school.

And next to him, the woman with almost a whole hand inside her came for the first time in months.

Next to her, the arsehole also came in his pants for the second time in a week.

As the lights came up Gary Sparks was busily wiping his hand on his trousers, it looked like he he'd been having his way with a jellyfish. He smiled as the girl turned around and winked at him and pulled up her hotpants. He glanced up and caught the eye of the punter. He winked again at Gary.

'She fucking loves me, mate, did you hear her? She fucking loves me...'

'Yes, mate,' Gary replied, 'You've got a keeper there. Take her home with you!'

The punter looked puzzled... then held up his left hand that displayed a wedding ring.

'Of course I'm taking her home, she's my fucking wife!'

Gary's eyes nearly popped out of his head and he downed his lager in one. He fucking loved Amsterdam!

## 2.21 Stripes and Spots

The pool balls were old school stripes and spots. The table, one of the big American ones with huge pockets. The white ball was massive and the cues were heavy. It wasn't ideal conditions for pool but there was chalk and chalk was the most important thing when playing pool. Even if when breaking you were in danger of giving your wrist a stress fracture. It was girls against boys and the Dutch girls were more than able pool players. The girls were fun and Tom had almost forgotten why they were here by the start of the third frame. Lassie looked happy too, even more so now he'd had a few vodkas and beers and was getting used to communicating with Abi again, who took it all in her stride. Another lovely young Dutch girl with a huge smile was pulling the beers. They were everywhere; maybe he should stay in Amsterdam. It seemed a good idea until he reminded himself of the situation he had to deal with first.

'So, ladies,' he ventured, leaning on his cue, 'what have you got planned for us tonight?'

Pascale said that after they'd played some more pool they were going to take the boys to a more local club for house music and dancing. Tom loved the idea, especially the idea of getting out of the way of the more touristy places.

'OK?' Pascale said.

'Cool with us, eh, Tom?'

Tom nodded in agreement and wobbled an empty glass at Lassie who wandered off towards the bar, returning in amazing time with another tray of booze. Abi held up two fingers on each hand and signaled for a decider.

'Last game! Come on, boys, you're getting worse as the vodka flows. Easy targets!'

Tom broke and potted nothing. 'Bollocks.'

'Abi's shot isn't it?' asked Lassie.

Pascale and Abi held a quick meeting that the two boys watched intently. Voice, sign language and angles with cues ended with Abi on the black ball to the middle pocket. She rolled it in with ease and stuck her tongue out at Lassie and then Tom.

'Top drawer that. A proper clear up, I think we've been had, Lass.'

Lassie agreed and laid his cue down and bowed in appreciation of Abi's prowess on the table. They all finished their drinks and stepped outside into the street. It was getting dark now and the neon was in full glow, music was pounding out and there were lots of people on the street and in the bars around the square. Lassie stood looking around, watching the trendsetters of Amsterdam coming out for a pose. He wondered if every night was as lively.

'Boys, are you OK to walk to the club?' As Pascale said this she took Tom's hand in hers and smiled at him.

'Lead the way, my dear.' Tom squeezed her hand and smiled. It was really nice to see these girls again and he felt he could tell her anything. She was a pretty cool chick.

They drifted off past small cafés and pubs and Tom noticed the change from the centre of town to the more residential areas.

'So Tom, how long do you intend to stay in Amsterdam?'

He pondered telling her everything but held back.

'Well, I'm definitely here until Saturday, then hopefully back to England for a bit. I'd really like to come and visit you again though, if you'd like me to that is!' He laughed nervously.

'I'd like that a lot, though I'm sensing you're holding back about something. Do you have a girlfriend back in England?'

'No girlfriend, just an MBA.'

'What's an MBA, Tom?' Pascale looked quizzically at him as she led them through a short tunnel.

'Oh sorry, an MBA is a major ball-ache. A big problem. A difficult situation.

Pascale laughed out loud, 'Major ball-ache, an MBA. I love the UK sense of humour, fucking brilliant. Though I'm guessing you're also using the skill of understatement?'

He did all but tell her then. He kept the forged money out of the tale, telling her they came over just to get a bit of headspace and that he could just about afford to pay the people he owed but that it would leave him skint and without options. He also left out the fact that the blokes chasing him were in Holland too and were actively looking for him and

Lassie and that he thought they would, if they caught them, probably maim or kill them and maybe the people they were with too.

'Well, I know we have only known each other a short while but you are welcome to stay with me in our flat for a while.'

The last thing he needed was to drag someone else into this fucking mess. 'Thank you, Pascale and I would truly love to spend some more time with you in Holland but...'

'Ahh yes,' Pascale interrupted Tom, 'I sense the understatement coming through?'

Tom smiled.

Tom turned to Lassie as they both picked up the sound of heavy bass thudding through the air. They rounded another corner and facing them was an industrial unit, with a line of windows running the length of the building but above head height. Through the windows they could see lasers and lights dissecting the air inside in rhythm to the now thunderous bass that was making the huge metal rolling door on the front of the building vibrate like it was dancing itself.

They joined the queue, and found to their amazement that the person in front of them was an old lady. An old lady with a dog.

'I fucking love Holland,' Lassie chirped, pissing himself laughing.

'Hello Boy.' Tom bent down to stroke the dog, a little West Highland Terrier, which happily yapped at him and tried to lick his face.

'His name is Benji,' the elderly owner said to Tom. 'He's four and a half, he loves treats, and I even give him chips on a Wednesday. He has a brother and a sister but he doesn't see them very often because they live in Delft.'

'He's a lovely little fellow – does he like house music?' Tom said, turning to the others and smiling.

She grinned back, showing off a healthy quantity of disco foam at the sides of her mouth, 'I'm not sure, but I fucking love it!'

It was at this point that Tom and Lassie took a deeper interest in the old lady, she was at least sixty and judging by her grinding jaw and chatter, was speeding her tits off! They turned to each other in disbelief and then to the girls who were equally entertained by the raving granny they had just met. The fun came to an abrupt end though when the queue shortened to the point where it was the granny's turn to get frisked. The bouncers were speaking in Dutch and Tom asked Pascale what was going on.

'I think they are refusing her entry.'

Tom went pulled out a wad of guilders from his pocket and pushed them into Pascale's hand.

'Tell them we'll pay for her if it's a problem, and also for Benji!'

The doormen were, unfortunately, having none of it though and when Pascale questioned them, calling them ageist, they calmly said her age wasn't the problem, she had been before, but that Benji got too excited and that he had done a poo on the dance floor last time he was there. Tom, Lassie and the girls said goodbye to the lady but all she would reply was, 'Benji's done nothing wrong, Benji's a good boy. He'd never do that.'

'She's caked,' Lassie said to Tom. 'Completely frazzled.'

Frisked and patted down, they found themselves inside. There was a stage full of speakers at one end, a huge lighting rig and a make-shift bar selling cold soft drinks and beer to one side.

Abi produced pills with a dove pressed onto each one which she dropped onto their outstretched palms. Nice work he mouthed as bottles of water were passed round to assist in getting the E down their throats.

They the throng of people dancing about and before long they were all having a little blow and rubbing the backs of their necks and the top of their heads. Eyes rolled, jaws wobbled, water was drunk and hugs and kisses were shared.

'I fucking love you, Lassie,' Tom grabbed his bestie and gave him a huge sweaty hug, which was returned with interest.

'I love you too, mate.'

'Sorry for all this bother,' Tom shouted, through his grinding jaw, but Lassie wasn't listening, he was nodding his head as the DJ cued up a song they both loved and they and threw their hands in the air. Altern8's 'Infiltrate 202' boomed out across the floor and Tom stood and looked towards the speakers as the bassline made his body shake. He could feel his eyes rolling and his chest heaving as wave after wave of euphoria swept through his body. He grabbed Pascale with a sweaty hand and attempted to dance. Unfortunately, the E had rooted him to the spot and he could barely stand. They stood hugging, holding each other up. These were powerful and he was actually looking forward to a lull so he could get his head together. Tom kissed Pascale's sweaty forehead as Lassie appeared in front of him with a laser backdrop highlighting his outline, making him look like an alien.

Lassie gave Pascale some money and said, 'Go get some more, baby, we'll get smashed tonight!'

## 2.22 Pour me a large one

'I don't fucking believe you, Gary, I just don't fucking believe you.'

Gary Sparks pointed down to the leg of his new jeans, jeans that were a real mess. As they were on the inside too... 'I'm gonna have to go back to get these changed and laundered George, they're disgusting.'

'Jesus yes, you dirty bastard. Go on, fuck off back and meet me in outside the pub opposite our hotel. I'm gonna have a wander, might get myself a massage or something.'

'A massage or something? Don't you mean you're going to get a brass?'

George turned to Gary, 'No, Gary, I mean a massage. Why on earth would I want to get a brass? Pay for sex? Fuck off.'

'There are some real stunners here though, George, absolute beauties.'

'Gary,' George said, 'one thing you need to remember, the first inch is bliss beyond belief, the rest is just raw meat. Now fuck off and I'll see you later.'

Gary skulked away into the night and George made his way back to the alleyway he had visited earlier.

'Hello, honey, looking for that special request still?'

George stepped inside, and the girl closed the door behind him and drew the curtain.

'OK, you pay me for the room, and you pay Thelma for the trick, Yes?'

Terms discussed, George felt oddly out of his comfort zone, he was usually the one in absolute control but this was so far gone it was mad. He handed over 150 guilders – clearly it was over the odds but his was a strange request and he needed the room too. He considered asking to see her first but then thought better of it as he was going to do it anyway so it didn't really matter. As the girl left her replacement slipped by her. She wasn't great, but he'd seen worse, and he felt she'd made an effort for him. Her hair was done up in a Mari Wilson beehive and her war paint was fresh on. She was dressed in a full-length PVC mac and was wearing black stilettos. She looked to be in her forties but was probably younger; it was, after all, a tough industry and she played to a tough crowd.

'Hello, Sailor,' she said cheesily. 'So you're the man with the specific tastes, eh?'

'It seems so, Thelma is it?'

'Thelma it is, but I can be anybody you want to be, it's your money, my dear.' She then began to undress him. While she was still fully clothed in her mac she knelt and took him in her mouth and started giving his cock and balls a good clean. This went on for a minute, and he confirmed his satisfaction with the odd grunt. She then pushed him back onto the bed. George sat up to watch her work. She looked up, teasing the end of him with one hand while the other played with her tits. She could feel his balls swelling and wanted to make sure she wasn't there for too long.

'You ready, baby?' She asked as he felt a finger in his arse, fuck it felt good. He wanted to fuck her right now.

'Yeah, turn over.'

'Oh no, baby, Thelma on top, Thelma likes it on top. You won't regret it.'

With this she took off her PVC mac and climbed on top of him.

'Watch out, baby, this will get messy.'

George Meachen was excited; exactly what he wanted was messy. Bloody messy. She unrolled a condom and put it on him, then positioned herself above, as if choosing her moment. Then she let herself drop onto him and let out a little squeal. Almost instantly George could see blood. She was riding him, massaging both tits, his hands on her hips to steady her. As he looked down the thought flashed through his mind that he could be in a slaughterhouse, this pushed him over the edge and he began to tell her he was going to come.

'Yes, baby, give it to me, give it to me.' He was looking at her, riding him, massaging and squeezing her tits, and he felt a huge groan coming up from his groin as he closed his eyes and emptied himself into the condom inside Thelma. He opened his eyes as the last surge left his aching balls.

He couldn't quite believe what he saw. Thelma had slid of him and was writhing her way up his body and moving towards his face. He pushed her off, stood up and looked at himself in the mirror. From the neck down he was covered in blood. He looked like he had just been fucking born.

'You like Thelma on top, baby? She stood, studying him as she buttoned up her PVC mac. Her choice of attire was clearly appropriate.

All George could do was nod. 'Yes,' he said. 'Thank you.'

Thelma disappeared through the little door and into the night. The other girl then called, 'I'll give you five minutes to clear yourself up and then I need the room, darling.'

George did what he could with the sink and the wet wipes, and put on his clothes back on... He thanked the girl loudly and let himself out into the night air. He needed to go back to the hotel and have a shower. He made his way back to the hotel in a contented state. He couldn't quite work out why he liked it but what he was sure of was that this was going to the grave with him.

At the hotel, he found Gary Sparks, propping the bar up waiting for him.

'Where have you been, George? That must have been one hell of a massage.'

'Shut up and get the drinks in, Gary. I'll be down in a minute.'

George disappeared into the lift, giving Gary Sparks two fingers as the doors closed. He was warming to the lad he thought. He showered, washed his hair twice, changed his clothes and headed back down to the bar where Gary had bought a bottle of Scotch and had two glasses and a bucket of ice at the ready.

'You can put your name on it and leave it for when you come back. Nice touch, eh?'

'As long as you don't put Mickey Mouse on it I don't give a fuck, now pour me a large one.'

'We can sit out the front to watch for them if you like, George?'

George admired Gary's tenacity, but he was spent.

'Let's leave it for tonight, eh, Gary, we'll have another couple of these, have a decent kip and start again tomorrow nice and early. Let's order some chips.'

## 2.22 Somewhere

'Come on, it's five in the morning. Let's go back to the flat, or go get some breakfast.'

The others, a heap of shabby, strung out humanity on the floor of the warehouse, obeyed without a murmur and followed Pascale out into the bright Amsterdam sunshine, squinting like rats when a manhole cover is popped for inspection.

Lassie stood nibbling at his bottom lip as he watched his left leg carry out a set of involuntary twitches. He mustered a sentence together and replied, 'I couldn't eat a fucking thing, man, but I'd love a milkshake, a proper one you know, not from McDonalds, a proper café. One with fresh raspberries.'

Abi clapped in agreement and mouthed 'banana' to her sister. She knew where to go and started to lead them back into town. As Tom wandered down the street he felt like he was in an abandoned city. There was no one about and the sound of the rave had been sucked into the buildings as they weaved their way back into the centre of the city. He wondered what had happened to Benji and his mad owner.

He turned to Lassie and grinned the grin of a man that had munched through at least five Es.

'Hope she got her rave somewhere, she was a top lady. And Benji. Though if he did shit on the dance floor I can understand them not letting her in again.'

'Stop talking bollocks, Tom.'

The other three all started laughing and Tom held up his hand as if to say, 'sorry, I get it' and trailed along behind wishing he could lay down somewhere as he was still getting mad rushes every few minutes.

It wasn't long before Tom and Lassie began to recognise streets and bar names and especially bureau de change kiosks they had visited only the day before. They passed a few street cafés before being led into one that seemed especially popular for the time of day, though the girls pointed out that Amsterdam rarely, if ever shut down completely.

'Hope it's because of the milkshakes,' said Lassie and wasn't disappointed when Abi got the menu and sat next to him and pointed to the pictures. Milkshakes of any and all varieties were on offer.

'Just what the doctor ordered,' Tom smiled at Pascale, he knew E heightened the emotions but she was fucking beautiful and kind and intelligent.

Pascale leant forward and spoke to Tom in surprise, 'Lassie's studying to be a doctor?'

Tom took Pascale's face in his hands and kissed her forehead. 'No silly billy, it's just a stupid English saying!' They both laughed at the thought of Lassie being any kind of doctor and focused on ordering some milkshakes.

Post Ecstasy, they kept drifting off to little private areas of their brain, trying to reform links and memories that would allow them to function as a human being again shortly. Tom sat and looked at the other customers in the cafe. He thought many of them had been at the rave. His gaze landed on one individual in particular. Fuck. Tom slowly kicked Lassie under the table, and nodded behind him. Lassie didn't seem to grasp the attempt at covert communication and just gave him a double Roger Moore with his eyebrows.

'What?' He mouthed silently.

Again, Tom motioned for Lassie to look behind him and this time he realised Tom's intention and the colour began to drain from his face.

'Relax, Lass, relax. It's not who you think it is. It's that silly bollocks Aky from Tollesbury, we just can't seem to shake him at all!'

Lassie looked around, with some relief, and laughed. It was indeed their battered friend from Essex and before Tom could say anything Lassie had called him over and was standing, arms open, waiting for a post rave hug. Tom then received one, but not before Abi and Pascale had the pleasure of a sweaty man embrace from someone they had only just met. They all sat down, both girls wafting their tops to get some air circulating around them. Introductions were made and as expected, the girls were told what top blokes Tom and Lassie were and the boys were told how beautiful the girls were.

'So, beautiful people, how's it going? I'm fucking slaughtered. Proper mangled.' Aky helped himself to the closest milkshake, which was Tom's luckily, as he wasn't feeling it. 'Fucking mental milkshake, man, it's like it's cooling my fucking brain down, eh?'

Tom laughed, 'In that case you'd better finish it.' He pushed his milkshake towards Aky nodding for him to take it.

'Cheers, mucker! You're a fucking legend!'

It turned out that Aky had been at the rave too. His eyes were like piss-holes in the snow and he looked completely off his head still. Lassie enquired as to what he had got down his neck to end up in such a state?

'Fucking mental, lads, fucking mental. You won't believe it. Turns out one of the lad's knows a vet and we were downing these horse tranquilisers. Fucking mental. But even before that we did what they called a green goblin! They take your head off at the shoulders!

'What's in one then?' They all asked, almost in unison.

'Well, it's like a shot of vodka and methadone downed in one. It's a massive hit. Fucking wiped me out for an hour at least, catatonic I was.

A DRM confirmed to Lassie what Tom was thinking about Aky's night.

'Well, glad you enjoyed yourself Aky, a Thursday night in Amsterdam – vodka, methadone, horse tranquilisers and a vanilla milkshake to finish. You, my friend, are one of a kind.'

## 2.23 A Sausage Sandwich

Gary Sparks woke with a slightly sore head from last night's session. He had a feeling today was going to be tough and so far he'd been shambolic on this trip. He needed to up his game. He showered and dressed and went down to the dining room. George was sitting at a table that looked out over the hotel garden and another sunny day in Amsterdam. Gary liked this hotel, a lot.

George had finished his breakfast and was busily checking numbers from some sort of local directory. 'Come on, get fed and let's get going,' he said to Gary.

'OK, boss. What's the plan?'

George looked around the room quickly. 'Don't call me fucking boss, it makes us look like cheap gangsters!'

'Sorry, George.' *Make you fucking mind up for fucks sake* Gary thought as he tucked into his sausages.

George nodded. He wasn't really irritated with Gary; he was irritated with himself and the goings on yesterday. He felt like he'd lost his grip. The day had been a mess. There was no structure, no plan. Just a fucking mess from the moment they'd got off the boat to the moment with Thelma... He was determined today would be different. He was going to find this Tom Adams and his sidekick and sort out this mess. He'd already been on the phone and found out that the funerals for the Stones brothers and possibly Patrick would be on the coming Monday, pending the results of the post mortem. He wanted to be back in Liverpool by then and that meant winding this up ASAP.

He told Gary he'd had an idea as he had showered earlier. They were going to call as many hotels as possible and say they were looking for their brother, Tom Adams, who was in Amsterdam on a stag weekend because they urgently needed to get in contact with him due to a family crisis. George was guessing that as most hotels needed to see a passport the boys would be booked in under their own names. If they did strike gold, they would take the car, watch and follow them to see what they were up to. He was convinced it was a better plan than wandering about looking for them, especially as Gary didn't even know what they looked like.

Gary shifted uneasily in his seat. 'Can I make a suggestion, George?'

'What's that, Gary?'

'Well, why don't we do both? I don't know the faces, you do. So why don't I stay here and bash the phones while you go out and look for the boys?'

George had to admit it was a good idea, although he'd be covering a lot of ground alone. But it was only reconnaissance so he didn't really need the man power. He said he'd head out but would call Gary's room occasionally to gauge his progress and he'd check back physically every two hours and see how things were going.

Gary had barely finished his breakfast, but got up with George, ready to go. He could easily order room service later and watch a film while he rang the hotels. George gave him the local directory. He and the waiter had gone through it earlier and crossed off all the expensive hotels as he guessed two little scallies wouldn't be staying anywhere posh.

'Start with A and remember the script, Gaz, he's our brother, family and we need to contact him.'

'OK, George, I'm on it.'

Twenty minutes later George Meachen was outside the hotel, he turned to the left and was instantly very nearly knocked over by a woman on a bicycle, ringing her bell madly as she swerved past him.

George managed to avert the crash but looking down the road as the woman disappeared into the distance shouted after her, 'Fuck me, you nearly killed me, love!'

Judging by the grins on the faces of the people sitting outside the café opposite the hotel, her response had contained a few choice words for him in Dutch. George walked towards one of the men sitting at an outside table. Seeing his approach the man began to cower back into his seat, assuming he was about to get his coffee poured over his head, at best.

'Excuse me, Sir... would you know where a gentleman might be able to hire a bike, such as the one that just nearly fucking killed me?'

A very shaky hand, holding an almond croissant that was busily shedding almonds and sugar, pointed to a shop just down the street with a sign proclaiming 'Bike Hire – By the Hour or Day'.

'Thank you very fucking much. Enjoy your fucking breakfast.'

As soon as George headed down the street towards the hire shop a very flustered man left a very good tip and rushed away from where he had been enjoying a leisurely Friday morning breakfast before work.

Being nearly killed by a Dutch bicycle had given George an excellent idea – hire a bike. This would allow him to cover more ground and look more Dutch and less like a bounty hunter, which essentially he, or they, were. His driving license and a hefty deposit were all that was required and before long he was cruising along the Dutch canals on his very own Dutch bicycle, much like the thousands of other bikes that were buzzing around the capital.

George had tried his story out on the very helpful chap at the hire place who been able to provide a map of the city and circle the hotspots where young people hung out, like clubs and bars and so on. He decided to make his way to Rembrandtplein first. It was early, but as the saying goes, the early bird strangles the fucking cunt of a worm. He smiled to himself and pushed down on the pedals.

Back at the hotel Gary was sitting at the little desk in room. He had the window open and the radio on. He was actually enjoying himself and had already got through most of the hotels beginning with the letter A. He put down the phone, picked it up again and called room service. He ordered a sausage sandwich with brown sauce and an Amstel. He might as well start as he meant to go on he thought, this could be a long day.

## 2.21 Dream Sequences

They left Aky, with his methadone dream state life and drifted off into the morning air. People were starting to go about their daily routine, which, it seemed for a lot of people in Amsterdam, was to go home and sleep it off. Unless, that is you worked in a shop, bar, café or bank, and even if you did it seemed most started late.

'You coming back to our flat, boys?' Pascale asked. 'We can just chill out and relax, watch a film or something. I have some Valium.'

'You had me at Valium,' Lassie laughed and caught a friendly slap on the arse from Abi. They walked down the cobbled streets that curved around the river and headed toward Centraal Station. It was a nice walk. This time it was Tom who took Pascale's hand and squeezed it lightly as they strolled along the bank of the canal.

'I had a great night, Pascale. Thanks for taking us out. I've loved it so far and I guarantee Lassie is having the time of his life.' They turned to look back at Lassie and Abi, who again, were snogging like teenagers.

'Why don't you boys get your stuff from the hotel and stay with us? You can stay as long as you want.'

Tom stopped and gave her a hug. 'Thank you, it's a lovely offer. I'll speak to Lassie and see what he thinks.'

'I think I know what he'll say.' Pascale laughed, and carried on walking.

They climbed seven flights of stairs before Abi opened the door to a huge, spectacular loft apartment that gave amazing views of Amsterdam in two directions. Lassie stood looking out of the huge front window at the view across the city. He felt like he was soaring above the rooftops like a bird.

'Fuck me, I think I'm rushing again,' He said and lay down on the sofa by the window.

'It's amazing, girls,' Tom said, 'fucking amazing. What did you say your dad did again? And when can we get married?'

The girls laughed and offered to show Tom around, as Lassie still couldn't get off the sofa as he was having a 'moment'. The apartment was beautiful, securely in the 'Benelux style' that Tom had heard about on those fucking irritating house shows at home. With the tour complete they sat, as couples, on two large sofas, each of which had a view of the large TV.

'Shall we crash then and watch a film? We've got a whole bunch of tapes we can choose from, well three…' Pascale said.

Abi laughed, got up and disappeared downstairs. Tom had crawled the short distance to the TV stand and was looking at the selection of the three films available to them when Abi returned tossed a bottle to her sister.

Pascale read the label and sighed, 'Ahh, Valium.'

'And the *Grapes of Wrath*,' added Tom. 'I can't think of a better way to spend a Friday morning in Amsterdam.'

'Never seen it, lad.'

'It's Dad's, I think.'

Abi shrugged her shoulders.

Tom pressed play on the video recorder, took his place next to Pascale on the sofa, and thanked her as she passed him some blackcurrant and a Valium, necked it and smiled as she rested her head on his chest to watch the film.

Pascale squeezed Tom's leg, 'You gonna come and stay with us for a while? Come on, we could have some fun, go up to the beach at Scheveningen, or go to a theme park and ride rollercoasters!'

Tom had been thinking about this since the café that morning and was slowly coming round to the idea. Nothing would go wrong to put the girls in any danger. Even if they bumped into the Scousers they surely wouldn't hurt two innocent Dutch girls, especially one that was deaf. He winced at himself for playing the disability card but it was the truth he thought, or hoped.

'That sounds cool, apart from the rollercoasters, I don't really like heights.'

'I didn't even know Holland had beaches,' Lassie said.

'We have beautiful beaches, Lassie, they are very long, wide and sandy. With cool beach bars and music. You would love it.'

Lassie felt his eyes roll as the Valium made his eyelids heavy. 'I'm sold, people.'

'OK, let's wander over to the hotel to get our stuff early afternoon. Check out isn't until two, I asked for a late one when we arrived.'

Lassie had already fallen asleep on Abi. Tom could still feel the Ecstasy in his blood, his heart still pumping over the odds. Though that could easily have been the effect of cuddling up with Pascale. It wasn't long before the Valium got the better of them both though and they were also off into the world of spectacular Ecstasy and Valium dream sequences.

## 2.22 Stay Safe, Son

The big red digital display read 08.30. The ceiling hadn't changed since the last time he had looked at it. He felt helpless. His body was weak and at its core was a thick rope of guilt that ran through him like a second spine. In fact, like it was his only spine. A backbone of guilt and regret that he had been party to the downfall, the suffering, and the fucking torture of all the people he loved.

They heard the screaming from the nurse's station and a nurse rushed into the ward to find Razor screaming and shouting.

'What's the matter, Raymond?'

'Sorry, flashback.' He was being careful to not let them know his final intentions. Another nurse approached with a sedative and a cup of water.

'Take this Raymond, it will relax you. It's only mild and won't make you drowsy.' The nurse's tone was soothing and kind. He had determinedly refused to take any painkillers or sedatives that made him feel off his head. He wanted to be able to read and to understand the news. Some of the drugs he had been given would have been superb with some rum and coke and a banging baseline but if you wanted to be able to read and recall information ten minutes they were a disaster.

'I want to move about, please,' he said the Nurse. 'Can I have a wheelchair?'

He still couldn't walk but if he was lifted into a wheelchair he could move about. He'd enjoyed getting out of bed and the staff had seen that it had noticeably lightened his mood. He had even made it to the day room and read a magazine by the window. This was seen as positive for a man who had a ninety-five percent chance of losing at least one of his legs, if not both, from the knee down.

'I'll ask the ward Sister, but I don't see why not.'

Razor lay back down on his bed, his half-eaten breakfast cast aside. He wasn't hungry. He felt like a spy in a film, trapped by his injuries. Had he been able to walk he would have been out of here days ago. He either had to get better, go home and face the consequences, or take more drastic action. He was at a crossroads. Losing one of his legs or both, would just add to the bleakness of his future. Scratching around for charity fucks or even spending his disability allowance on a cheap fat brass to get his rocks off. The future was bleak – he didn't need anyone to tell him that. Perhaps he could tell the girls he been in the Gulf War and get a sympathy shag, but only if he was living on fucking Shetland. Anywhere else and he was sure he'd be known as the scally that robbed his own and ended up the spam in a car sandwich. Fucking loser.

He wondered what was happening at home and what the fuck had happened to Tom in Harwich? That poor cunt was up against it now and he'd need to seriously get the fuck away from George Meachen and his crew, or he'd end up in the boot of a car... all he'd done was try to help them, and now he was caught up in all this. And what about his Mum and Dad? All he wanted to do was see them and make sure they were all right, why the fuck would someone do that to a person? A cunt... He thought deeply about this question but could only come up with one answer. Perhaps if someone had stolen 40K from them?

This, it seemed was all his and Paddy's fault. He pulled his pillow up over his face and began to cry, not for the first time this week. Razor could sense his mind was melting, but he told himself to stay calm, if he got sectioned that would be it. Strapped down and over medicated. Useless to everyone and that was unforgivable. He had to do something.

He pulled the pillow away from his eyes as he heard his name being softly called. In front of him was a nurse, with a metal trolley with a big yellow payphone mounted on it. She held the receiver out towards him, with the curly yellow lead all twisted from over-use by stressed out patients and spoke again, 'Raymond, you have a phone call. I think it's your Dad.'

Raymond sat upright in shock. His Dad? Fuck. His Dad. He quickly tried to get himself together, rubbing his face and pushing the pillows back to get himself upright. His legs still hurt and he flinched as the nurse attempted to help him.

'Sorry,' he said, acknowledging that she was only trying to help, and once ready held his hand out to take the receiver from her.

'Hello? Dad? Is that you?'

'Hi, Son, it's me. How are you?'

Raymond bypassed the question, 'I love you Dad, and I'm so sorry for everything that's happened to you and Mum.' He began to sob uncontrollably. 'I'm so, so sorry. I hope you can forgive me.'

'Listen, Son, pull yourself together. Mum and me are OK. Don't say anything that will get you into trouble. You need to get yourself better and get home. We can sort all this out when you're back. You hear me Raymond?'

'OK.' He couldn't believe his Dad was being so composed. He was such a lovely, gentle man. 'OK, Dad.'

'The police have been round to see your Mother and I, that's how we knew where you were. But they haven't told us much.'

'Dad, have you heard anything about Paddy? The police said...'

The other end of the receiver went quiet for a few seconds before Razor's Dad spoke again, 'There was a car crash, the other day, Son, late evening. A car left the road just off the M62 and hit a concrete post on the underpass. Three people were pronounced dead at the scene, there aren't too many details being released but I've been told it was the Stones brothers.'

'Fucking good job,' Raymond interrupted.

'Hang on, Son, there's more. They haven't said who the other person in the car was, but rumour is that it was Patrick. I'm sorry, Son, it all adds up. You've got to get well and get home. Goodness knows what George is doing at the moment and who to, just stay safe, son, and come home soon.'

With that, Raymond gave the receiver back to the nurse, grabbed the pillow again and began sobbing into it. He had never felt so completely alone in his entire life.

## 2.23 Amsterdamage

George had decided, after looking at the map of the city to cycle backwards and forwards across the fan shape that grew out of the central station. That way it would be easy to pop in and see how Gary Sparks was getting on. He was enjoying himself and had stopped at a small café for a coffee and a toasted cheese sandwich. He sat, waiting for his coffee to cool down to a temperature where he would be more inclined to drink it, scanning the people on the street. He imagined he was too early for Adams and his mate, unless of course they were on their way home from a night out, like a lot of the other people on the streets seemed to be. He had even heard two men walking past saying that they'd forgotten where their hotel was. How the fuck could you get so wasted, he thought? Then he remembered where he was. He leant back into his chair, took a bite of his sandwich and a small sip of is coffee and told himself the answer again, this time out loud. 'Amsterdamage.'

Some people were on their way to work: the beggars and homeless were setting up shop for the day. Across the road he had seen a drug deal happening as a young mum with a child in a seat behind her cycled past. It really was a huge social experiment in tolerance, George thought to himself. One that he, unfortunately, couldn't be a part of. Tolerance in his game led to weakness and weakness led to failure.

He finished his coffee and climbed aboard his iron horse. He crossed over a small bridge scanning the crowds as he went. Backwards and forwards he cycled, at a steady but slow pace, allowing him time to check faces in the street and outside bars. He was hoping for a breakthrough. If one didn't come this wild goose chase would become a waste of money, time and effort. He had thought about travelling back to Essex and attempting to extort the monies owed from family members, but Essex wasn't Liverpool and he was pretty sure turning up and demanding money from people who truly had no idea what he was on about would bring the whole of the Essex constabulary down on him and he had no help, or underworld jurisdiction there. He was also worried that this was becoming some kind of vendetta or a matter of pride. It irritated him that the little shit had the balls to fuck off abroad and he was interested in why he had. He was pretty convinced that Tom

Adams was actually trying to raise the missing 6K. In which case he had definitely understood the gravity of the situation. Seeing the state of Razor Wilkins must have made the lad shit himself. George actually quite admired the little tosser, though that wouldn't save him from his fate. Even if he was enjoying this little holiday, people were dead because of this situation, and he couldn't rule out there being a few more bodies before it was over.

He drifted around a bit more then popped back to the hotel. The morning was ebbing away and it seemed like no real progress was being made. Gary was having some small success with the hotels in that they were offering the information under emotional pleading but no one under the name of Adams had booked into any he had checked with so far. He stopped for a quick drink, lager this time as it was now after eleven and then took to his bike again, this time he found himself at Leidsplein, another little area of debauchery he thought as he saw the clubs and bars dotted around the streets in front of him. This seemed promising. He parked his bike without locking it as no one else seemed to bother either and took a seat at an outside café called Eat me inside-out. He was presently greeted by a waitress and ordered a BLT and an Amstel. He settled in and started to scan the crowd. There were many more people out now and the outside bars were beginning to fill up with Hen and Stag parties, twenty-first birthday parties and even the odd fortieth. He even saw a balloon with 'sixty and still fucking' on it! He crossed his fingers and thought *I bloody hope so* and smiled.

Back at the hotel Gary Sparks, a grown man of forty-one was walking around punching the air. 'Yes,' he said, 'Yes. Fucking Yes!' After what had felt like a lifetime of having the same conversation, a young receptionist at the City Hotel, Rembrandtplein had confirmed that a Mr. Adams and one companion had booked in Thursday morning for two nights, with the option of two more. He grabbed his city map and looked up Rembrandtplein. It wasn't too far at all, a ten-minute walk, if that. George would be over the fucking moon and he would be golden-balls for at least a couple of days, he may even forget the debacle on the boat on the way over after this! Gary grabbed the phone, ordered a large bottle of Heineken and opened the windows. The beer arrived and Gary Sparks sat, feet out in the Amsterdam morning, waiting for George to get back.

By one, George and Gary were sitting in the Vauxhall Astra watching the entrance to the hotel. Gary had been applauded, the bike had been returned. They had both showered again and had clean clothes on, courtesy of the hotels rapid laundry service. In the car, they had snacks, drinks, papers and magazines. George was determined not to let this one get away.

'Gary,' George said, nodding at the shop across the road from them, 'go and buy a camera. Not an expensive one, just a little click and go. It might come in handy.'

## 2.24 Post E

Tom and Pascale woke up in each other's arms. He couldn't help but think, after all the grief, that something truly good had come out of the scariest situation he had ever been in. He looked at Pascale. Was it the post E feeling or was he in love? It had to be the E he mused. Must be. He kicked Lassie's leg, but it took another dig to the shins before he came round from what had been a spacey and sweaty dream.

'Fucking weird, Tom, I dreamt I was kissing this big fat bird and as I was kissing her, her lips went from covering my mouth to the bottom of my chin and top of my nose, then basically my head was in her mouth and then she swallowed me and I was inside her stomach and it was all red, but I could breathe and could even see out of her belly button. No one could hear me but I could hear them, and then you kicked me so I have no idea how it would have ended.' Lassie looked slightly put out that he had been robbed of the end of his dream.

Tom laughed, 'Fuck off, Lass, I can tell you how it ended – with you ended up being shat out an hour later, covered in shit and all thin and tall from going through her sphincter!'

Their laughter woke Abi, who laughed along after the whole dream had been explained to her.

They all showered and Pascale opened the windows, which allowed the glorious sunshine in and dispersed the stink of four sweaty post rave casualties. Tom stood and looked out of the window across the city. What kind of job could he do here he thought, tourism? Could he go to college here? Would it be in English? Could he teach English? Now that was an idea...

He felt a hand on his bum and a little pinch. 'So, Tom, where about is your hotel again? We should start out soon, it's a lovely day. When we've got your bags we could have a drink somewhere nice.'

The tram was almost silent, just sounding the odd bell to remind pedestrians of their presence as they approached. It was barely a five minutes journey to Rembrandtplein.

'Wow, cool. Look at that!' Since they had checked into their hotel the day before a fun fair had been assembled in the middle of the square. Lassie was over the moon. 'We've got to spend an hour or so here, Tom, I wanna win Abi a stuffed toy!'

'Course, we can do that.' Lassie was such a top bloke, Tom thought. He dragged him all over the place and the sight of a funfair he was away with the fairies again.

'Let's sort out the bags first, it's nearly one and we had to be out by two at the latest.'

Hand in hand, both couples made their way over the road, past a big nightclub, past the pub and around the corner to the entrance to the hotel.

Chapter 46

'Click'.

## 2.26 Let's get out of here

They waved at the receptionist.

Tom said, 'Do you two want to wait down here? It won't take us long to get our stuff together.'

OK, no problems.' She said and the girls took a seat in reception.

The boys made their way to the stairs, ignoring the lift, which was in use.

When they were in the room, Tom said to Lassie, 'Let's get out of here ASAP. And don't say anything to the girls about the money, OK?

'I'm in love though, Tom, can't we just stay and share it with the girls?'

Tom rolled his eyes, he fucking wished. 'Get out of the clouds, Lass, this needs sorting out. And when it is, maybe we can come back?'

Both boys got changed into clean clothes and Tom, borrowing Lassie's idea, stashed half of the guilders inside some socks, and then inside a plastic bag of dirty washing. He left Lassie about a grand to stash in his bag.

'You OK with this Lass? One more night at the girls, back on the Saturday day boat to settle up with those psychos.'

'You're about a grand short though, Tom, what are you going to do?'

'Hope they'll suffer it for a bit…? I might be able to raise a bit of cash when we get back. We'll see. I've got to try though mate. Then that's fucking me. I'm never going to talk to a stranger in a bar ever again.'

Tom was counting out the cash to pay for their room when the receptionist said, 'Mr. Adams, in sympathy for your problems I have waived the cancellation fee. You had taken the room for two nights, but we understand that in the circumstances you have to leave early. I hope everything is OK when you return home.'

Puzzled, and immediately apprehensive Tom asked what she meant.

'Your brother rang this morning, he explained that there had been trouble at home and he was trying to get in touch.'

Feeling faint, nauseous and mildly rushing from the E again Tom grabbed the counter. 'Yes, of course, thank you. A terrible mess.'

'Good luck.'

Tom looked in the reflection in the mirror behind the reception; luckily the girls had wandered out of earshot and were standing by the door, discussing restaurants for lunch. He turned to Lassie. 'They know where we are staying, Lass. They've rung and been told I am staying here. We need to get the fuck out of here, now. Keep your head together though and follow my lead.'

With this, Tom and Lassie slung their bags over their shoulders and walked over to Pascale and Abi.

'All done, come on, let's get out of here!'

Chapter 48

'Click, click, click'.

## 2.28 The Tram

'OK, ladies, lunch?' Tom stood, looking over their shoulders, scanning the streets, he could feel his legs shaking in his jeans and he was glad his bag gave one of his arms something to concentrate on, he imagined Lassie felt the same.

'We were thinking the Mexican, just along the road there, and then the fair for Lassie?' Pascale said as they started giggling.

This didn't work for them Tom thought. He needed another plan.

'Lass, err, Mexican?' The double Roger Moore Tom was sporting at this moment would have won the raised eyebrow world championships, if such a thing existed.

'Err, to tell the truth, I'd rather get back on the tram and go somewhere we haven't seen, what do you lot think? I'm really not bothered about the fair.'

The girls seemed surprised by the sudden change of heart but had a quick sign conversation and suggested a tram home to drop of their bags, and then a walk up to the park.

'Sounds cool. Let's go.' Tom set off towards the tram at a brisk pace and broke into a jog when he saw the tram arriving. 'Come on, let's not miss it!'

When they had caught the tram, the girls laughed at them for running, explaining that there were trams every ten to fifteen minutes and there was no need to rush. But Tom and Lassie were just glad the tram was moving, taking them away from the hotel.

## 2.29 It's an Automatic

'Click'.

'Got it, Gary. Slowly now, stay back, easy now...' The Astra pulled away and followed the tram. George was beside himself with joy. The camera was a masterstroke, and as for those poor lemons, bringing those beautiful little lambs to the slaughter was the icing on his fucking cake. He would have grabbed the cunts as soon as they had walked out but when he saw they were with some girls he had started to formulate an even better plan. He just needed to find out where they were going next. Letting them run was definitely a gamble, but one he was sure would pay off.

'Do not fucking lose them, Gary. Do not, under any circumstances lose these two thieving little fucking cunts. Each time the tram stopped Gary Sparks pulled up a way back. Very conscious of the British plates on the Astra, as was George who was now upset they not hired bikes again or at least a Dutch car.

'Fuck it, Gary, if these plates blow our cover I'm gonna fucking burn it. Cunts. A bike would have been perfect, those trams are slow and stop every thirty fucking seconds!'

Gary reassured George as the tram slowly pulled away and the car followed.

'Stop, stop, it's stopping again!'

Shut the fuck up, cunt, Gary thought as George jumped around in the passenger seat. He'd already had three large Heinekens and didn't want any undue attention. George should've driven actually, but who was he to tell this psycho maniac what to do?

'There they fucking are Gary, they're getting off the tram. There!' George had them in his sights now. He watched them get off the tram, the boys looking about. 'They haven't got a clue we're on to them.' George was in charge again. For the last couple of days he had felt like a spare wheel running about looking for them, now though, he was back in the game.

'Should we ditch the car, George?' Gary asked.

'I'll stay with the car, Gary, you're going to follow them. Quick, out of the car. They're waiting to cross the road. I'll park it over by the hotel and wait for you. George pointed to a Golden Tulip hotel twenty metres up the road from the tram stop. 'Don't lose them. Go, now!'

Gary grabbed his jacket, jumped out of the car and set off behind the group as they crossed the road. He followed them for about half a mile before they crossed again and walked up towards the big train station. They looked happy he thought as he sauntered along, a hundred metres or so back. He kind of felt sorry for them. George was an evil bastard and he now had something he could really get his teeth into. It was his favorite game: terrorising people by threatening their family or friends who had nothing to do with the situation. Just like these two young girls. He stopped as he saw them go up some stairs into a residential building. He waited and after about five minutes saw a window open on the top floor and one of the girls and one of the boys looking out pointing at something. He knew what he had to do. 'Click, click, click' went the shutter of the camera. He then stood directly opposite the building and took some shots of the front of the block. Jesus, part of him just wanted to throw the camera in the canal and fuck off somewhere and get away from this situation. He was done snapping, he popped the camera back into his jacket and walked back towards where George was waiting in the car.

George had sat patiently, looking at the city map, a traffic warden had asked him to move on but he had explained they had broken down and his friend, a mechanic would be back later. He saw Gary and wound down the window. 'Well?'

'Beautiful,' George purred when Gary had told him what he'd seen. 'Couldn't have worked out better. Now have a pawn, Gary, a bargaining chip. Leverage, Gary, beautiful, golden leverage. In fact, I'd go as far to say we're on our way home.'

Gary handed over the camera.

'Lovely Gary. Let's just hope you had the fucking shutter open, eh?' George joked. 'You did though, right?'

'It's an automatic, George. Can't really fail.'

'Anyway,' George said, ignoring Gary, 'this is what we do next.'

George explained that Gary was going to walk back to the apartment block, watch it and follow them if they went out. In the meantime, George would go and get the pictures developed and take the car back to the hotel. Once they were settled somewhere like a bar or a restaurant Gary was to call George at the hotel and he would take it from there.

'Fine with me, George.' Gary got out of the car and walked back the way he had come. At least they were going home soon, though he still fancied getting a brass before he left. That bloke's wife had given him the taste and he needed to feed that pony. He walked back to the apartment and found a café across the street, ordered a large Heineken and settled in.

## 2.30 The Most Beautiful Lips

Pascale took Tom's hand and led him straight out onto the tiny balcony.

'Look how lovely it all looks from here!' They looked out across Amsterdam, Pascale pointing out the different landmarks.

'It is beautiful, Pascale.' Tom felt relaxed. No one could get at them up here. It was a place of safety. He put his arm around her.

'So, what was going on at the hotel? Is someone looking for you? Are you in trouble? You were acting so weird. Sorry, too many questions.'

Tom shook his head. 'No, not too many, and they all deserve an answer. It's just a bit of a mess,' he said with unintended understatement.

'Tell me, Tom. It will be OK. Let's go back inside, sit down with a drink and talk it through.'

They found Abi teaching Lassie some sign language on the sofa. Pascale went to get them all beers from the well-stocked fridge.

'Lass, Pascale noticed how odd we were when we left the hotel, so I've decided to tell her what's going on. They deserve to know, don't you think?'

Lassie agreed with a single Roger Moore, which Tom took to mean to maybe not tell them absolutely everything. But he wasn't sure how to leave bits out, or even which bits.

'So,' Tom said, ready to start. Lassie sat across from him looking very pensive indeed.

'Slowly,' Pascale said, 'for Abi.'

Tom and Lassie both looked at the girls, waiting for them to say something. Abi began to sign for Pascale and both watched as Pascale concentrated intently, nodding along in agreement as the speed of her signing increased. She finished with the universal hands in the air 'what the fuck do you do?' motion that everybody understood and the boys then looked to Pascale.

'You poor boys. You're fucked,' she said sadly. 'It seems to us that none of this is really any of your fault. Meeting people, being kind, taking them shopping, having a good time, and then you end up with all this mess.'

Tom and Lassie nodded in agreement and said in unison, 'Fucking scary!'

'So, you think it was them who had found you at the hotel?'

'Yes. No one else knows we're here, apart from you two,' Tom explained.

Abi signed and Pascale said, 'But you have their money now, so it's not that much of a problem, no?'

Tom made a murmuring sound, he hadn't told the girls about Razor being crushed by the car or Lassie being punched and his firm belief that he was going to get a hiding at the very least... 'Not all of it. Some of it is back in England. The plan was to see if this worked and then go back and try to sort it out.' He smiled and then carried on, 'Then we met you two and just wanted to spend time with you.'

Abi signed again for them and Pascale spoke. 'She wants to know if have you put us in danger?'

Tom and Lassie looked at each other.

Tom answered. 'Honestly, I'm pretty sure not. If they'd seen us they would have grabbed us and we've been in a warehouse raving and then sleeping. You two are fine.' Tom paused.

'Go on,' Pascale said to him. 'Is there more?'

'Of course not, Pascale, no. It's just that I really like you, we really like you,' he said nodding at Lassie. 'And I think we need to get this sorted sooner than later. So, time spent here with you is time for them to get angrier, even if, as you say it's not our fault, and if we do bump into them here, which I'm pretty sure we won't, I wouldn't, or we wouldn't want to drag you into it, would we Lass?'

'Fuck no!' Lassie said, adamantly, grabbing hold of Abi and giving her a kiss on the cheek. 'That would kill me.'

Pascale still looked worried, Tom gave her a hug. He fancied her so much but at this point he didn't feel like he had a sexual atom in his body. He was pretty sure they all felt the same, except maybe Abi who seemed to be up for it 24/7. He wondered again what had happened to Paddy and Razor.

'Pascale, listen... don't worry. We don't want you two involved.' Tom gave her a kiss on the lips. She had the most beautiful lips, he thought.

## 2.31 Both Vials Empty

Razor sat in his wheelchair. His food, largely ignored, remained on his lap on a scratched beige plastic tray. Since he had spoken to his dad he hadn't really been able to function. It seemed that what had begun as a stupid idea had transformed into something terrible, and he felt he was largely to blame. He could have told Paddy it was a crazy idea and he had, the voice inside his head answered. He could have refused to be part of it then, maybe? He should have done something to prevent this fucking mess. He sat up and watched as the nurse pushed the medicine trolley up the ward. She stopped at the bed next to him.

'Come on now,' the nurse said calmly as she pulled the man's pyjama top up. 'You do this yourself all the time, seeing your belly is no great hardship and you'll have your insulin then.'

He hadn't really spoken to anyone on the ward but understood the bloke next to him had diabetes and had to inject Insulin every day. He knew about diabetes because he'd had a teacher who was diabetic. He would pop into the nurse's room to inject himself and always had a little bloodstain afterwards. He'd always had a good stash of Twix or Mars bars too, which would sometimes become rewards if they had done any good work. He was a nice teacher, and he was definitely in the minority in that. It must be tough having to do that every day he thought.

The nurse had finished in seconds, and without any thanks, cleaned him up as other staff began clearing away the dinner things. He looked down the bed at the metal pins and plaster that decorated his leg. All he needed was lights he thought and he'd be like a twisted Christmas tree. He wondered how he'd end up. What about the money? Would their debt be transferred to him? Or worse still, his parents? What would be become? Wheelchair bound? Smack head? Drugs Mule? After all who would stop a cripple? He couldn't stand the thought of his parents being dragged into this mess. That was even worse than being crippled; at least it was his actions that had got him in this position. He sat as he contemplated the thought that had been creeping around in the dark recesses of his mind all day. He began to cry again. He felt a hand on his shoulder.

'Is it pain your legs again, Raymond? Hang on and I'll get you some painkillers.'

The nurse came back with two yellow and green capsules in a meds pot and a glass of water. He wasn't in physical pain but any respite would do he thought and swallowed them quickly.

She used the hoist to lift him out of the wheelchair and back into bed, fluffed his pillows, adjusted the back rest and then retreated off the ward. He lay back and was soon drifting about in a mash-up of consciousness. He hit the red button and soon received the items he has asked for. He had decided to write some letters and the nurse had brought him down some stationery and a pen. He wanted to say sorry to his Dad and he wanted to say something to Paddy that could go into his grave with him. He felt he wanted to say goodbye, and he had been robbed of the chance. This made him feel sad and so he wrote to Paddy first. This was tough, especially as he wasn't sure who would read it, if anyone. As he finished he hoped it would go straight into the grave and wrote these instructions on the envelope. He felt so sad, he had truly lost a great friend and to lose him like that made him angry. It didn't matter though, there was nothing he could do about it and it wouldn't matter soon at all. He then picked up the pen and began, his next letter. 'Dear Mum and Dad...'

He sobbed quietly to himself throughout. This was much tougher than he had anticipated. He was full of apology. For what he had embroiled them in and for the action he was about to undertake. He tried to explain that he felt there was no other way out and signed off with a single kiss. Any more may suggest he was unsure about what he was planning. He sealed that letter too and addressed it, like the other one to Liverpool. He put the pen, pad and spare envelope to one side. He hoped that he hadn't made any mistakes. He had always been shite at English and his spelling was awful.

He now had to put his plan into action. He'd watched the rounds for the last two days trying to work out who had what medication and what it did. From blood pressure pills to gastro-resistant pills, to painkillers and anti-viral, he just wasn't sure what they would do to him or whether they'd have the desired effect. He did though, have a fair idea that if he could get his hands on enough of next-door's insulin he could achieve his goal relatively easily. The problem was how to get it. The little glass bottles of insulin sat in a buff cardboard tray on the drugs trolley with the syringes. Razor thought his best opportunity had to be the last call for the night – sleepers, painkillers and insulin after a drink and a biscuit.

He woke from a light sleep and rubbed his forehead. He was sweating. He lay back and tried not to think about it. He'd had enough, of that he was sure. It should have been him with Paddy in that car, or them together in Morocco or somewhere away scot-free. Not here, stuck in hospital with nothing to look forward to except prosthetic limbs, or worse in the very near future. It felt stuffy, and as his bed was by the window he decided to try and open it himself, as the guy across the ward had done. He was able to do it relatively easily and he relaxed as the warm breeze entered the room, the smell of outside being a refreshing change from the smell of the hospital ward.

The evening began to close in and he began to think that he may not get the chance to carry out his plan while still in the hospital. Would he still do it? Would things be different outside? Would his injuries and the death of Paddy be enough to tip the scales of justice in his favour? His thoughts were playing games with him, games he didn't want to play. Another wave of emotion hit him as his mind raced and he realised he wanted revenge. They had nearly killed him with that car! He wanted them dead now. The cunts. He also wanted revenge for his parents, for Paddy, and for the boys, who would no doubt be in all sorts of trouble at the moment. He struggled for ideas. He hated them all and wanted to hurt them, but how? Then, a broad smile broke out across his face as he remembered the A Team from when he was a kid. Hannibal always had a plan...

A while later he heard the wheels of the trolley approaching, he looked up at the clock. He must have drifted off, as it read 22.00. And the nurse was on the ward, attending to the troops. He watched as she made her way towards his end of the ward. The trolley, and his quarry, were in sight. He imagined it was going to speak, with its flaps on the side making it look like a metal mickey, but with special fizz bombs. He smiled to

202

himself, was he happy? How could he be planning his own death if he was making fucking jokes? There, he thought, at least he'd looked at the words in his mind. His own death.

The nurse arrived at next-door's bedside with a smile and a polished bedside manner.

Razor listened as the nurse carried on talking about the need to change his Insulin pump, this didn't mean much to him as he lay looking at the trolley, wondering how he could get to it. She started to do something he couldn't see but was immediately distracted by the sound of the alarm going off. A nurse shouted cardiac arrest the one attending to next-door's insulin pump grabbed her keys and closed the trolley before running to assist in the emergency.

Razor had winced at the professionalism – even as she panicked she had closed the door of the trolley. He then realised that she had missed one flap through which he could see insulin vials and a syringe.

'Now or never,' he told himself and leant over to grab the trolley, it was too far away. He wanted to scream and realised he didn't have long. He looked around and saw the pole he had used to open the window; he grabbed it and swung it around so the hook was facing the trolley. He hooked the leg of the trolley and pulled it towards him. Should he take it all, or just some? His mind raced as he considered his position. All of it may make her think she had put it away; some of it may raise suspicions? He decided to take just some and a syringe, hoping that she wouldn't notice. He hid them in his bedside cabinet and pushed the trolley back into position before closing the window and putting the window pole away. The emergency over, the nurse returned. She was now so behind with her rounds that she opened the trolley and carried on without a second glance.

Razor watched her finish and walk back out of the ward. The lights went out and he turned on his night-light. He lay on the bed, thinking. This was not the time to think, he had to be decisive. He really didn't see that he had much to hang on for. This would seem to be the best for everyone involved. He was sad and would miss his mum and dad, but the shame he felt about involving them and the hatred he felt for the people that had hurt them and his best mate gave him no real option. He said a prayer for only the third time in his adult life, raised the glass vial and pulled the syringe down, taking in the entire contents. He carried out this exercise twice more, each time injecting into his cannula. He had watched with morbid curiosity as the nurses had done this to him on numerous occasions with antibiotics for his leg wounds. With all three vials empty, he relaxed back onto his pillow, his arms crossed, holding on to three letters, hand-written on beautiful cream Conqueror stationery that had been given to him so kindly by the same nurse that he had now taken advantage of to end his life, and probably her career.

## 2.32 Another Stakeout

Gary had read his magazine, drunk his lager and eaten his carrot cake. It looked to everyone there like he had been stood up. What he was waiting for hadn't arrived and the waiter was giving him a look that said 'Laugh it off mate, tomorrow's another day.' He'd paid his bill a while back and realised he'd passed his sell by date here. He needed to keep the house in his sights though and a slip up now would be catastrophic. In fact, he'd probably join them on the run! Much to the waiter's relief, he was sure, he left the café and scuttled across the road to a small bar.

He went through a set of small double doors into a dark, wood covered space with only one other customer. 'A large Amstel, please.' Gary took in a window seat and hoped the barman would bring over his drink. He did and Gary gave him a note and waved away the change to a deep nod of appreciation. The stakeout recommenced, albeit from a different and more pleasurable location.

## 2.33 The Summer Evening

They all agreed with Tom's suggestion that Tom and Lassie would stay with the girls that night and take the night boat to

Harwich on Saturday. When they'd sorted out the mess they were in they'd return for a proper holiday with the girls, and head to the beach. They all toasted the plan with the remnants of a bottle of wine. 'To end of a nightmare and a beautiful summer!'

'Now for tonight?' Pascale enquired, 'What would you both like to do?'

Lassie dived in, 'I'd like to just have a nice meal. I really don't want to be hungover tomorrow.'

'Totally agree. Let's just have a nice relaxed evening and eat some good food.'

While the girls got ready to go out, Tom said to Lassie, 'It'll be over soon, mate, don't worry.' Tom could feel his own worry as he muttered the words to Lassie. Not only had he dragged Lassie into this fucking mess he was now staying in a flat with two utterly innocent, lovely Dutch girls. He fucking hated himself but couldn't show it. If he did Lassie would smell it and then panic.

'They know we're here, Tom. They know we're here somewhere.'

'Yes, but they don't know we know they know, Lass, do they?' He thought about this and it didn't seem to matter much either way. If they knew that they knew, they might think they would have fled, would that be better? If they didn't know that Lass and he knew that may just take their time and watch the hotel? He told himself to shut up.

Lassie looked equally confused. 'Jesus,' he said. 'Fucking deep.'

## 2.34 A New Pair of Jeans

Seeing the group leaving the building, Gary gulped down his lager and left the bar. What bad timing! He was bursting for a piss. He made sure he kept a good distance from the group but had them well in his sights.

He tried to forget about it as he trailed them but couldn't help but obsess about his increasingly swollen bladder. It felt like he was carrying a water balloon that was on the point of collapse. He followed, now bent over double and in growing pain.

As he waddled along, Quasimodo style, he was approached and asked if he was OK, he beat the concern away, trying to keep an eye on the group ahead.

'I'm OK. I'm OK,' he exclaimed, but then caught sight of his refection in a window. He had seen this before in Liverpool. People bent over from a bad hit, in agonizing pain looking for help or an ambulance. No wonder he'd been asked if he was alright! He struggled on and then waited as he watched the group go into a restaurant across the street. Staying on the opposite side of the road, he edged nearer until he could see inside. They were beginning to remove their jackets, a sure sign they were stopping, he heaved a sigh of relief.

Unfortunately, as he relaxed he felt his bladder join in and in a blind panic he struggled to release himself from his jeans in time to piss behind the bins next to him. But his body had taken over and as before he could get his fly undone he felt hot piss begin to flow with some power into the crotch of his jeans, seconds later he was free and was aiming at the bin and wall but the damage had been done.

He was still squeezing the remnants from himself when he saw two policemen turn the corner and make their way towards him... He finished with seconds to spare and nodded a hello.

'You do know it is an offence to urinate in the street in the Netherlands, don't you?'

The two officers now stood in front of him, staring. Both were showing off their pistols and pepper spray in the shiny evening light. One reached for his torch and spot-lit the offending area.

Gary Sparks nodded. If he got nicked now it would be a fucking disaster.

'I dropped something, I was just looking for it,' Gary said, apologetically while pointing at the area where there now was a large puddle of urine.

'Really?' The policeman smiled, turned to his colleague and pointed at Gary's puddle. 'What were you looking for? Your fucking nappy?'

Both policeman then spoke in Dutch before laughing at Gary Sparks.

Gary stood, telling himself to suck it up while wanting to batter both of them with their own torch. He needed to be able to move on and get to a phone. He had to suck this up.

He shrugged again. 'Sorry, I was desperate.'

The policemen laughed and one wagged his finger at Gary. They were clearly enjoying themselves.

'Go back to your hotel and change, Sir, it's a hot evening and you will soon be smelling like a, how do you say it? A tomcat?'

With this they both laughed and walked off down the street. Gary Sparks' first instinct was to throw both of the cunts into the canal but he managed to rein himself in, after all, they were right. He could smell his piss already.

He made a note of the restaurant and the street name, now all he had to do was call George at the hotel and wait. He wondered how George would take his request to bring him a spare pair of trousers. Not well he imagined but he hoped he would see he was in a desperate spot and needed to keep eyes on the situation. He walked up the road and soon found a phone box. He called the hotel and was put through to George's room.

'Gary?'

'Yes, George, got the little fuckers cosied up in a restaurant with the two girls we saw them with earlier, I'm across the road.'

'Well done, Gaz, great fucking work. Let me grab a pen. OK, name of restaurant and street name.'

Gary told him where he was and asked George to bring him his shell suit bottoms, which he also had to explain. Luckily, this brought laughter from George.

'You dirty bastard. That's fucking disgusting! But, it does show true commitment to the cause. See you shortly.'

Gary put the receiver down and shuffled back to his vantage point and the humid summer air began to cook his jeans.

## 2.35 Beirut Delight

'What are you having then, Tom?' Pascale asked, touching his hand.

He looked up to see the friendly face of the waiter. 'Hi, may I have a beer? Is Almaza a Lebanese beer?'

The waiter nodded. 'It is, Sir, and very good if I may say so.'

'OK, one of those, the shish taouk and a fattoush salad, please, oh and a hummus snawbar. Thank you.'

Soon, they had all ordered and bread, breadsticks and a selection of dips were on their table along with four Almazas. They each raised a glass and toasted a lovely evening. The food brought a thumbs up from Abi and everyone agreed. Lassie looked at Tom and smiled.

'Things will work out, squire, they always do!'

'I hope so, Lassie, I truly hope so.' Privately Tom was worried. The Scousers had caught a whiff of them at the hotel. Surely they wouldn't be giving up that easily?

## 2.36 Have A Look

The porter had been happy to open Gary's room for George when he had heard about the need for it. Carrying the shell suit trousers and a brown A5 envelope he went down to the hotel foyer and asked the doorman to get him a cab. He sat in the back seat, trying to remain calm. He was feeling very excited, in a very dark way.

The voice of the cab driver brought George out of his twisted meditation. He pointed across at the Beirut Delight and said, 'Is that it?'

'Yes, that's it, my friend.' George peered out of the window, looking for Gary, but it was getting dark now and he assumed that as he'd pissed himself he would be in the shadows somewhere. The cab driver pulled up but George waved him on past the restaurant and stopped him at the next corner. He didn't want to get out in view of the restaurant.

George walked back and stood under a streetlight, allowing his considerable frame to be seen. Within seconds Gary appeared and George threw him the bag.

'There you go pissy knickers. Get them on sharpish.'

'Thanks George, give me two minutes.' Gary retreated to a little refuge he had found behind a line of parked vans and changed into the dry trousers.

Relieved, he returned to where George was waiting for him. 'Thanks, George. Fucking lifesaver. Couldn't help it though, they left the flat just as I was going to go for a piss...'

George raised his hand for to shut Gary up and said, 'Well, now you're decent, you're going in there for a meal. They don't know who you are so they won't notice you. You wait until one of the lads goes to the toilet. Then you follow him and give them this envelope. The most important thing tonight is that they get the envelope. Once you've done that you leave the restaurant and meet me. We'll take it from there. Is the restaurant busy? It looked it as I drove past.'

'Yup, people in and out all the time I've been here.'

'Then go and do some damage, Mr. Sparks.'

Gary Sparks nodded. Just one question, George. What's in the envelope?' Gary had his suspicions but wanted them confirmed.

George smiled and handed the envelope to Gary. 'Have a look' he said with a dark grin.

As Gary had expected the envelope contained the pictures he had taken. They were just snaps of young people having fun, two lads who were out of their depth and about to pay for it.

'Now, Gary, make sure they get them, eh?'

## 2.37 Brief Encounter

Lassie was enjoying himself and felt relaxed. He looked across at Tom and said, 'This place is superb, I love Lebanese food. let's open a Lebanese place back home, it'd be rammed mate!'

Tom smiled at his enthusiasm but he really couldn't imagine the racist pricks back in Essex going anywhere near a Lebanese restaurant, the only thing they knew of Lebanon was Red Leb hash! They had even tried to turn the kebab van over when it first appeared in town.

Tom and Pascale started discussing the merits of opening a restaurant specializing in a different cuisine from your own.

'What about cafés though? They do all sorts of food: pizza, sandwiches, pasties, milkshakes.'

'That's exactly my point, Tom,' Pascale said. 'They aren't specializing, are they?'

'Mmm, I suppose not...' He liked her a lot he thought. She was bright and sexy...

Lassie stood up, excusing himself, 'Just off to the toilet, this beer is going straight through me.'

'Perhaps a little too much information, Lassie?' Pascale smiled.

'Sorry.' Lassie laughed and walked towards the two doors to the toilets at the back of the restaurant. They were signposted with pictures of chickens – one with enormous breasts and the other with a huge penis. It would be hard to misread those. Once in the toilet he stood at the far end of three urinals. Just as he was congratulating himself on getting the urinal to himself a guy wearing a shell suit walked in and stood staring at him. Lassie hadn't ever been propositioned before and decided he should say something to clarify what was happening, but before he'd worked out what he should say shell suit spoke.

'This is for you.' He placed a brown envelope on the sink and then the man carried, 'Look at it first and then I then share it with your mate, and your mate alone, if you catch my drift?'

Lassie stood, rooted to the spot as the bloke turned and walked out of the toilet without another word, punch or kick. He stood, blinking in shock as he methodically put himself back in his jeans and approached the sink, staring at the brown envelope. He squirted some hand wash into his palms

2 1 0

and nudged the faucet with the back of his palm. He slowly washed his hands, still staring at the envelope. As the water increased in temperature he realised he had been washing his hands for ages. He stopped, dried them and then with one hand picked up the envelope. He turned to the cubicle, went inside and closed the door.

The envelope was lightly glued and opened easily. Inside it were photographs, four in all. He sat looking at them as the gravity of the situation began to make his arse twitch. One was of the girls' flat, clearly showing the number. One was of Pascale and Tom on the small balcony and one was of him and Abi kissing at the bottom of the steps of the apartment. The last one was of Abi, signing to Pascale as they stood on the bottom step of the apartment.

Lassie could barely control his panic and his mind was racing. This was serious. He then realised there was writing on the back of one of the pictures. He read it, spun around, pulled up the toilet seat and puked his gorgeous dinner and Almazas into the pan. He carried on retching until the tears in his eyes became tears of fear.

'You in here, mate?' Tom asked. Lassie had been a while and he seen people come and go.

The door of the toilet opened and Lassie stood, looking at Tom. He stretched out a hand holding the pictures and offered them to Tom to look at. 'We're fucked.'

Tom Adams looked at the pictures in disbelief and then read the messages on the back.

'*It's time to come home and face the fucking music. You need to catch the 2pm ferry to Harwich tomorrow. Any fucking about will incur a penalty. The pictures should leave you in no doubt about who will pay that penalty. We'll meet you in the front bar of the boat.*'

'Who gave them to you?'

'A bloke in shell suit trousers. Just came in, fronted me and told me to show you.'

Tom didn't know what to do so he just gave his best mate a hug. He wasn't going to cry but he was close to it. This was entirely his fault, no one else's. Not Lassie's, nor the girls. Just his. He tried to steady himself. He had to manage this situation carefully.

'Nothing's changed, Lass, nothing at all, don't worry. The most important thing is to protect the girls. We'll go back tomorrow and sort out the cash, just like we were planning. We're just going a little earlier.' Tom was trying very hard to be convincing even if he was close to breaking point. 'Let's just keep it together, eh?'

'And do what mate? And do fucking what?'

Tom shrugged and began laughing, 'Pack, mate?'

Tom picked up the photos and put them in his back pocket thinking they might potentially come in handy when they were back. He was trying to formulate a plan but hadn't got very far with it yet.

Lassie splashed some water on his face and they both returned to their table where the girls had finished and were sitting chatting.

Tom spoke first as they both took their seats. 'Don't ask. You'd accuse me of giving you too much information.' With this he winked at Pascale, who returned the wink and laughed, knowingly.

'Anyway, boys, we've paid the bill, and before you argue we insist, we've had such a lovely time, even with everything you two have going on, so let dinner be on us please?'

'Anyway, boys, we've paid the bill, and before you argue we insist, we've had such a lovely time, even with everything you two have going on, so let dinner be on us please?'

The boys accepted the offer with thanks. 'What now then, ladies?'

'We're both shattered. How about grabbing some wine and heading back to the flat?'

Tom thought this was probably the safest option. 'Sounds cool, eh, Lass? In fact it sounds perfect. Lead the way ladies.'

The four strolled back to the flat, the two couples hand in hand, stopping on the way for the boys to buy wine.

Back on the sofas with glasses of wine and the TV on, it wasn't long before they were all fighting the urge to let their eyelids collapse. Before they crashed, Tom raised the idea of travelling back on the day boat, mostly under the premise of getting out of the girl's hair and sorting their mess out. He didn't understand sign language but he was sure both girls wholeheartedly agreed. Maybe a little too enthusiastically he thought, but who could blame them? Lassie and he had been on edge since the meal and he was sure Pascale could feel it. He had been half expecting to be kidnapped or worse on the way back to the flat and he had been scanning the streets all the way. Luckily though, nothing had happened. He imagined there was no need. They had made their intentions known and were probably sat in a bar somewhere laughing and discussing what they would do with them when they got back to the UK.

Tom picked up the bottle of wine and replenished the glasses on the coffee table, then he sat back and dozed, hand in hand with Pascale, in front of *Brief Encounter* subtitled in Dutch. It seemed to please everyone and fit the mood. He was woken by Pascale. She stood up and walked him downstairs to her bedroom. He glanced behind him and grinned as he realised that Lassie and Abi had already vacated the sofa.

# 3 The Green, Green Grass of Home

## 3.1 Smug

George and Gary had melted into the shadows. Gary had delivered the bomb and George was happy with the way things had gone. He sat and sipped his whisky; a decent single malt with two ice. He was content, was prepared to admit to himself, smug. Smug that he had fucked with those boys. Mind control and power, suspense and the sense of imminent threat were his greatest tools. That was what scared the shit out of people, and George was a man who enjoyed issuing the threats as much as he enjoyed delivering on his promises. Gary had asked if they should wait and follow them again. George told him there was no need. He had walked off, found a nice bar and had ordered them drinks. He understood the worm had very much turned and he was now in charge. He couldn't help but pat himself on the back. His plan had been cruel, vindictive and arbitrary in its creation. The girls coming into the picture had done nothing but present him with an opportunity.

Gary's thoughts had been running along a very different line. He really wanted to know what they would do when they got back. Or even on the boat. They had the lads within their grasp now but what if they didn't come up with anything? He wasn't sure he wanted more violence now, especially after hearing about young Paddy and the Stones brothers. The whole week had taken its toll on him and he wasn't sure he fancied it anymore. He thought it was all getting a bit out of hand, though he wasn't sure how he would explain that to George. So he stuck with, 'So, what now, boss?'

'It all depends on what they have for us, Gary. If they scrape together the 6K it'll show the little cunts have some balls, and then I've got a plan. If they don't come up with it, well then we'll break their fucking fingers for putting them anywhere near my pie and put them to work with our gear, for free, until we get bored of them and then, when the smoke has settled waste them. The old bill won't bother too much. Just little boys who got in too deep.'

George smiled and sipped his drink. 'Come on, Gaz, I'm knackered. Let's get back to the hotel. We've got a big day tomorrow.'

Gary Sparks, puzzled as he finished his whisky, left a note on the bar and followed George out into the street.

'So your saying if they come up with the 6K you'll let them off?'

'I didn't say that at all Gary.' George put his huge arm around Gary's shoulders and gave him a squeeze that was slightly uncomfortable in a non-violent way. 'I said I had a plan if they did.'

It was simple. If the boys did in fact come up with the 6K it would be a bonus because George was fairly convinced that they hadn't taken it anyway, and that it was probably his nephew and his stupid sidekick who had spunked the cash on their little holiday. But, if they did come up with the 6K it would show that were, at the very least, resourceful. So he'd use them to do some leg work, maybe a couple of runs up and down the country. He'd would still see them punished for what he saw as their part in the Stones brothers' and his nephew's death – when he was bored with them he intended to have them arrested, either with drugs or credit cards and enough gear to have them put away. He'd have plenty of time to plan that part. He could probably make sure they would suffer in the nick too.

Gary wasn't shocked by George's confession that he was pretty sure they hadn't stolen the cash, but was worried that he blamed them for the death of the Stones and Paddy. Paddy, after all, had lifted the cash in the first place and the Stones brothers worked with George. He couldn't help but feel sorry for these two lads. They looked barely into their twenties and hadn't done anything wrong yet were probably going to die or spend a long time getting raped in prison. He stood in the street, taking in what George had said. He had honestly thought there was a bit of honour amongst thieves. A kind of 'values set' that the people he knew had, a set of moral guidelines they should follow. It seemed to him that George was actually blaming these two lads for things that he had essentially made happen himself. It dawned on him that he was in fact, just a horrible cunt of a man.

'So, you honestly think they didn't take the cash then, George?'

They stood, no more than two feet from the canal's edge, and Gary Sparks could feel his fist, tucked in his jacket pocket curling into a fist.

'It doesn't matter what I think now, Gary, the wheels are in motion and we are nothing but soldiers doing our duty.'

Gary felt angry. He was close to knocking George Meachen into the canal, hopefully to drown, but was stopped by the realization of what would happen to him if it went wrong. Gary felt a cool breeze from the canal glide across his face as he unclenched his fists. He couldn't believe what he had nearly done, yet regretted not doing it. Something had changed in him as he had listened to George and he didn't know what to do apart from bury his thoughts for the time being at least.

The two set off back towards the hotel in silence.

'You OK, Gary?'

Gary wasn't. He had been looking at every dark alley, every road with poor lighting. Every skip with rocks or wood in that could be used to crush a head. Every little bridge they walked across, talking to himself about killing George Meachen and going home alone. It would be easy. A fucking mercy killing almost. He might even get a fucking knighthood.

'Yeah, I'm OK, George, just tired.'

## 3.2 If You Make It

Tom opened his eyes and had a split second of thinking *Where am I?* He stood up, pulled on his clothes and opened the bedroom door. He could hear 'Fools Gold' by the Stone Roses playing in the kitchen. Abi and Lassie were already up and at the table eating breakfast. Lassie nodded, away in the music somewhere, Abi beamed a smile and carried on eating.

Pascale was cooking eggs. 'Morning, are you hungry?'

He was and they were both soon tucking into scrambled eggs on toast, rocking along to the tunes.

'It's just after nine boys, but with a tram and then the train and checking in I'd say you need to be on your way by ten. We're going shopping so will come with you as far as Centraal Station.' Pascale made a sad face at this then smiled. 'You'll be back soon though?'

'Yes, we will, I promise.'

Tom glanced towards Lassie, they had struck gold with these two and if all went well they would be laying on a Dutch beach very soon. And if it didn't, well he wasn't ready to think about the alternative.

Tom swallowed hard as he felt tears well up and a lump push into his throat. 'But now we have to pack.'

It was a bright Amsterdam morning and the tram arrived promptly. Tom and Lassie sat quietly through the whole journey, both looking out of the window as the city swept by. Abi began busily signing to Pascale who sat nodding and occasionally signing back and nodding quickly. Abi pointed ahead as the tram pulled alongside the huge façade of the main station and Lassie gave Tom the nod as they pulled past the car park where the whole Dutch leg of the adventure had started.

'I know, mate, what a mental week, eh?'

Once off the tram Pascale grabbed Tom's arms and began to speak as tears welled up in her eyes. 'You're both very quiet and look very sad. You're scared. Abi and I are worried. We think you should tell the police. They will help, please. Do this

for us. Abi is scared she won't see you both again and so am I.'
She flung her arms around Tom and Abi did the same to Lassie.

Tom kissed Pascale, and whispered into her ear. 'Hey, calm down, its only *au revoir*. We'll see you real soon.'

'Really?' Pascale asked. She Looked as though she didn't believe it any more than he did.

'Go and have a nice time shopping. I'll ring the flat UK time nine, so ten here, OK?'

'OK, promise?'

'I promise.'

Abi and Lassie were still hugging as Tom picked up his bag, gave Pascale a final kiss and told Lassie to hurry up. They had to get moving and this goodbye was killing him. Lassie gave Abi a final kiss and then he followed Tom into the station.

The train pulled into Hoek Van Holland just after midday. Tom had half expected them to be waiting for them but they weren't and he heaved a great sigh of relief. He really didn't want to see them any sooner than he had to. Lassie seemed equally anxious as he scanned the station.

'Tom, look, there's a little café. Better than going straight into the terminal.'

They sat outside and looked at the menu. A local in a Hell's Angels jacket who clearly owned the massive hog parked nearby recommended the local delicacy, called kibbling, which was fried pieces of white fish, usually cod, with a special sauce. The last thing Tom wanted to do was upset anyone else so they both ordered kibbling with chips. It turned out to be very tasty and the boys both nodded their thanks to the biker.

Tom saw Lassie flinch, beckon him closer and began whispering very quietly. 'Don't turn around, Tom. Stay where you are.'

As he spoke Lassie maneuvered himself so he could just see over Tom's left shoulder out into the street.

The position of the café gave them a direct view of the vehicle queue for ferry. As they had been chatting Lassie has spotted the shell suit drive into the queue in an Astra.

'It's them, Tom. They've just pulled up in an Astra.'

'Well that's not exactly a shock is it, Lass? After all, they did insist we were on this fucking ferry.'

Yeah yeah, just made my arse twitch though. I'm fucking scared now, Tom. Actually scared.'

'So am I, mate, but there isn't much we can do to the change the situation is there? Now come on, we might as well get on board.'

'What about the cash?' Lassie asked.

'It's in my socks Lass, and its legal tender. If we do get stopped, we'll say we won it in a poker game, or at pool, or in a casino. It'll be OK.'

Lassie laughed, 'I've never been in a casino!'

The boys slowly walked back up the platform and into the terminal. Tickets were checked, customs passed through and in less than twenty minutes they were walking along the gangplank and onto the ferry.

Tom was feeling it now. His legs were shaking and sweating. He headed for the nearest toilet, closely followed by Lassie, and into the first cubicle, he quickly whipped down his trousers before his stomach fell out of his arse. Lassie was in the stall beside his, he could see his Reeboks under the partition.

'You OK in there, fella?'

'Yeah. I'll meet you outside. If you make it.' Lassie chuckled nervously as he pulled up his jeans and left Tom to his own devices.

## 3.3 For The Foreseeable

Gary had felt odd since the night before. He felt like he'd had an epiphany. The very fact that George had essentially admitted this wild goose chase was some kind of vanity project and that he didn't really care that he was ruining innocent people's lives had turned him inside out emotionally. Usually it was easy. Someone in the game owed money and knew the rules and consequences. Or someone who knew the game had broken the rules. Those were easy jobs. There was no malice and usually the recipients understood the deal. This was different though. These two poor little fuckers didn't have a clue what George was planning or what he was capable of, and to top it off they hadn't actually done anything wrong. It was just wrong all over. Rotten from the middle, and he didn't fancy it anymore.

He'd been mulling these thoughts over in his head as he drove back to the port. His position had moved from grudging respect and slight fear of George to utter loathing. Each time they had approached red lights or a bridge or any other potential accident spot Gary Sparks had considered crashing the car. He imagined a head-on collision that would kill them both instantly. Would it be worth it? He couldn't believe the answer that kept popping into his head. It was yes, it would be potentially be worth it to rid the planet of this horrible psycho cunt of a man next to him. He just couldn't bring himself to do it, at least not yet.

His mind wandered and as George dozed next to him they drew ever nearer to the Hoek Van Holland. Another crossroads appeared in the distance and Gary Sparks' hand drifted towards George's seat belt. If he released his seat belt and then crashed he might have a chance of killing George and surviving himself. The tension in his mind grew as the crossroads approached and at the last moment he again sighed and put both hands back on the steering wheel as George's eyes popped open.

'All OK, Gary?' George asked.

'Yes, George, only another thirty kilometers.'

## 3.4 Good Work

Tom and Lassie had seen George and Gary coming. Neither of them knew what to say so they both decided to say nothing.

The shell suit nodded at the boys but didn't speak.

George said 'Afternoon scumbags.' He smiled. 'My name is George, and this gentleman to my left is called Gary.'

Tom spoke for them both. 'I'm Tom and that's Lassie.'

'I fucking know your name, shithead. Lassie? Like the fucking dog? Well pleased to meet you again, Lassie, how's your nose? George was enjoying himself.

Lassie nodded, it was still sore as fuck.

'Well, boys, I hope you left your lady friends in good health.'

Lassie and Tom remained silent and rooted to their chairs.

'Now, the last time I saw you two chaps poor young Raymond had managed to get himself stuck between two cars, the daft cunt. He's still in Colchester General at the moment. He'll probably lose one, maybe both of his legs.'

George looked at the boys; they were shitting themselves and looked on the verge of tears. He was fucking loving every minute of it. Get them desperate, struggling to breathe. Like his sister's goldfish. When he was a kid he'd pulled it out of the tank and watched as it gasped for air.

'You see, little boys, that's what happens to dirty thieves where we come from isn't it, Gary? Nasty things happen to them. Almost like it's fucking karma. Do you understand what karma is, little boys?

Tom and Lassie nodded.

Gary couldn't help but wonder whether it was karma that had killed the Stones brothers and Paddy Wherry or George's ego? He kept his mouth locked though.

'So, as I recall, after our brief phone conversation. You owed me 6K and were given a strict timeframe for payment. You then decided to piss off to Holland on a jolly, which landed me with a predicament, as I was worried about my 6K. I had to follow you little twats to keep an eye on you. Unfortunately, this means I've incurred extra costs that I have now decided to transfer to your ongoing debt, which as it stands, due to the rather nice hotel we stayed in over in Amsterdam, stands at around 8K.'

George sat back in his chair and smiled smugly to himself. He then leant in to the boys and whispered,

'How would you like to pay?'

Lassie and Gary sat in silence. It was Tom who spoke, clearing his throat, but unable to stop his voice from shaking and involuntarily notching up in pitch. 'OK, just to be clear. First, I didn't take any of your money. Not one English pound.'

George sat listening to the little upstart. He wanted to glass him right there and then but also had a grudging respect for his bravery in standing up to him. Especially when he placed the plastic bag on the table.

'In that bag, is £2,800 in Dutch guilders. In Harwich I have another 3K. In terms of your incurred costs I'm prepared to go 50/50 with you. Seeing that I didn't know it was on my bill and if I did you'd have been staying in the YMCA... I'd need some time to raise the other grand too, and then it's done. No more me and you.'

Tom was shaking inside and the only way he knew to calm himself was to make light of the situation. He crossed his fingers at his attempt at humour and hoped it wasn't badly received.

Lassie could hardly breathe. He knew Tom didn't have 3K. Gary couldn't help but be almost impressed by the lad in front of him. His courage was probably largely due to the fact he didn't know George Meachen, if he did he would have probably jumped overboard at the first sight of him, but fucking good on him Gary thought.

The silence was tangible as all at the table sat and watched George pondering his next move. It would be an important one. In the back of his mind he already knew that Tom probably hadn't taken the money but he had got involved with Paddy and Razor, which was a mistake and due to all this mess three of his people were dead and this little toe rag and his dog were very much alive. The money was immaterial really. They had recovered the bulk and this youth was now offering him the missing 6K in less than six hours when the boat docked. It was really a win/win in that sense. He still felt he wasn't getting full retribution though and he considered his earlier discussions with Gary.

Lassie sat intrigued as he watched Tom actually having a discussion with this maniac. He felt so sorry for him. He hadn't done anything apart from have a few beers with those boys and look where it had ended up.

Gary fully expected George to strangle Tom at any moment. He watched as George began to speak again.

'A debt is a debt and yours is eight thousand, sonny.'

'I haven't got 8K.'

'I know, that's where I come in again.'

Tom had expected this and had to concentrate hard on not throwing up as George began to explain what was going to happen.

'Your shortfall will be made good by doing two little jobs for us. You don't need to know the details but you'll either be importing something or exporting something. Each time you will reduce your debt by a grand. Everybody's happy.'

Tom stared into empty space and knew he was fucked. This was an impossible task. He wouldn't even know what he was carrying or doing, it could be fucking anything! At least Lassie seemed to have gotten away lightly, that was some small consolation.

'Is there any alternative?'

George smiled; he knew he had him by the balls. 'Not unless you can give me the 8K with an hour of getting off this boat.'

Tom shook his head. 'No. I can't.' There was absolutely no one he could ask, he felt crushed, but then realised he wasn't dead, yet...

'OK lads. I'm going to retire to my cabin, you enjoy your uncomfortable seating arrangements and we'll meet dockside. We'll pick up you outside the main entrance when we come off with our car. Again lads, don't do anything silly, we know where your girlfriends are and it's a cheap flight to Amsterdam. Come on, Gary. Let's go.'

George picked up the plastic bag of cash, winked at Tom and said, 'Good work.'

Gary followed George back towards the accommodation decks. He wanted to strangle the evil cunt right there and then.

## 3.5 She Was Rock Solid

'Well that's me fucked, Lass. Might as well have a few beers.'

'We're still here, mate.'

'For the moment,' Tom replied.

'And what the fuck is he going to have me doing to pay off the rest. I imagine there will be interest on what I owe until I do the jobs, whatever they are. I'll owe this psycho cunt forever. Never trust a bin dipping Scouser, Lass, they'll meet your friends and burgle their houses the week after!'

'Kill him?' Lassie looked serious. 'I'll get some drinks.'

He returned with two pints and began to quickly devour one himself.

'Looks like we're not going back to Amsterdam in the very near future, eh?'

'Relax, Lass, we've only just left. I want to know what he wants me to do.'

'Obvious: drug runs.'

'Not the end of the world then.'

Tom shrugged his shoulders and slouched back into his seat. This would be an awful journey and he didn't feel like drinking either. He was already numb from the ankles up.

The boat was unusually empty and the main bar was quiet. They both tried to get some sleep on the way back but the seats didn't help and neither of them managed more than fifteen to twenty minutes of unbroken sleep.

Soon the Essex coast came into view. Car and freight passengers were asked to return to their vehicles and foot passengers were loudly told that they could make their way to the exits. The boys remained in their seats. It was not worth queuing. They were in no hurry. They sat and watched as the huge ferry came alongside the quay and began docking manoeuvres. The footbridge opened, they grabbed their stuff and made their way off the boat onto dry land. Neither of them felt ecstatic to be back.

'I feel like I could sleep for a week, Lass."

'You reckon? without nightmares?'

Tom nodded at the passport control officer and offered his I.D. Oddly, the guy glanced up at him and then quickly down again and handed over his passport with a curt 'Welcome back to England and have a pleasant onward journey', which Tom thought odd as he was sure he recognised him as the brother of someone he played football with. He waited for Lassie and they went through the 'Nothing to declare' area of the customs hall without a hitch. An overzealous customs officer was busy destroying a man's perfectly packed bags. The owner of the bags was dressed in an African robe and sported a matching hat, all very colourful. Tom nodded to Lassie and back to the gentleman.

'Racists Lass, all bloody racists.'

The pair snaked their way through the walkways and presently found themselves standing back in the main area for departures and arrivals. They slowly moved towards the exit, Lassie could feel Tom's reluctance about going outside.

'Don't feel like pressing the green button for go again then, mate?'

'I'm spent, Lass. Last week started in fucking court and now I feel like I've been given a life sentence. All I did was talk to those fuckers! I'd decided to sort my life out, and look how that's going! I'm completely fucking screwed.'

Tom stood with his bag at his feet, his hands on the top of his head. He looked towards the exit and considered what was beyond. He wondered if he could kill somebody. Of course he couldn't and did anybody get away with murder nowadays, especially with programs like 'Crimewatch' on TV? Nothing seemed to get past Nick Ross and Sue Cook! He'd have no hope. He laughed at himself for even considering the option.

Lassie watched as he saw Tom start laughing, his hands on his head. Was he cracking up he thought? He wouldn't blame him. He didn't know what to say, or do that wouldn't potentially upset Tom more. The reality of the situation was that Tom, his best mate, was in a horrible mess and he didn't know what the fuck to suggest.

'Listen, lad. We'll go down and wait for them. We'll go and sort out the cash you can cobble together and give it to them. At least then hopefully they'll fuck off back up north for a bit and give you, well us some time to have a think and hatch a plan, eh?'

'Yes, Lass, a bit of space, I might even be able to raise a bit of cash and try to pay him off before he asks me to do anything for him.'

Lassie didn't say so, but he thought that was as a long shot. Those cunts had their claws into Tom and he honestly couldn't see them releasing him soon unless something dramatic happened. 'Come on Lad, let's go. We can't stand here all day.'

Tom picked up his bag and walked out of the station, he took a large breath of fresh air and began the descent to the car park. They reached the bottom of the stairs and a small walkway deposited them at the front of the station. Harwich Parkeston Quay, as it proudly announced itself on the signs. Tom put his bag down and looked around for the white Astra. Lassie stood beside him and did the same. It was just before nine, a warm summer evening and still light. The ferry stood proudly behind them, it's bow doors open. Both boys sat down on their bags and watched the boat slowly empty its belly onto the dock in front of them. They recognised a few locals as they poured themselves, post hen night into a waiting taxi. The cab lurched into life and crept down the road into the town.

They didn't have to wait long for a white car to slowly pull into the car park and methodically snake its way around the stationary cars and pull up alongside them. The car, however, although a white Vauxhall Astra, didn't carry Tom's nemesis, inside were two policemen. The window came down and the passenger spoke to the boys. 'Evening, lads, waiting for somebody?'

Both shook their heads and said, 'Na, no one.'

The two men in the car looked quizzically at each other as if they were a comedy double act.

Tom looked at Lassie and offered a single Roger Moore. The car hadn't moved and the two occupants seemed to be having some kind of extra sensory conversation. Lassie looked back at Tom and returned the SRM. He looked back at the car and beyond into the car park. He couldn't handle the stand-off much longer.

Tom realised that he actually quite fancied asking them for a lift, or if they would lock him up for a year or two. He watched, surprised, as they both men got out of the car. The driver came around the side of the vehicle and stood with his colleague against the passenger side of the car.

'Where have you two chaps been then?' Asked one of the policemen.

'Amsterdam,' Lassie replied. 'You should go, it's fun.'

'Could I see some I.D. please?'

Tom stood up, wondering what the fuck all this was about. All he needed was for the Scousers to see them having a chat with the Old Bill. That truly would be the last nail in his coffin!

'Why are you giving us grief, fellas? We've just been through customs and you're welcome to have another look in our bags, even though I'm not sure if you're allowed to. We're just waiting for a lift to go home and get our shit sorted.'

The second, policeman now turned his attentions to Tom.

'And what's your name, my friend?'

'Tom Adams. What the fuck is going on here?'

'Tom Adams, I am arresting you on suspicion of failing to stop at a road traffic accident, you do not have to say anything, but anything you do say will be taken down and could be used in evidence against you. Do you understand?'

'What the fuck...?'

As Tom tried to work out what was going on he heard a different charge being read to Lassie, perverting the course of justice! They were both put in handcuffs and placed in the back of the police car, the doors shut on them and the engine started. Tom was panicking as he craned his neck to see if any white cars were in the car park as they drove out and towards the town. He strained across at Lassie, who was equally surprised at the goings on. Both had realized it was the accident, Razor... something had happened and it had been traced back to Harwich.

Lassie looked across at Tom, his eyebrows fixed in a double Roger Moore position. 'Razor?' he whispered.

Tom nodded. They had driven off and left the poor cunt at the mercy of George and the others, but how the fuck had they traced the incident to them? It didn't make any sense. How did they know they were in Holland even? And if they had been nicked, what had happened to George and the shell suit? It dawned on Tom that this could be extremely bad.

The driver of the police car couldn't help himself and looked into the rea- view mirror before curling his lips and smirking, 'You boys seem to have gotten your young selves in a right fucking pickle, haven't you?

Prepare yourselves for a bit of a stay boys, this could take a while.' Again, sarcastic laughter emanated from the front of the car.

Tom and Lassie sat back and contemplated their current helplessness. Tom pondered the future as they made their way up the main road and through the town. They soon pulled into the car park at the back of the police station, where they were escorted into the charge room and interviewed by the custody sergeant. Their fingerprints taken, they were walked down a narrow hallway and placed separately in individual cells.

Tom waited until he heard the main door close before shouting to Lassie, 'You OK mate?'

'Yeah, I'm OK,' Lassie shouted back as he sat down on the blue plastic cushions inside the cell.

Tom sat on his bed and stared at the walls, hard paint covered them and he could see people's vain attempts to leave their mark. The seat-less stainless steel toilet, took pride of place in the corner next to a tiny hand basin. The thick glass bricks that gave the incumbent a suggestion of the outside world only reminded him that it was now dark outside and another day in this disastrous week had passed and he wasn't any closer to daylight, or understanding, or emancipation from the problems that had seemed to have swept over him and Lassie like the waves crashing on the beach less than a mile away from where he sat. He was exhausted and felt like he must be on the verge of an emotional breakdown. He couldn't take it anymore. He decided to lay down and close his eyes. Perhaps it would all go away.

As his head hit the tough blue plastic the first door opened and he heard the custody sergeant approaching. The door opened and a gruff voice spoke, 'Someone wants to speak to you.'

Tom stood up, and was led back up the passageway and left, into an interview room where he was offered a seat at a barren table. In the room were two police officers in plain clothes. In ugly plain clothes, he couldn't help but notice. One was female, the other male. They introduced themselves as DS Cook and DC Barnes.

'Hi, Tom,' said the female. 'We'd like to have a quick chat if we may. You are of course, allowed to get in the duty solicitor but that will take time and we'd love to get you out of here ASAP if poss. What do you think?'

Tom nodded tacit agreement and was invited to take a seat. Tapes were placed in the recorder and the two officers introduced themselves again before introducing Tom who acknowledged his presence and waived the right to legal representation for the time being.

'So Tom,' DC Barnes said, 'I'll tell you where we are. Over the last week lots of incidents have happened. Incidents in relation to which your name and your friends' name have popped up again and again. What we need to clear up is what part have you played in these incidents and how involved you are with a man we now know is called George Meachen.'

Tom's face twitched even at the sound of the name. 'I don't know any George Meachen.'

'Tom, I haven't got time for this bollocks, I know you're small fry but definitely connected somewhere.'

At this point, DS Cook handed DC Barnes a plastic bag with a letter in it. Tom looked at the letter, written on nice beige paper in quite neat handwriting.

'This letter, Tom, names you. It was written by a man called Raymond Wilkins, on Friday we believe, and it attempts to explain, to some extent the goings-on with which you seem to be connected. It appears that Raymond and Patrick stole some money from Patrick's brother-in-law, George Meachen. They fled from Liverpool to Harwich where they met a lad called Tom who had a laugh with them for a couple of days before things went a bit awry and they realised Uncle George wasn't too happy. You still following me lad?' DC Barnes looked across at Tom, 'Need some water?'

His mouth was stuck shut, and very dry indeed and he nodded at the offer. Where the fuck was this leading?'

The DC continued, 'It seems that this George then ran his car, a black BMW 5 Series into young Raymond, nearly severing his leg and putting him in hospital. Now Raymond luckily remembered the car type he and Patrick had hired. A Ford Orion, and put this in the letter too. He names you as being there, apparently on a bit of a day trip. Fancied yourself as a bit of a tour guide for thieves and gangsters, eh, Tom?

Raymond then goes on to explain George Meachen's nefarious activities in his hometown of Liverpool and the fact that he's a psychopath.'

Tom put his hand up and the DC stopped.

'Yes, I do know most of this story, but why would Razor, sorry, Raymond write all this down?'

'Well, it seems that later in the week Raymond spoke to his parents, who were in shock both from realising where their son was and from the brutal attack carried out on them in their own home by George Meachen. During that phone call he also found out that there had been a car crash that had unfortunately killed the Stones brothers and Patrick Wherry.'

'Why would he write all this down though? I still don't get it.' Tom was confused.

'Because it was the last thing, apart from two other letters found on him, that he ever wrote. He committed suicide in Colchester hospital.'

Tom sat stunned. Gutted. Four people were dead now and he was pretty sure he could be next. None of them could be tied to George Meachen though. It was fucking crazy. He now had a question of his own.

'Where are George Meachen and the shell suit guy, Gary, I think?'

'They are also in custody, but with much less chance than you of getting out. We traced the BMW back to the crash in Essex. It ended up in a compound, amazingly, with a Glock handgun under the spare tyre. The Orion we then traced in Harwich, parked on the seafront, luckily bits of Raymond were still all over the front of it. Wilhire gave us the Astra and the manifest on the boat gave us Holland, we just had to wait for you all to get back. We arrested you on suspicion of failing to stop and that still stands, I have to decide whether to charge you, as I am sure you were probably taking the best course of action in fleeing the scene. Which leads me to my next question. How come you two fools seemed to have survived this one-man hurricane, and what the hell were you doing in Holland with Meachen and Sparks?'

Tom was slowly beginning to realise that with George Meachen and Gary Sparks in custody and everyone else dead there could actually be a speck of light at the end of the tunnel. What were they charging him with he thought? The same as them? Attempted murder?

'I was scared, scared shitless. Apparently when Paddy gave back George Meachen's money it was 6K short. George decided that I owed him that money because he knew I'd been with Paddy and Razor. I haven't got £600, let alone £6,000, what did you expect me to do? I wasn't really aiming on coming back, I have a few friends in Amsterdam and I was going to look for work, then they found us and threatened to hurt my friends unless I came back with them today. I was going to have to work off the 6K by doing jobs for him; I imagined they weren't thinking along the lines of building work or taxi driving and I didn't know what to do. That's it, honestly. I just didn't know what to do. I feared for my life and for the lives of my friends too.'

Tom was doing his best to sound the innocent victim but didn't want to over-egg the pudding.

DS Cook interrupted, 'You prepared to write that down in a statement Tom? Potentially modern slavery or bonded labour charges there?'

DC Barnes nodded in agreement. 'The more charges the better. Less chance of seeing him again, Mr. Adams.'

Tom refused. 'No way. No statement, I just want to forget him and the past week.'

The DS spoke for the benefit of the tape and paused the interview. Tom was to be taken back to his cell while they followed up other enquiries and he imagined, spoke to Lassie and or the Scousers. As he was escorted back he listened to the cells, he was on one end and Lassie the other. There didn't seem to be anyone else there, he wondered where George and Gary were being held.

Back in his cell Tom lay on his stiff and uncomfortable mattress and reflected on what he had just been told. The whole story was mental, from start to finish and Raymond Wilkins had, essentially just saved his life. He made a promise to himself that he would visit Razor's and Paddy's graves wherever they were buried and pay his respects. His thoughts turned to Pascale, he'd said he'd phone her this evening and it was past his promised time. Should he buzz and ask for his phone call? Would they even let him call abroad? He wasn't sure. That one would have to wait until tomorrow. She was rock solid. She'd be OK and he was gambling that he and Lassie would be out of there by the morning at least. He just hoped George and Gary wouldn't be. That would be heartbreaking having being given this little lifeline. His senses picked up a noise, the door creaked open and he heard a key slide into a locked door at the end of the corridor, they must be questioning Lassie he thought, and decided to try and get some sleep.

## 3.6 Roaring Red Rockets Racing

The key turned in the door of Tom's cell. Tom woke as he heard the noise and opened his eyes to the sight of the custody sergeant, DS Cook and DC Barnes standing by the bed. The custody sergeant then left the two plain clothes police in the cell with him.

'Well, Tom.' DS Cook sounded very tired herself, 'We're letting you go without charge. We are happy with your account of your involvement in what has been going on over this past week.'

Tom sat up, stunned. Not really knowing what to think or do.

The DS continued, 'What I would say is that, with all the tragedy surrounding this mess, your friend Raymond did the right thing, despite the utterly tragic outcome. He gave us a number of other lines of enquiry and George Meachen is not going anywhere anytime soon. Now, I think you should go home, lesson learned. Keep your nose clean and try to put this all behind you. And of course, if you think of anything else that could possibly help us further get in touch straight away.'

Tom felt a tidal wave of relief wash over him.

Tom was led to the custody desk where Lassie was waiting with the sergeant. They had their belongings returned and then were formally released without charge, taken through to reception and let out into the moonlight of very early Sunday morning.

As they walked towards the cab office Tom said, 'I feel like I've been on the shittiest rollercoaster all week, Lass. What happens next? Or when they get out? It's all a bit surreal, they just let us out, scot free and locked the two of them up for us. It's just fucking weird.'

Lassie didn't want to think about it, but indulged his mate one last time 'In jail, out of jail. He's not going to come looking for you or us. They have bigger fish to fry probably holding on to their turf up there, and to be fair, who actually knows the story? Everybody's fucking dead. It's like a poisoned chalice mate. Whoever touches it seems to meet a sticky end.'

'I hope so Lass, I really fucking hope so. Apart from us of course.' With that he managed a wry smile. 'I just had a beautiful thought, Lass, I've still got a little over 2k stashed at mine! Result!'

The taxi arrived at the office and whisked them away home. They both knew the driver but were well and truly beyond conversation. Soon they were both lying on their beds, Lassie fast asleep and seconds from snoring, Tom wide awake, his head racing. The tongue twister about roaring red rockets racing round ridiculous rabbits was spinning around in his head, refusing to let his mind rest...

## 3.7 Soaking Up The Rays

It was four o'clock on Sunday afternoon before even opened his eyes and the first thing he hoped was that the last week had been one mad awful dream. His damp sheets and sweaty body suggested that it probably wasn't, and when he looked at his bag laying where he'd dropped it last night the nightmare was complete.

He sat upright in bed and leant over to pull the curtain open. Sunlight exploded into the room and he immediately closed it again. A couple of minutes later, more composed, he got up and opened them again. He went downstairs wondering when the front door was going to get smashed in and those two mad bastards would drag him off somewhere and hang him from a tree. He told himself to calm down; his imagination was wringing him out.

'Hello! You up then... lazy fucker!' Lassie was sitting outside in a garden chair soaking up the rays with a massive spliff. 'How goes it my friend? Seems you needed that kip.' Lassie offered Tom the joint but was waved away.

'Very much so. I just can't believe that it all actually happened. It's fucking mental. And is it even over?'

Lassie nodded in agreement, and tugged hard on the spliff causing its tip to burn a dark orange. He spoke through a huge cloud of white smoke in a very matter-of-fact way. 'Well the Old Bill seemed pretty sure they had them bang to rights and as much as I dislike John Law, at this given point in the proceedings I am more than happy to concur with our local constabulary, young man...'

'Fucking stonehead,' Tom said, laughing. He couldn't actually believe Lassie had been so subdued in Amsterdam with all that gear about.

'"Fucking stonehead"... Do you know, that is exactly what that Meachen fella called me when they turned up here and smashed my nose and my vinyl?'

Tom now understood the mess in the front room and promised Lassie to replace all of his records. They really were fucking animals and he was crossing everything he had that neither he nor Lassie ever saw them again. He heard the Top Forty countdown in the background on Radio One as they announced that Crystal Waters' 'Gypsy Woman' had moved five down to number eight.

'Come on, Lass, I'll take you to the pub. My shout.'

Lassie stood, slid into his flip-flops, finished his spliff and was ready for the pub. In a moment of clarity stopped and looked at Tom. 'Have you rung Pascale?'

'No I haven't, we'll do it from the call box on top of the hill. I've got some change and their number.'

They left the house and walked purposefully towards a drink. They talked as they walked and Tom suggested they give up their tenancy and move house. Lassie agreed. 'Great idea, lad. Back to Amsterdam?' He proposed hopefully.

'Great idea,' Tom replied as they approached the call box. Once inside the smelly cubicle they called the girls, it rang for ages before going to an answer machine. Tom left a message, explaining last night and that he had just got up. They sent their love and carried on to the hotel bar. The sun was out and they decided to sit upstairs and look out onto the coast. It wasn't long before they had moved downstairs and had begun to get steadily pissed at the bar. Tom had insisted to Lassie they shouldn't talk about what had happened to anyone else. It was much safer that way.

Last orders soon rang resoundingly at the bar. 'Soon be time to go boys,' one of the bar staff shouted at them.

Lassie sat up, grinning. 'Hang on, this is a hotel too isn't it?'

It was, he was informed, but the smallest room, a twin was still £55 a night and a cab home was in fact only a fiver.

Tom's decision however, was made. He owed his mate more than a night out and they booked the room, ordered two pints of Stella, two Smirnoff Ice, two whiskies and two burgers and then staggered upstairs, past the parrot to collect their key before being shown where the room was. The night porter met them with a smile, 'OK, you two bloody drunken idiots. Last chance. You sure you don't just want me to ring you a cab?'

The boys politely refused the offer and were soon at the door of the room.

'OK, I'll put the grill on... arseholes,' he murmured sleepily.

They sat on the beds and waited for their drinks to arrive. Something suddenly struck Tom and he told to Lassie that this was the exact room the two lads had stayed in last Monday, where they had sniffed E and the whole sorry fucking affair had started.

'How fucking weird fella, total full circle.'

'Bizarre eh? And now they're both dead. Fucking tragic.'

The drinks arrived and the two boys toasted absent friends and downed the whiskies. When they woke up the next morning the Smirnoff Ice and Stella had been left untouched, and the burgers were cold and looking very unappetising.

'Fuck me, my head is pounding.' Tom made his way to the small bathroom and threw cold water over his face.

'Come on pal, time to get up and out of here before I have a bite of that burger.'

Lassie was making horrible noises from his bed and refused with a grunt to come from under the pillow he had over his head. With no toothpaste Tom decided to scrape his teeth, front and back with a flannel he had found in the bathroom. When as clean as could be expected he strode back towards his single bed, considering a twenty minute snooze before trying to raise Lassie again. As he paced across the room a creaking noise oozed from the floorboards close to his bed. He dived onto it and, kneeling on the floor, pressed on the area that produced the noise. Something seemed loose under the carpet. He pushed the bedside table to one side and began to tug at the carpet, the ease with which it came away from the skirting board gave him a twinge of excitement. He pulled the carpet back to the point where the noise had come from and found a loose floorboard. He hands began to sweat and he looked up to see if Lassie had offered any interest in his endeavors. He hadn't and was lightly snoring. He carried on, wobbled the floorboard loose and felt it, with a bit of resistance come away from the joist.

Tom looked around the room, checking for inquisitive eyes. There were none and he gingerly looked inside, expecting nothing. He then sat back down on his arse, leaning against the bed as a smile began to grow on his face. In the floorboard cavity nestled a wad of notes, mostly twenties and fifties. He guessed that when counted they would probably add up to around six thousand pounds.

The End

# About the Author

Martin Doohan was born in Essex in 1970 to Thomas and June. At this point in time, he works in Education.

Lightning Source UK Ltd.
Milton Keynes UK
UKOW04f0828231217
314970UK00002B/365/P